writer of penny dreadfuls

a prima ballerina

a coffin maker's daughter

a physician

"For I have
all the instincts of . . ."

a stockbroker

a trapped miner

a secret agent

a caterpillar

a princess in a tower

a postmaster's daughter

a prized stallion

a junior Sherlock Holmes

a prima ballerina

a Buddhist monk

"For I have all the instincts of . . ."

a princess in a tower

a writer of penny dreadfuls

a stockbroker

a five-star general

a coffin maker's daughter

an assistant librarian

a physician

a sedated cow

a caterpillar

a postmaster's daughter

a highland hermit

a secret agent

a startled rabbit

a lion

a trapped miner

a cheese-maker's niece

SOMEBODY STOP
Ivy Pocket

By CALEB KRISP

Illustrations by
BARBARA CANTINI

SOMEBODY STOP Ivy Pocket

By CALEB KRISP

SNAGSBY'S
ECONOMIC FUNERALS

SNAGSBY'S
ECONOMIC
FUNERALS

GREENWILLOW BOOKS
An Imprint of HarperCollinsPublishers

Somebody Stop Ivy Pocket
Text copyright © 2016 by Caleb Krisp
Illustrations copyright © 2016 by Barbara Cantini
First published in 2016 in Great Britain by Bloomsbury Children's under the title
Somebody Stop Ivy Pocket.
First published in 2016 in the United States by Greenwillow Books.
The right of Caleb Krisp to be identified as the author of this work has been asserted
by him in accordance with the Copyright, Designs and Patents Act, 1988.
www.epicreads.com
The text of this book is set in Spectrum MT Std.
Book design by Sylvie Le Floc'h

Library of Congress Cataloging-in-Publication Data is available.
ISBN 978-0-06-236437-1 (trade ed.)

16 17 18 19 20 CG/RRDH 10 9 8 7 6 5 4 3 2 1

Greenwillow Books

For my grandfather Plantagenet Krisp,
who never saw it coming

1.

"What have you got for us this time, Ivy?"

I patted the pocket of my dress. "'Petals on the Wind.' It's frightfully touching—all about dropping dead and floating away on a warm breeze."

Ezra Snagsby gave a nod of his head, which caused his heavy jowls to flap about gloriously. "Very good." Then he peered at me rather anxiously from beneath the untamed jungles of his bushy eyebrows. "You will read it as *written*, won't you, Ivy?"

"Yes, dear. Every dull word."

He nodded again—but this time at Mother Snagsby, who

was *terribly* dignified. Even when the carriage hit a pothole, shaking us like rag dolls, Mother Snagsby barely moved an inch.

"I have Miss Carnage to thank for 'Petals on the Wind,'" I said, smoothing out my very best royal-blue dress (with the white sash). "She took over after Mr. Abercrombie vanished— he was last spotted somewhere between Greek myths and French fiction. All very mysterious. Miss Carnage has only been at the library a few weeks, but she's already frightfully fond of me."

"That's very interesting, Ivy," said Ezra with a long sigh. He leaned his head against the side of the carriage. His heavy lids shut. The old man was snoring almost instantly.

"Faster, driver!" bellowed Mother Snagsby, hitting the top of the carriage with her parasol. "We haven't got all day!"

Before Miss Frost had sent me to London to live with the Snagsbys three months ago, I had little experience being a daughter. I remembered nothing of my real mother. I only knew that she was dead. That Miss Frost had found me quite by accident, curled up in my mother's lifeless lap, in some ghastly house. But it turns out, I'm a natural.

"You have a whip, man! Use it!" thundered Mother Snagsby, sticking her head out the window. "Or must I come up there and do it myself?"

The Snagsbys were a delightful pair. Ancient. Heads like lightly beaten melons. Matching back humps. But wondrously affectionate. Deliriously cuddly. Their daughter, Gretel, was at finishing school in Paris, so they had oodles of love to lavish upon me. It would be fair to say that I was the apple of their eye. The sun brightening their days.

"Stop squinting, young lady," snapped Mother Snagsby, showering me with a warm scowl. "It makes you look like a pickpocket."

Mother Snagsby was always heaping these tiny morsels of motherly advice and affection upon me. Pointing out how I might improve. Or be slightly less horrendous. Which was lovely.

"Sit up straight," she ordered. "When a girl isn't blessed with pretty features or fetching hair, she must employ other skills— good posture, refined speech, impeccable manners."

"And you use them to great effect, dear," I said, flashing my most understanding smile. "Your generous use of powder is a marvel. Never has so much been done with so little."

Mother Snagsby shook her head as if I were a nincompoop. "Whatever was Miss Frost *thinking*, lumping you on our doorstep?"

"Miss Frost is a wonder," I replied. "Somehow she knew we would be a perfect match."

Mother Snagsby shook her head again. No doubt trying to stop the tears of joy that threatened to burst from her beady eyes and drown us all. The Snagsbys hardly ever mentioned Miss Frost. They only knew her in passing and believed her to be some sort of traveling governess. Somehow Miss Frost had gotten word that they were in the market for a daughter. They never asked how I came to know her or what I was doing at Butterfield Park. In fact, the Snagsbys had no interest in my life before I came to live with them.

"Fix your braid," said Mother Snagsby. "Your hair looks as if you've been out in a windstorm."

"Which is true enough," I said, getting to work on my hair. "While I was out this morning, fetching the milk, buying the bread, picking up the bacon for your breakfast, and taking your shoes to be mended, there was the most violent gust of wind. I saw a fruit peddler lifted off his feet and thrown against a nearby carriage. The poor man broke into three pieces. Utterly tragic."

"Complete nonsense," growled Mother Snagsby.

"Not to him, dear," I said gravely. "And just think of his wife and their eleven children."

The Snagsbys knew nothing about the Clock Diamond. It was monstrously tempting to tell them—a secret as delicious as it was tragic—but I had promised Miss Frost. Besides, the Snagsbys were simple folk. Unworldly. All the sophistication of a scrambled egg. It would terrify them to know that I was wearing a priceless and deadly necklace.

"This is not a leisurely drive through the park," bellowed the old goat. "Get a move on!"

We were in something of a hurry. And it was all on account of death. My best blue dress. The poem in my pocket. The tape measure around Ezra's bony neck. The Snagsbys made coffins for a living—Snagsby's Economic Funerals was a thriving business, specializing in generous discounts for premeasured coffins.

"The viewing chamber was in a ghastly state this morning," said Mother Snagsby, eyeing me with motherly affection. "When our business is concluded, you will clean that room until it sparkles. Am I understood, young lady?"

"Hard to say, dear," I replied. "You tend to mutter a great deal. I find it easier just to *imagine* what you have said and go from there."

Before Mother Snagsby could explode with merriment, the carriage came to a sudden halt. Ezra was thrust forward, his bony body landing in a heap at my feet. The poor fellow woke with a start and immediately let out a painful groan. He clutched at his back, slowly picking himself up.

"Get a move on, Ezra, we haven't got all day," snapped his wife, peering out at a depressing row of houses.

"If your back is troubling you, I have an excellent remedy," I said as the carriage door opened. "All I require is a cup of lard, a ball of yarn, three carrots, and a field mouse."

Ezra began to chuckle, which was terribly unnecessary. Mother Snagsby rolled her eyes and pushed her husband out of the carriage. Then she fixed her eyes upon me.

"This is a house of death," she said sternly, "so you know *exactly* how I expect you to behave. Stay out of the way until you are needed, do your job when you are called. Understood?"

I nodded my head.

Mother Snagsby stepped out of the carriage, and I hurried after her.

"Thank heavens you are here!"

Mrs. Blackhorn was a marvelous creature—round of belly, fat of cheek, bad of breath. But it was what sat atop her head that really made an impression. A glorious crown of golden ringlets that would slip down her brow as she fussed around her husband's sickbed. She was forever yanking it back up.

"I have been counting the minutes!" she bellowed, clutching at her perfectly dry handkerchief and ushering us into the darkened bedroom chamber. "Poor Mr. Blackhorn is not long for this world . . . the doctor says his heart has finally given in. I've nursed him day and night—an angel, that's what he calls me."

"A devil's more like it!" barked the dying man, lifting his pasty head from the pillow. "I'm doomed to die in this filthy bed, full of fleas and lumps, while you spend my money on your fancy ribbons and foolish curls."

Ezra took off his tape measure and began the beastly task of taking the dying man's measurements.

"Hush, my dear," said Mrs. Blackhorn, covering her husband's head with a damp cloth. "It's the fever talking, you see. I will love him until the end of time, as you would expect, but once he is gone, I feel it only right that I treat myself to a few of the finer things. Have my lovely hair done and such." She patted her locks as if they were spun gold. "The curls are natural, of course."

I laughed. Rather loudly. Mrs. Blackhorn spun around to glare at me. But her curly locks did not. As such, her delightfully round face vanished behind a pile of tangled ringlets. While the poor creature adjusted her hair, Mother Snagsby pulled me toward the deathbed.

"The young lady has selected a poem that may provide some comfort, Mr. Blackhorn," she said loudly. "It is a service we now offer to all of our customers, free of charge."

Mr. Blackhorn pulled the cloth from his face. The candle

beside his bed cast ghostly shadows upon his skin. He had sunken cheeks. Gray whiskers. But his eyes had a certain spark. "Haven't I suffered enough?"

His wife looked mournfully at him. "It will comfort his sister when I write and tell her that the last words George heard were a few lines of lovely poetry. Go ahead, girl."

"Last words?" spluttered Mr. Blackhorn. "I'm not dead yet, Martha, so you can tell these blasted coffin makers to clear off! I'm feeling better than I have in days."

"You are not!" scolded his wife with some force. "You're dying, George, so stop fighting it." She dabbed at her eyes and her bosom heaved. "I just want my dear husband to be at peace."

Mother Snagsby nodded at me, and I fished the poem from my pocket and began to read:

"As my true love fades away in the dying of the light,

I know his soul will scatter, petals on the wind.

In any life there are seasons and we all must submit

Surrender unto death, petals on the wind."

It was a ghastly poem. So dull and worthy and bleak. It was

monstrous! Which was why I continued with the following:

"Mrs. Blackhorn vows that her love will never die,

But the poor cow hasn't shed a tear, though she really does try."

Mrs. Blackhorn gasped and covered her mouth. Mr. Blackhorn began to chortle and clap his hands. Which was terrifically promising!

I went on:

"Poor Mr. Blackhorn shall find peace beyond his flea-ridden bed,

And his dear wife a new wig, once old Gloomy Guts is dead."

"Stop it this instant!" hissed Mother Snagsby. She turned to Mrs. Blackhorn. "I do apologize for the girl. She has been warned about making up her own verses."

"I thought it was grand," declared Mr. Blackhorn.

His wife had fallen to the bed, shrieking something rather unkind in my direction. Mother Snagsby tried to comfort her, while Ezra ushered me over to a chair in the corner of the room. "Sit here, Ivy," he instructed, "while we finish up."

When Mrs. Blackhorn stopped bleating, she left the room to straighten her wig. A maid came in carrying a pot of tea for the Snagsbys and a glass of warm milk for me. I hate warm milk as a general rule. Revolting stuff. But for some reason Mother Snagsby always *insisted* that I drink it while she and Ezra conducted the last part of each sickbed visit—discussing particulars with regards to the coffin and whatnot.

"Shame on you," scolded Mother Snagsby, handing me the glass. "What you have done is unforgivable. Drink the milk and button your lips."

For once I did as I was told.

"Wake up."

I was shaking. Or rather, a hand had grabbed my shoulder and was rattling it.

"Wake up, I say." It was Mother Snagsby. "Wake up this instant!"

I opened my eyes. Felt a burning in my chest. Looked about, blinking a great deal. Then yawned like an infant and stretched my arms. It took a moment or two to realize where I was: Mr. Blackhorn's dreary bedroom. Except that it was no longer Mr. Blackhorn's room. For he was dead. A sheet covered his lifeless body. His wife was sobbing real tears at his side.

"But I thought . . . Mr. Blackhorn said he was feeling better," I said softly.

"He was mistaken," came Mother Snagsby's reply.

"How long was I asleep?"

"Long enough," said Mother Snagsby, picking up the empty glass from the table beside me. "You are making a habit of this, young lady. Are you not sleeping at night?"

"I sleep like a log, dear," I said, getting to my feet. My head spun furiously, and I sat back down again. I *had* drifted off to sleep several times in the past few months. Right after reading a poem at the bedside of a nearly departed. Which was odd. And another thing. My chest felt terribly warm. I lifted my hand to my heart. But it wasn't my chest that was hot. It was the Clock Diamond. I felt certain there was a perfectly reasonable explanation. I just couldn't think what.

Ezra shuffled over to Mrs. Blackhorn and offered his condolences.

But Mother Snagsby did not. She handed Mrs. Blackhorn the bill of sale. "My men will be along to collect the body within the hour." Her tone with the grieving widow was cool and businesslike.

"Death acts quickly, Mrs. Blackhorn, so I would advise against looking under the shroud. Remember your husband as he was, and Snagsby's Economic Funerals will take care of the rest."

Mrs. Blackhorn nodded her head.

"He's at peace," said Ezra. "That's got to be a comfort."

"I thought it would be," said Mrs. Blackhorn meekly.

Mother Snagsby grabbed her parasol, then motioned to Ezra and to me.

"Let us go," she said, already striding toward the door. "Our work here is done."

2

The Snagsbys disappeared every Sunday morning at nine o'clock sharp. Which was a great relief. It was all on account of Adelaide Snagsby, Ezra's favorite sister. Once a week the Snagsbys would put on their finest clothes and set off for Adelaide's boardinghouse in Bayswater. But I wasn't invited.

For I didn't exist.

Apparently, finding out that her brother had adopted a twelve-year-old maid of dubious origin would upset the narrow-minded nitwit. Therefore, I was kept a secret. Left behind with a list of chores while the Snagsbys went off to shovel cream cake into their pie holes and chat about the weather.

Sometimes I threw a thrilling tantrum. But not today. Mother Snagsby was still cross with me about Mr. Blackhorn's poem. Two days had passed, and she had barely uttered a word in my direction.

"We are running late," muttered Ezra as he shuffled in from the workshop. Ezra made all of the Snagsby's discount coffins in the carriage house out back, though he spent a great deal of time snoozing under the almond tree.

"Mother Snagsby is in the kitchen," I said, moving my dustpan and broom to let him pass.

The Snagsby's home was narrow and tall and terribly fond of dust. The downstairs was devoted to the funeral business—the viewing chamber and consulting room were handsome and elegant. The upstairs was for living—these rooms were faded, worn, and bleak (with the exception of Gretel's room).

Ezra looked toward the kitchen. Scratched at his jowls. "Bacon?"

I nodded my head. "She's on her third plate."

Mother Snagsby had an unnatural fondness for bacon. Ate it by the bucketful. Poor Mrs. Dickens (the housekeeper and cook) was forever sending me to the butcher for another pound.

The old man sighed and sat down in a chair beneath a portrait of his daughter, Gretel. There were paintings of her in every room of the house, including the kitchen—one for every year, from a little girl up until the age of eighteen, when she was sent off to finishing school in Paris. Mother Snagsby had painted each one. She was very gifted with a brush. In the picture above Ezra's bald head, Gretel looked to be about ten or eleven, sitting atop a horse and looking rather delighted.

"It cannot be good," said Ezra softly, "all that bacon."

"I wouldn't worry, dear," I said, wiping my hands on the

beastly apron Mother Snagsby insisted that I wear. "Back when I worked for the Midwinters, Miss Lucy ate nothing but turnips for a whole winter." I gave Ezra a reassuring smile. "It did her no real harm. Well, apart from her skin turning green. And I seem to recall she lost all feeling in her face. Other than that, fit as a fiddle."

"Get up, Ezra!" snapped Mother Snagsby as she bustled into the narrow hall.

Ezra jumped to his feet—he was frightfully obedient.

Mother Snagsby wiped some bacon grease from her chin and regarded me coolly. "Why are you sitting there, young lady? The hall will not dust itself."

"I feel I must point out that as your *daughter*, it isn't proper that I should dust and polish and sweep like some sort of pint-sized Cinderella. Not to mention answering the door, fetching endless pots of tea, and cleaning your monstrous bloomers."

"And where would you be if Ezra and I had not taken you in?" Mother Snagsby slipped on a pair of pale green gloves (which matched her pale green dress). "This house is a place of work, and everybody must play their part, even *daughters*."

It was hard to say exactly how old Mother Snagsby was. She

had a most interesting face. Lumpy skin covered by a thick layer of white powder. Fine lines scrunched around her bright blue eyes and tiny mouth. Black hair with a streak of white at the temple. And a stupendous mole sitting above her upper lip like a Christmas pudding.

"But there must be more to life, dear," I said, picking up the dustpan. "Why can we never have company over? Haven't you any friends?" I gasped with great commitment. "I know! We could throw an enchanting afternoon tea and invite some girls my own age. Just think how nice it would be to have people in the house who haven't come to view a dead body."

"Out of the question," came Mother Snagsby's stiff reply. "But as you are keen for company, young lady, once you have finished your chores, you may go to the library and select a few *suitably* somber poems—no more making things up. It's unseemly."

Ezra put on his cap and opened the front door. "Be sure to walk the main roads, Ivy," he instructed, same as always. "No shortcuts, you hear?"

"Yes, dear," I said with a sigh.

Then the Snagsbys passed out into the morning sun and were gone.

The long trek from Paddington to the library always went by in a blur. It was my thinking time. And I had a great deal on my mind. Secrets aplenty. The Snagsbys hadn't a clue about my adventures in Paris, or the journey to England with Miss Always, or the events of Butterfield Park. Mother Snagsby disapproved of the way I dusted, so I could not imagine how she might receive the news that I was dead. Or *half* dead.

And then there was the Clock Diamond. That cursed and magical stone that should have killed me when I had first worn it, all those months ago. For that is its great power. It steals souls, leaving behind the withered husk of the innocent fools who put the necklace on. Just as it did with poor Rebecca.

The necklace also offered visions of the past, present or future. But ever since I had arrived at the Snagsbys' front door, it had been something of a disappointment. Not a single vision. Nothing . . . *until* I woke up in Mr. Blackhorn's bedroom chamber and the stone felt warm against my skin.

It had occurred to me that the diamond might have something to show me. So I had hurried up to my bedroom the moment we got home, and peered into the stone. Was I about to be shown a glimpse of my tragic past? Or my glorious future? Perhaps it would be a tantalizing clue about why the Clock Diamond hadn't killed me as it did everyone else who wore it. But no. All I saw was the present—the afternoon sun setting over London. It was a cruel blow.

But I let those worries fall away as I passed through the imposing doors and entered the cool of the London library. It was a hive of bookish activity. People reading with tremendous relish. Others carrying bundles of books, speaking in whispers. I scanned the room. I did this everywhere I went. What on earth was I looking for? Certainly not Miss Frost. I didn't expect her to appear and whisk me away on some thrilling adventure. At the train station in Suffolk, she had promised that although I would not see her, she would be around. But I had my doubts.

Even the dangerously bonkers Miss Always had vanished. Hadn't set eyes on that mad cow since she jumped off the roof at Butterfield Park. If she really believed I was the Dual—the great hero who would heal the plague killing her people—then why hadn't she appeared? Or tried to grab me and drag me into her world? Perhaps Miss Frost had been right about London being the one place on earth Miss Always would not think to look for me.

"You are in the wrong place, Ivy."

I smiled. "Am I?"

Miss Carnage motioned to the sign in front of me—MYSTICISM AND THE OCCULT. "The poetry section is upstairs." She poked me playfully in the arm. "You of *all* people should know that."

I had only known Miss Carnage for a few weeks, but she was everything that one could hope for in a librarian. Poorly dressed. Frightfully thick spectacles. Graying hair pulled back in a no-nonsense bun. Hooked nose. Enormous chin. Teeth that looked big enough to carve an inscription on. She was plump and walked rather like a duck, taking short, waddling steps.

"You are right," I said. "My mind was elsewhere."

"It worries me that you spend so much time looking at morbid poetry," said Miss Carnage with great certainty. "It isn't my place to say, but I do not think it healthy for a young girl to be reading poems to the dying. Not healthy at all."

I sighed and nodded. "It's not nearly as much fun as you might think."

Miss Carnage peered down the narrow corridor of books. "And I do not think it was an absent mind that brought you to *this* section of the library. Mysticism and the occult must hold a certain fascination for you, Ivy, given the nature of your parents' work."

I shrugged. "Not really, dear."

"The books here concern dark matters indeed," said Miss Carnage, completely ignoring what I had just said. "Things you would not have any experience of—such as communing with the spirit realm, cursed objects, ghostly visitations."

"No experience?" I huffed. "Miss Carnage, I've had more ghostly visitations than you've had lonely evenings by the fire."

"Heavens." Miss Carnage pushed the spectacles up her bent nose. "You have seen ghosts? *Real* ghosts?"

"Dozens," I told her. "Vengeful ones. Sad ones. Lost ones."

"How fascinating!" Miss Carnage pulled me down the aisle, scanning the endless spines as we went. "In that case, there are a few books here that will interest you greatly. Of course, some books are so revolutionary they are frowned upon." She looked up and down the aisle as if she was expecting a train. "I believe that the library has a few such books hidden away, though they are long forgotten, concerning ghostly matters, worlds within worlds . . . that kind of thing."

Miss Carnage stared at me expectantly.

"Honestly, dear, I'm not at all—"

"Here!" she declared, pulling out five tomes with lightning speed. "If ghosts are troubling you, then the only answer is to arm yourself with the tools to get rid of them." Miss Carnage piled the books into my arms with great enthusiasm. "This top book is most interesting—*The Great Ghosts of Scotland and Wales,* by Miss Geraldine Always."

"She's beastly," I heard myself say.

"You know the author?"

I nodded. "The truth is, I thought we were friends, *bosom* friends, but I was horribly mistaken. Has that ever happened to you, dear?"

Silence.

I looked up. Miss Carnage was nowhere to be seen.

Just at that moment, I heard the floorboards creak behind me. I spun around, expecting to see the tenderhearted librarian. But the aisle was deserted. Which was rather odd. Perhaps it was because I had been thinking of Miss Always, or perhaps it was being alone in that vast, dim corridor. Whatever the reason, I began moving swiftly out of there.

A shameful thrill of relief surged though me as I reached the end of the aisle. My eyes were fixed on the welcome buzz of the crowded reading tables. Which is why I didn't see the foot shoot out. Tripping me up at the ankles. I tumbled to the floor. The books scattered all around me in a thunderous symphony that shattered the quiet.

As I climbed to my knees, I spotted a pair of black boots and the hem of a fine lilac skirt.

"Honestly, dear," I said, hastily collecting the books from the floor, "you really should watch where you are going. If I wasn't the beloved daughter of a pair of violently upstanding coffin makers, I might slap you about the head with a book on vengeful ghosts."

With tremendous dignity I got to my feet and looked my attacker in the face. There wasn't time to control the gasp that flew from my mouth.

Matilda Butterfield was smiling at me, but her pretty eyes glistened darkly. "Hello, Pocket."

3

I placed the books on a long reading table swarming with poorly groomed history professors and stared at Matilda in bewilderment. I'm certain I looked gorgeously gob-smacked. "What on earth are you doing here?"

The girl scowled at me from beneath her fringe of dark hair. "Not that it's any of your business, but Mother and I are in London to escape Butterfield Park—we simply couldn't stand it a moment longer."

I nodded as the sadness bubbled up inside of me. "You miss Rebecca."

"Rebecca?" Matilda frowned. Then sighed. "Oh, *that*. Yes, it's all terribly sad, but people die every day and there's no shame in it. What's really made life unbearable is my birthday ball, and we *both* know whose fault that is, don't we, Pocket?"

"You mustn't blame yourself, dear," I said.

"Myself?" spat Matilda, stomping her foot (which attracted a great many disapproving looks from the history professors). "It's you, Pocket! I should wring your neck! What sort of idiot falls from a chandelier into a birthday cake? Now the entire county is laughing behind my back."

"I admit that I may have caused a *slight* disruption, but that is what made your party so special. For it now has something money cannot buy—infamy."

The girl's gaze narrowed. "I'm listening."

"Well, it's really very simple. Your birthday will be talked about for decades to come. I'm almost certain it won't be the last party to have a heartbreakingly pretty girl falling from a great height into the birthday cake, but it will always be the *first*, and that makes it terribly unique."

Matilda's eyes began to dance. "I see them whispering when I go into the village. Yes, they stare and gossip, because *my* birthday ball was the most exciting thing that has ever happened in their dreary little lives."

I shook my head. "I'm almost certain they stare and gossip because you're hideously unpleasant. But they won't soon forget your birthday, and surely that is all that matters?"

The history professors were now openly pointing at us and muttering to one another. Talking was frowned upon in the reading room. And as the library was my one refuge from funerals and deathbeds, I grabbed Matilda by the arm and made a hasty retreat.

The midday sun shimmered over the grand building's stonework, causing the ground to sparkle like gemstones as we walked down the main stairs. Matilda was grumbling about having to meet her mother at a nearby hotel for lunch.

"Is Lady Elizabeth with you?" I asked.

Matilda stopped at the bottom of the stairs. "Grandmother said she did not feel well enough to travel . . . but I do not believe her."

This provided me with an opportunity to ask a question that

had been troubling me a great deal. "How is she?"

"Broken," came the faint reply. Then the sharp edges returned to her voice. "Butterfield Park is closed to visitors, and Grandmother won't see anyone apart from her doctor. Mother says she is just sad, but I think she's selfish. My cousin is gone, and she isn't coming back. Must we all wear black and bow our heads forever?"

"You do miss Rebecca . . . don't you?"

Matilda looked over the parklands beyond us. "Do you still have it?"

"Have what?"

"The necklace."

"Oh. I have it somewhere or other."

"Mother thinks the stone killed Rebecca, but what do you think, Pocket?"

A peal of laughter flew from me. (I hoped it was convincing.) "Whoever heard of a diamond killing someone?"

"Why don't you sell it, then?" said Matilda, looking scornfully at my dreary apron and hobnail boots. "If you bought some new clothes and fixed yourself up, someone might actually *want* you in their family."

I shrugged. "I already have one of those."

"You do?"

"Oh, yes. Lovely couple. Successful in business. Pretty house. They shower me with so much love and affection I'm practically gasping for air. I even have an older sister. Gretel's in Paris right now, at finishing school, and I expect Mother Snagsby will send me there too when I come of age."

A sly smile creased her ruby lips. "Things turned out rather well for you, didn't they?"

"Splendidly well, dear. Couldn't be happier."

Then Matilda walked away. Without so much as a good-bye.

"Perhaps we could meet for tea?" I called after her. "Or a walk around Hyde Park? I'm frightfully busy, of course, but I just happen to have the next seven or eight weeks free!"

Matilda didn't even turn around. "I don't think so, Pocket," I heard her say.

The walk home was rather bleak. On most days, Rebecca was never far from my thoughts—but now, after seeing Matilda, it *all* came back in hideous detail. Her death had been so beastly. All she had ever wanted was to see her mother again. That was why she had put on the Clock Diamond. But Miss Frost had made it clear that Rebecca's soul had been spirited away to her world, and that even in death, there would be no reunion between mother and daughter. Knowing that I had brought that cursed necklace to Butterfield Park was a knot in my stomach that would never untangle.

I was feeling so sorry for myself that I nearly walked straight past the old woman crying up a storm in the middle of the footpath. She had white hair beneath a lace cap. A bruise on her temple. Milky eyes. And she was rather dead.

The frazzled creature shrieked when I asked her what was the matter.

"You can hear me?" she cried. "But I've talked to Mrs. Denton next door and Miss Wilcox at the grocer, and they looked right through me! But *you* . . . you can see me." She threw her arms toward the sky. "Thank the stars! I thought I was dead!"

"You are. Dead as a fence post."

She gasped. Looked rather unconvinced. "How can you be sure?"

I looked down at the ground and pointed to her feet. "You're floating, dear."

The ghost looked down and saw that she was indeed hovering just above the cobblestones. "Well, I never," she muttered. "The last thing I remember is stepping up on a chair to reach the pickled herring on the top shelf. Ohh, I do love a pickled herring."

"I'm almost certain you fell off the chair, bumped your head, and promptly died."

The ghost gasped again. Spun around. Stopped. Looked rather crestfallen. Pointed to the sky. "I always imagined that when it was my time, I'd go up there."

"I'm no expert, but it seems to take longer for some spirits than for others. Eventually you will see a light of some kind. It will be gloriously warm and inviting. Go to it, and I think you will find what you are looking for. Until then, why not visit the theater?"

She seemed rather thrilled by the idea and hurried off, leaving a puff of starlight in her wake. I went on my way again, the street crowded with peddlers and vendors haggling with customers over the price of apples and bread and flowers. I checked my watch—the Snagsbys were soon to be home from visiting Ezra's sister, and I hadn't finished any of my chores. So I decided that a shortcut was in order.

I stepped off the footpath to start across the street, just as a carriage came charging down the road toward me. I halted. Stepped back. As I waited for it to pass, my gaze traveled to the other side of the road. Which is when I saw her. A woman staring back at me. Her glare was of the ravenous kind. Her fierce eyes fixed on mine. The carriage tore past me in a blur, blowing a violent gust of wind in my face. I blinked. Then desperately searched the footpath opposite.

But Miss Always had vanished without a trace.

My bedroom door was locked at night. From the outside. This was done for my protection. Apparently Paddington was teeming with criminals—robbers, kidnappers, assassins. All very unpleasant and dangerous for a newly adopted daughter. So I was locked in. Mother Snagsby kept the key around her neck. A second key was kept by Mrs. Dickens (the housekeeper), in a bunch that dangled from a hoop attached to her belt.

That evening I had been sent to my room without supper. Punishment for not completing my chores. I wasn't bothered. My mind was a tempest of worry. Miss Always. I had seen Miss Always across the street. How on earth had she found me? Did she know where I lived? Was she coming?

I heard a key turn in the lock. The door opened, and Mrs. Dickens came in carrying a tray. On it were four potatoes, half a pumpkin, and a slice of chocolate cake. God bless Mrs. Dickens! She had worked for the Snagsbys since the beginning of time and was suitably plump. Face like a walrus. Drank like a fish. But beneath her chubby cheeks and purple nose beat a heart of gold.

"I expect you're hungry, lass," she said, putting down the tray. She looked around the room and shook her head. "I might ask Mrs. Snagsby if we could put up some pretty curtains or a bright cover for your bed. A girl your age needs a little color."

My bedroom was at the back of the house on the third floor. Just a small bed, a chair, a chest of drawers, and a plain side table with the battered silver clock I had taken from Rebecca's bedroom atop it. Exactly what you would expect for a treasured new daughter. It was *true* that there was a very pretty bedroom on the second floor, right next to the Snagsbys'. It had bright red wallpaper, a marble fireplace, a glorious brass bed, and its very own dressing room. But that room belonged to Gretel. And no one was allowed inside.

"A touch of color might be nice," I said.

"Of course Mrs. Snagsby might not agree," said Mrs. Dickens, running her apron over the top of the dresser, "though I can't see how she could object, as this room hasn't had a lick of paint since Miss—"

The housekeeper stopped suddenly. Cleared her throat.

"Since Miss *what*, dear?" I said.

"Well . . . your parents let out this room a long time ago," said Mrs. Dickens rather quickly, "and the last lodger who stayed here was Miss . . . Miss Lucas."

"Did she have red hair?"

Mrs. Dickens turned around. "How did you know that, lass?"

"Found her hairbrush in the drawer along with a pair of black gloves." I sighed with just the right amount of melancholy. "Mrs. Dickens, I knew a woman with the most ghastly red hair. She was grim and sour faced, and I disliked her very much. At least, I *thought* I did."

"You best eat your supper and get to sleep," said the housekeeper. "And mind you don't let your mother know I sneaked in this food, you hear?"

But I didn't reply right away. For there was a sudden heat radiating against my chest like a splash of midday sun. I hurried Mrs. Dickens from the room. Promised her I would eat my supper and get a good night's rest. I could hear the door being locked as I raced back to the bed and fished the Clock Diamond out from under my nightdress.

A thrill rippled through my body as I stared deep into the heart of the stone. At first all that I saw were the stars in the moonless sky above London. But I waited. I knew, absolutely *knew*, that something was coming. Perhaps it would offer a vision about Miss Always. A clue of some sort.

The diamond throbbed in my hand. Heat pulsed from it

like a furnace. Then a white mist churned in the heart of the stone, swallowing the night sky. In its place, a forest of dark trees appeared. A frost-covered ground. The mist blew with a fury and the trees began to bleed white, seeping up from the roots to the ends of the bare branches. In moments the whole forest was a ghostly white woodland.

Something streaked between the trees. A girl. She wore a lavender dress. Blond hair fanned out behind her. I recognized her instantly. Which is why I cried, "Rebecca!"

It was her. Unmistakably her. Was this some fragment of her past? She was running. Twisting through the pale trees. Stealing looks behind her. *Terrified* looks. Then the trees began to move. No, not trees. Locks—those hooded henchmen in dark cloaks who worked for Miss Always. They moved as one. Dozens of them, spreading out through the forest.

The girl stumbled. Fell. I saw her flinch with pain. She got to her feet and took off again.

In a flash, her face filled the stone. Just for a second. Cheeks flushed. Brow knotted anxiously. Eyes crackling with fear. And then it hit me. Rebecca was wearing the same lavender dress she had worn to Matilda's birthday ball. Her *new* dress. Which could only mean one thing—Rebecca was alive! Somehow. Some way. She was alive. And something more. Something monstrous. Rebecca Butterfield was being hunted.

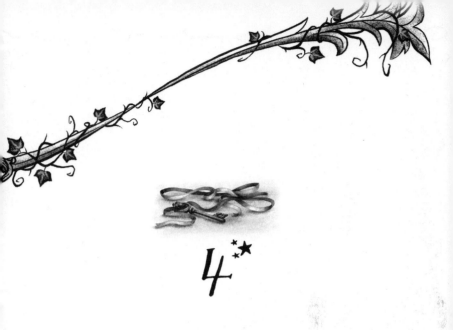

4

Mother Snagsby eyed me with considerable suspicion. "You do not look sick to me."

"That's only because I have a naturally radiant complexion," I said, holding my stomach for good measure. "But I assure you, Mother Snagsby, I am as sick as a dog. Or at the very least, a badly neglected house cat."

"I suppose we should call for the doctor," said Ezra from the doorway.

"There is no need for that," said Mother Snagsby, circling the bed like a lion eyeing its supper. "Ivy can come with us to

Mrs. Quilp's. If she is *truly* unwell, the fresh air will do her a world of good."

This discussion had been going on all morning. When Mrs. Dickens came to unlock my door, she found me still in bed, looking gloriously feverish. The plan only came unstuck when Mother Snagsby marched into the room and declared me perfectly healthy.

"But *why* must I go?"

Mrs. Quilp had infected lungs and was expected to die any day now. And for reasons that I could not understand, the Snagsbys seemed determined to drag me to every deathbed in London. And while I wasn't *exactly* unwell, I was certainly sick with worry about poor Rebecca.

"The dying and their loved ones find it a comfort to have a child recite a suitably meaningful poem as the hour of death approaches," said Mother Snagsby sharply.

"You've been awful good for business, Ivy," said Ezra, scratching at his flappy jowls. "Since you've joined us, profits has shot up fifteen per cent."

Which was delightful. What daughter doesn't want to hear that she's been good for business?

"I'm sorry, but I cannot come."

Mother Snagsby glared down at me, her splendid mole twitching above her lip. "Is this the sort of daughter you wish to be? Rude and defiant?"

"Only in a pinch, dear."

Mother Snagsby turned her back on me and let out an exasperated sigh. Clearly this poetry-reading nonsense meant a great deal to the Snagsbys and their business. Therefore, I felt it was my solemn duty as a treasured daughter to take full advantage.

"Death is wearing me down," I said with a sigh. "I have it on good authority that it's hideously traumatic and unhealthy for a girl of my age to be reading poems to the dying—and my source is a librarian, so we cannot doubt her credentials."

Mother Snagsby turned back and lifted her head regally, the streak of white through her black hair giving her all the charm of a skunk. "Is that so?"

"Yes, dear, I think it is. Now it seems to me that I could simply refuse to attend another deathbed. I might make a great deal of fuss. Embarrass you in front of the customers. Unless . . ."

The old crow's mouth curled into a sneer. "Unless?"

"Well, that's not for me to say, now is it? Of course, you *might* like to consider letting me rest today and regain my strength."

"Rest, you say?" said Mother Snagsby.

"That's right. And it may be that you decide to let me have some company at the house. Nothing fancy. Just a few girls my age. I'm practically positive that these *small* concessions would be enough to lift my spirits and get me back to work."

Mother Snagsby made no rely. Her craggy face was set in stone.

"The Roaches," she said at last.

I frowned. "The Roaches?"

"We have buried several of their kin," said Mother Snagsby frostily. "They are respectable folk and always pay on time. It is possible I could extend an invitation to Mrs. Roach and her two daughters to come for tea."

The urge to squeal with delight was awfully strong. But I resisted. It didn't seem right, in light of Rebecca. Instead I nodded my head and said, "That sounds lovely."

"But I expect much in return," said Mother Snagsby. "You

are to come with us to every appointment without complaint after today. And you are to perform your household duties without complaint. While Ezra and I are seeing to Mrs. Quilp, you can *recuperate* by dusting the viewing parlor from top to bottom."

"Surely my time would be better spent lazing about eating crumpets?" I said hopefully. "Or perhaps you might wish to paint me as you have Gretel?"

Mother Snagsby grabbed the cleaning rag out of Mrs. Dickens's hand and pushed it into mine. "Dust," she barked.

"Where on earth are you going, lass?"

"Important business, dear," I said, opening the front door. "Frightfully important."

The housekeeper looked positively alarmed. "But you promised Mrs. Snagsby you would clean the viewing parlor."

"Fear not, Mrs. Dickens," I said. "They will be at poor Mrs. Quilp's all morning, and I will be back in plenty of time to do my chores." I pointed to the portrait above her head. "Did Gretel have many chores to do around the house? Before she went to Paris, I mean."

It was as if a cloud passed overhead. The housekeeper looked grave, then she jumped up as if she had felt a sudden urge to polish the brass door knocker. "Miss Gretel was always so busy with this and that." She pointed to the street outside, and I suddenly became aware of the sounds of carriage wheels and chatter. "You best be getting along, lass."

I stepped outside as the sky began to rumble. "We should go on strike, Mrs. Dickens. Let Mother Snagsby discover the delights of cooking and cleaning for herself."

"You might be shocked to know that your mother was once a keen cook—at least I *think* she was."

"Mother Snagsby a cook? Surely not."

Mrs. Dickens nodded. "She has a book of family recipes, carries it with her everywhere she goes—guards it like the pharaoh's gold, she does."

"Whatever for?"

"I expect the recipes mean a great deal to her."

"But how do they *taste*—surely that is the question?"

"Well, that's the queer part," said Mrs. Dickens, her voice dropping to a conspiratorial whisper. "In all the time I've worked here, Mrs. Snagsby's never cooked a single recipe from that book."

I was befuddled. And felt it frightfully unfair of Mrs. Dickens to burden me with suspense.

"Well, why does she carry it around with her, you great lump?"

Mrs. Dickens chuckled. "That's a very interesting question."

Then the housekeeper hurried me along, muttering something about the feathers of a chicken not plucking themselves.

As I set off down Thackeray Street, any thoughts about Mother Snagsby's curious book of recipes fell away. I quickened my step, my mind swirling around a single image—Rebecca being chased through those ghastly white woodlands by a pack of vicious locks.

The rules of the Clock Diamond were very clear. The stone offers visions of what was, what is, and what will be. It was clear from Rebecca's lavender dress that the vision had taken place on the night of the ball. And I was certain that Rebecca had not been chased through any such forest *before* she had worn the necklace and perished.

Which only left one possibility. The stone was showing me a glimpse of Rebecca after she put on the stone. Therefore, that haunting forest must be a place in Miss Frost's world. But hadn't she told me that only Rebecca's soul passed into her world? And that she was dead? Gone? Hadn't I seen her wither to a husk before my eyes? Yet Rebecca had looked very much alive in the vision.

Miss Frost had lied. And if that was true, what else had she kept from me? But no, I would not think of that tomato-headed scoundrel for the moment. Rebecca was all that mattered. Finding a way to help her. To reach her.

So lost was I in my thoughts that I ran straight into a lanky fellow walking the other way. We collided in glorious fashion. I reeled back. He staggered sideways, the sandwich in his hand dropping to the ground.

"Watch where you're going!" he snapped.

"I haven't the time," I told him quite reasonably. "Much too busy trying to save the day." I shrugged. "Besides, I think we can both agree the fault lies with you."

"With *me*? You just about knocked me over." The young

man pointed at his sandwich in a most judgmental fashion. "I've lost my lunch thanks to you!"

Which was a scandalous accusation. I was on the very brink of telling the unpleasant gentleman to prepare for a firm thrashing when my eyes were drawn to the small hooded figure zipping along the crowded footpath behind him. The figure was remarkably short and wore a brown cloak. My blood seemed to stir from its slumber, rapidly picking up speed and tearing through my veins. It was a lock!

Which is why I set off in pursuit.

"Hey, come back here!" the young man hollered behind me. "You owe me two shillings!"

The little monster was a good twenty feet away from me now. He had passed under the shade of the shop awnings, which formed a dim tunnel stretching almost to the end of the street. The villain was zigzagging between the other pedestrians with great skill, and owing to his size, he vanished from view on several occasions.

The path was swarming with people, and I feared that he would disappear completely before I could catch him. But catch him I must. The locks worked for Miss Always—and they were sure to know where Rebecca was being held. I would do whatever it took to get the truth out of that murderous little scoundrel!

Drastic action was required.

I darted off the footpath and onto the road—an empty apple cart in my sights. With audacity that would make a five-star general weep, I jumped up onto the cart. Leaped onto the wheel. Pushed off and flew toward the shop awning above my head. Clutching the edge of the awning with my left hand, I hoisted myself up. Got to my feet and started running.

As it turns out, navigating a series of shop awnings is a rather difficult business. They hang from above the shop fronts at a sharp angle, which makes dashing across them most challenging. But I was equal to the task.

I quickly found my footing and was soon bolting along. The thick canvas had a certain spring and I was able to leap from the Atlantic Shoes Company to Provincial Home Investments, then across to Harding Progressive Tailors. As I jumped onto the last awning (a cigar manufacturer), I prayed that I had been fast enough to overtake the diabolical lock traveling beneath me.

Being partly dead has supreme advantages in a situation such as this—falling and breaking my neck wasn't a concern. So I dropped to the canvas, gripped the edge of the awning, and flipped over. I arched through the air like a trapeze artist with a death wish and hurtled toward the footpath. My landing was terribly graceful. Well, apart from a slight tumble to the ground. A small amount of searing pain in my hip. And some rather salty language.

When I got to my feet, the bustling shoppers seemed to have stopped in their tracks. Some of them gasped in my direction— ogling me like there was something unusual about a girl leaping from a shop awning. Others pointed rudely and whispered. I scanned the crowd. No sign of the lock. Had he been faster than me? Had he gotten away? I refused to believe it.

Perhaps he had darted into one of the shops and was hiding there. Yes. I would search each one until—

My eyes suddenly flew back toward a woman in a red-and-black dress. But she wasn't my target. What had caught my attention was the flutter of a brown cloak behind her.

I pushed my way through the crowd. Shoved the woman in the red-and-black dress aside (she gave a startled cry and fell against an old man clutching a loaf of bread). And gazed hungrily into the void where she had been standing. There it was. Tiny. Long brown cloak. Face concealed by the shadow of that odious hood.

A lock.

If I felt fear, it was no match for my wrath, which was the cold glint in my eyes and the furious hammer of my heartbeat. The lock moved toward me. Which is why I grabbed the loaf of bread from the old man and swung it—bashing the little devil in the side of its head. The hideous hooded henchman stumbled sideways and yelped. Cries flew out from the bystanders.

"She hit him, she did!"

"Horrid girl!"

"Someone fetch the constable!"

"Tell me where Rebecca is!" I rushed toward the lock. "Why were you chasing her through the woods? Where are you keeping her? Answer me, you pint-sized jackal!"

"Leave him be!" shouted the old man (though I'm certain he was just grumpy because his battered bread loaf was lying on the pavement).

"I won't!" I shouted back. Those ninnies would thank me when I unmasked this monstrous little rogue. The creature swiftly found its feet and prepared to take off. I lunged without mercy. Grabbed his hood and threw it back in magnificently dramatic fashion.

"See for yourselves!" I cried, eyeballing the crowd. They would scream in horror when they saw the monster I had unmasked!

Except that they didn't. They just stared daggers at me. Shook their heads and tut-tutted like I was the nastiest girl who ever lived. Why were they not running for their lives?

I turned to look at my captive. What I saw was a rather well-dressed dwarf. He had a thatch of wavy blond hair. A thick mustache. Dimpled chin. And he looked extremely cross with me.

"What's the meaning of this?" he thundered in a wondrously thick accent (German, I think). "I have traded coffee in some of the deadliest corners of the world, and *never* have I been attacked in the street like this!"

"Awfully sorry, dear," I said quickly. "I thought you were a violent henchman from another world. But it turns out you're just a very short coffee merchant with a fondness for hooded cloaks." I tried to pat him on the head, but he slapped my hand away most unkindly. "No harm done, then?"

He sneered at me (probably his way of expressing complete forgiveness), while the angry mob looked as if they wanted to tie me to a tree and throw rotten vegetables. It was time to make a hasty retreat. I apologized to the furious fellow again (I may even have curtsied), then took off down the street, hoping they would not give chase.

There was some agitated shouting in my wake—the old man demanded I buy him a new loaf of bread. The dwarf wanted my name and address. A rather shrill woman suggested I fall in a hole. But their voices dulled as I took a sharp left, vanishing into the back streets.

I had destroyed a loaf of bread, a sandwich, and very nearly an international coffee merchant. Not exactly a successful morning. As I slowed, trying to catch my breath, the fear and excitement of my slightly violent frolic gave way to disappointment. I had hoped that capturing one of Miss Always's locks might lead to Rebecca. But it was not to be.

I crossed the pavilion and mounted the library steps two at a time, Rebecca's terrified face burned into my mind. I had to reach her. Had to find a way to save her. Most recently adopted daughters wouldn't have a clue what to do about such a problem. But I certainly did. It was help that I needed, and I knew just where to get it.

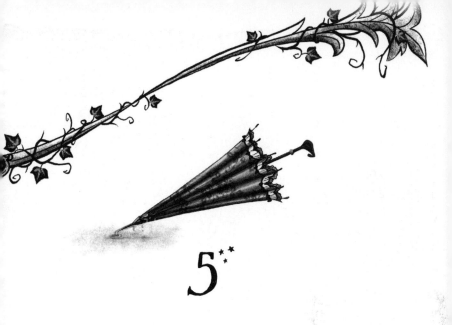

5

"Vanished?"

I nodded. "One minute you were talking to me about ghosts, and the next you were gone. What on earth happened?"

Miss Carnage pushed her spectacles up her gigantic nose. "It's really very simple, Ivy. There was an emergency in the reading room that required my immediate attention."

"What sort of emergency?"

The pudgy librarian waddled out from behind the borrowing desk and walked with me toward the library's large windows. Clouds hung low in the sky outside, shrouding the vast room in a gloomy half-light. "Well, Ivy, there was an altercation between two elderly women over a copy of *Wuthering Heights*."

"Did it get violent?" I asked hopefully.

"It might have, if I had not gotten there in time."

Which was frightfully disappointing.

"I am delighted to see you again so soon after your last visit," said Miss Carnage, "though I couldn't help but notice you left the books I selected for you behind. Were they of no interest?"

"None at all, dear," I said tenderly. "I know all I need to know about ghosts. I am here on another matter."

Behind Miss Carnage's thick spectacles, her dark eyes seemed to swell. "Oh?"

"I have a friend who needs my help. It's terribly complicated—you see, my friend is in a place that is rather hard to find, and I fear that if I do not reach her, she will meet a most unpleasant end."

"Your friend is in danger?"

"Frightfully so."

Miss Carnage had the good sense to gasp. "Is it life and death, Ivy?"

I nodded. "The situation is *most* unfair, as my friend has already died once."

The librarian's mouth dropped like a trapdoor. "That sounds terribly . . . unusual . . . and very dangerous. Would you like me to come with you to report the matter to the constabulary?"

"My friend is not in England, dear," I said carefully. "In fact, she is somewhere far, *far* away."

Miss Carnage clutched her throat. "You don't mean . . . ?"

"Yes, dear, I think I do." I stepped closer to Miss Carnage, signaling the importance of my next declaration. "Last time I was here, you mentioned certain books that the library keeps hidden away. Books that deal with ghostly matters and worlds within worlds. Isn't that what you said?"

Miss Carnage paled wonderfully. Nodded her head.

"You see, I know where my friend is—at least, I *think* I do. But I have no idea how to get there, having little experience in such matters. Miss Carnage, you are my first and last hope."

"Heavens." She tapped her pointed chin. "This is terribly unexpected, Ivy, what . . . what would you like me to do?"

"Show me the books you spoke of."

"Book," said Miss Carnage firmly. "On the matters that concern you, there is only *one* book."

She looked about, then took me by the hand and led me to a far corner of the library, rarely visited by anyone—AUSTRALIAN

LITERATURE. "I haven't seen it myself, but I have heard rumors," she explained in hushed tones. "The manuscript is the work of Ambrose Crabtree, a rather eccentric scholar who devoted his life to the study of mysticism and faraway places. He donated his research to the library, all contained in a single book called *Lifting the Veil*. The powers that be felt it was the dangerous ravings of a madman and ordered it locked away in a vault deep under the library."

"How thrilling," I said.

"As I explained earlier, it belongs to a small number of works considered too radical to be on public display. Some people fear what they cannot understand." Her eyes seemed to bore into my own. They were filled with unbridled admiration. "But not you, Ivy."

"No, dear, not me. Nerves of steel. Courage of a hangman." Then a perfectly sensible thought occurred to me (I am prone to such notions). "If this book is so dangerous, why did they not destroy it?"

The librarian's eyebrows lifted. "Perhaps they thought it was *too* dangerous to destroy?"

Which made perfect sense!

"I cannot pretend that I fully understand what has happened to your friend or where she is," said Miss Carnage. "But I feel that if there is any book in the world that might be of assistance, it is *Lifting the Veil.*"

"I quite agree," I said. "Now be a dear and fetch it for me."

Miss Carnage shook her head. "Impossible. Ivy, I hope you did not think that I told you about this mystical manuscript—which would perfectly suit your particular needs—with the intention of *giving* you the book."

"Actually, dear, that is exactly what I thought."

"Mr. Crabtree's book is *much* too dangerous for you to be experimenting with. No, it is quite impossible."

I sighed. "That's violently disappointing, but I suppose I understand. I will just have to find another way."

"As I said, Ivy," said Miss Carnage hastily, "I couldn't possibly help you. The manuscript is hidden away in a vault, under the library. To get there, you would have to sneak through the back office, go down the stairs, and walk all the way to the far end. The safe is concealed beneath an old printing press so as to avoid detection."

Miss Carnage threaded her arm through mine, and we headed back the way we had come.

"Even if someone managed to find it," she went on, "they would not be able to open it without the key." Then she pointed casually at the borrowing desk and the office behind it, visible through a glass partition. "And even though it is kept in the bottom drawer of Mr. Ledger's desk, he is always about—except for Monday mornings, when he takes his mother to the teahouse across the park." She looked very solemn all of a sudden. "I was foolish to even mention the book. Please forget I ever told you anything about it."

I smiled at the deluded nincompoop. "Already forgotten."

After a morning of disgruntled rumblings, the bruised clouds finally reached breaking point during my walk home from the library. A rather heavy shower began to fall just as I turned into Thackeray Street. It was past noon—no doubt the Snagsbys had returned from Mrs. Quilp's and were furious with me—but for the first time since last night, my heart was light. For I had hope. And it was all thanks to Miss Carnage.

As she had prattled on, listing the reasons why Ambrose Crabtree's book was beyond my reach, Miss Carnage had no idea that I was listening with terrific intensity. Picking up clues left, right, and center.

I was now in possession of all the information I would need to get my hands on *Lifting the Veil*. Waiting a whole week would be torture, but that manuscript was the best chance I had of finding Rebecca. Stealing it would take some doing, but I was equal to the task—for I have all the natural instincts of a cat burglar.

Quickening my step in a vain attempt to outrun the rain, I crossed the street and noticed for the first time a girl pacing back and forth in front of the Snagsbys' house. She was holding an umbrella above her head and looked very smart in a dress of pale pink with a white feathered hat.

I bypassed a pooping horse tethered to a lamppost and was nearly at the door when the girl stepped in front of my path and called me by name. Which was most unexpected.

"I'm awfully sorry to bother you, Ivy," she said, glancing toward the house, "but I was very much hoping to have a word with you."

"Some other time, dear, I'm running late, and Mother

Snagsby is certain to have discovered that I haven't dusted the viewing parlor."

"Of course, how rude of me," she said, her voice full of music. "It's just that I have been waiting rather a long time to see you and it is most important."

She was terribly pretty—heart-shaped face, rosy cheeks, blue eyes, silky brown hair piled most fetchingly atop her head. Without my noticing, this dazzling stranger had moved her umbrella to shelter us both.

"Then you had better come inside," I said. "We can talk while I dry off."

"If it is all right with you, I would prefer that we talk out here."

I was keen to get out of the rain, yet my generous nature won the day.

"All right then, spit it out."

"My name is Estelle Dumbleby, and I need your assistance." Tears pooled in her eyes, and she began to weep. She looked gloriously sad! "Forgive me, I am rather emotional these days, having recently lost my mother, Lady Dumbleby. I suppose you have heard of her?"

"Wouldn't know her from a boiled cabbage," I said kindly. "Were you after a discount coffin for Lady Dumbleby? We have a special offer this month—two for the price of one."

Estelle looked startled. (No surprise there, the special offer was a wonder!) "I am an orphan now," she said, lips all atremble, "which may seem an odd thing for a young woman of sixteen, but a girl always needs her mother, don't you agree, Ivy?"

I shrugged. "I've done very well without one."

"But were you not recently adopted by the Snagsbys?"

"Oh, yes. Wonderful day. We blubbered from sunrise to sunset."

"When one suffers a great loss, it is very hard to know who to trust." Estelle Dumbleby smiled sadly. "The vultures begin to circle when an heiress comes into her fortune."

"I suppose you're shockingly rich?"

The young woman let out a peal of laughter. "Yes, I suppose I am."

"I know just how you feel. Several months ago I came into a large fortune of five hundred pounds." I didn't think it was necessary to mention that Mother Snagsby had taken the money. For safekeeping and such. "Great wealth is a burden."

Estelle nodded. "My mother was the one person in the world I could depend on, and now . . ."

"Haven't you any other family?"

"A great-uncle," said the heiress solemnly, "though he is very old and frail. I had an older brother too—Sebastian. He vanished when I was just a little girl, but I remember him well."

"How magnificently heartbreaking."

"It's about Sebastian that I wish to speak with you, Ivy. My mother spent the past thirteen years trying to discover his whereabouts, but she was unsuccessful. Upon her death, I gained access to all of her papers—and among them I made a remarkable discovery." She looked at the Snagsbys' front door, and her voice quivered. "In the days before my brother disappeared, he visited this house on several occasions."

"That's very mysterious! Why don't you come inside and ask—"

"I cannot do that," said Estelle, interrupting. "The investigator my mother employed interviewed the Snagsbys, and they denied ever having met my brother. Without proof, the matter was dropped—but I believe there is more to the story."

"You want me to ask the Snagsbys about Sebastian, don't you, dear?"

"I do not." She reached out and grabbed my hand. "I want you to do something far more devious, Ivy. I want you to dig—to dig deeply, look through their papers and records, keep your ears open, and see if you can discover a link between my brother and your parents."

"Why should I help you do such a thing?"

"Because you know what loss is," came the mournful reply. "And I believe that if you were in my shoes and you had the chance to find the one you loved, you would move heaven and earth to make it happen."

My mind flew to Rebecca. She was not family. Yet I desperately wished to reach her.

I found myself nodding. "Let me see what I can find out."

"The Snagsbys must not know what you are up to," said Estelle firmly. "If they were to suspect anything . . . it could be very bad for you." The rain began to fall harder, thundering upon the umbrella above our heads. "Thank you, Ivy. Your help has given me hope. Oh, dear, I must let you go inside."

"How will I reach you?" I said, shamefully eager to keep Estelle a moment longer.

"I will be in touch. Good-bye, Ivy."

Estelle hurried away, and although I was now being pummeled by rain, I stood there and watched her go. Which is when a rather troubling question dropped into my head.

"How do you know so much about me?" I called after her.

But the pretty girl was already too far away, and she seemed not to hear me.

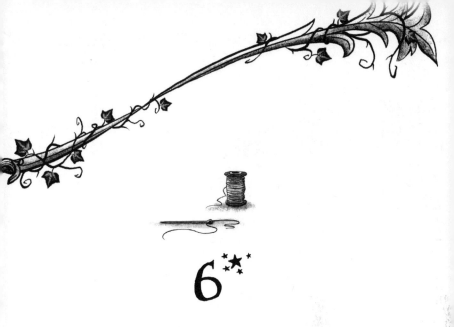

6

Mother Snagsby pulled the curtain shut, settling back in the carriage with a huff. "Foolish driver," she grumbled. "Perhaps he has all day to amble across town, but I do not!" She struck the roof with her parasol. "Hurry, you bumbling slowpoke or we won't reach Mayfair before noon!"

When I first stepped through the front door after my clandestine chat with Estelle Dumbleby, soaked to the bone and terribly late, I had expected the worst. But to my complete shock, Mother Snagsby did not throw anything remotely unpleasant at my head.

In fact, apart from asking why I had ventured out without permission, she seemed to accept my explanation—that I was researching suitably uplifting poetry—without suspicion. Even more shockingly, she had not inspected the viewing parlor to see if it had been dusted.

Her good mood had sprung from the visit to Mrs. Quilp's sickbed. As luck would have it, Mrs. Quilp had dropped dead just minutes before the Snagsbys got there. Better yet, her husband had ordered several high-quality accessories for the coffin.

When I had dried off and changed my clothes, Mother Snagsby announced that tomorrow she was taking me to be fitted for a new dress.

"Mother Snagsby, you must not listen to those who gossip unkindly about you—neighbors, customers, anyone who's ever met you," I said, when we set off for Mayfair the next morning. "Buying me a pretty new dress—which is sure to be of the finest silk, orange in color, with pretty lace trim and a white sash—is the act of a thoroughly generous soul." I patted her arm. "You are living proof that a person can be far more pleasant than they look."

The carriage came to a stop, allowing a flock of schoolgirls and their teacher to cross the street.

"Your new dress will be black—black, plain and somber," declared Mother Snagsby. "We have several important appointments in the coming weeks, and the blue dress simply will not do."

I had a sudden urge to push Mother Snagsby from the carriage. Or at the very least, grab her lumpy nose and twist it viciously. Instead I said, "Very well."

My mind flew to Estelle Dumbleby and her mysterious and sorrowful request. Sneaking about and going through the Snagsbys' papers and records seemed like a great deal of effort. Estelle's story was perfectly tragic—dead mother, missing brother—but a girl only has so many hours in the day. And I had my hands full with poor Rebecca.

Besides, I was frightfully crafty in the art of digging.

"Lady Dumbleby is dead," I said casually. "The whole city is talking about it."

"Who?" said Mother Snagsby.

"Lady Dumbleby," I said again. "She was from a

frightfully important family. I seem to recall reading that there was an older brother. I believe his name was Sebastian. Apparently he vanished in most mysterious circumstance many years ago."

"I don't listen to gossip," came the sharp rebuke, "and neither should you."

Things were going wonderfully!

"You know, dear, if you have any secrets of the deep and unpleasant variety, you can share them with me, your loving daughter. For example, if you *happened* to have met a young man once or twice, who just *happened* to have vanished into thin air— and who hasn't?—well, now would be the perfect time to spill your guts."

"Who have you been speaking with?" Her voice hissed and the lines around her eyes scrunched into a tight map of valleys and peaks. "Listen to me very carefully, young lady—I do not know what became of Sebastian Dumbleby, nor do I care. I will not speak of this matter again, is that perfectly understood?"

"Don't pop a cork, dear. I was merely trying to pass the time."

Mother Snagsby took a deep breath. Parted the curtain again to look briefly at the streets passing by. As she released the air from her lungs, the anger seemed to lift from her stern and rugged face.

"When we return from the dressmakers," she said evenly, "you can accompany Mrs. Dickens to the market. You eat such unreasonable quantities of potatoes and pumpkins, the poor woman cannot carry them all home by herself."

Which was the perfect moment to talk of something far less controversial. "Mrs. Dickens mentioned that you carry around a recipe book—which is wonderfully bonkers. Perhaps you might make something for our dessert tonight?"

"Mrs. Dickens should hold her tongue."

Oh, dear. Had I stumbled upon another forbidden subject?

"I adore family recipes," I said brightly. "The Pockets had a great many, passed down from one generation to the next. Most were destroyed following the tragic alligator pie incident of 1842. Uncle Mortimer did not realize that the beast had to be dead before wrapping it in pastry. We lost seven Pockets that day."

"Do you *ever* talk sense?" snapped Mother Snagsby.

"Only in extreme emergencies, dear. Did it belong to your mother—the recipe book, I mean? Might I have a look at it?"

"I sent a note to Mrs. Roach yesterday afternoon," said Mother Snagsby, choosing to ignore my question, "and her reply came by the morning post. She and her daughters have accepted our invitation, and they will come next Tuesday at three."

I may have whooped with delight. But not for long. I could see the hint of something sad and troubled at play on Mother Snagsby's unsightly face. There was a story behind her book of recipes, I was sure of that. One that might explain a great deal about her sour nature.

And it gave me a rather glorious idea.

Our visit to the dressmakers did not get off to the greatest of starts. The dressmaker, Miss Upton, had a shocking pallor, dull eyes, and rasping breath. Naturally, I assumed she was dead. Urged her to float away and head toward the light.

"What on earth are you talking about?" snapped Mother Snagsby.

She knew nothing of my ability to see ghosts. "I do not want to alarm you, dear," I said, pointing at Miss Upton, "for you cannot see the hideous apparition before me. Skin like a corpse. The stench of death about her. I would say more, but I'm much too refined, having all the natural instincts of a young Snow White."

The dressmaker took offense. Said I was unspeakably rude.

"She's an orphan," explained Mother Snagsby as I was told to step up onto a stool and keep utterly still. "Entirely unwanted and without blood relatives. Mr. Snagsby and I took pity on the child, as she had nowhere else to go."

Miss Upton threw a sheet of black fabric over me. Fortunately there was a hole cut in the top for my head, so I was able to look through the shop window onto the busy street.

"You are a good woman," said the dressmaker as she began sticking pins all around me, "to let a stray child into your home and treat her as your own."

"Indeed," said Mother Snagsby gravely, "we must all do our part, as the girl would be in the poorhouse if not for us."

"You're wrong there, dear," I said. "I would be very welcome in the village where my mother is from. They think the world of us Pockets. Every winter one of the local women carves a statue of the entire family from frozen pig fat. It's erected in the village square, right next to the one of Napoleon."

Miss Upton and Mother Snagsby were gawking at me.

"Foolish girl!" fumed Mother Snagsby.

"Excellent point, dear." Then I looked at my watch and shook my head. "Come, Miss Upton, do hurry along, my legs are starting to—"

But I never finished the sentence. For I had glanced out the window. And as I did, a slim woman dressed in a gray coat passed by. Brown hair. Spectacles. Head high. A brisk, purposeful stride. She appeared to be in a great hurry.

"Where are you going?" bellowed Mother Snagsby when I tore off the black fabric and leaped from the stool. "Come back here this instant, young lady!"

I charged across the shop, threw open the door, and bounded out onto the footpath.

"She's lost her mind!" declared Miss Upton.

Their frightful squawks quickly faded. I was already storming down the street, weaving between the passersby. I had Miss Always in my sights, and this time I would not let her get away.

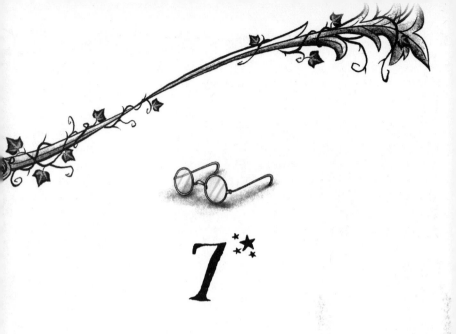

7

"Excuse me, ladies," I said, stepping between two women prattling on about hats. Miss Always had turned left at the end of the street and was no longer in view.

"What's the hurry?" said one of the women.

"Chasing a villain, dear," I called out, not looking back. "All very dangerous."

I broke into a sprint, tearing along the busy footpath. At the corner I stopped. Looked to my left. Miss Always had made great headway—she was already a good thirty feet in front, a grim figure in her long coat. The last time I had chased after someone, it had turned out to be a perfectly innocent dwarf. This time, there was no doubt. It was most definitely Miss Always. I would know that face anywhere.

A large posse of Bible-carrying vicars, talking eagerly, fanned out before me. Zigzagging with breathtaking skill, I was soon upon my target again. Miss Always slowed. Turned her head slightly.

In a flash, I threw myself against the wall. Kept utterly still. Which was no trouble for me, having all the natural instincts of a lamppost. I held my breath. Prayed that Miss Always would not turn fully and see me. She didn't, and quickly took off again.

About halfway along the avenue, Miss Always made a sharp right into a narrow lane. I got there just as she crossed the tiny street and disappeared inside a dull red building. Rather grimy. Windows darkened by soot and neglect. I had two options—follow after the dastardly hag, or wait outside until she emerged again.

Having a mind that would be the envy of a Scotland Yard detective, I swiftly determined that the building probably had a back entrance. And that Miss Always might use it to make an escape. In a display of eye-popping courage, I hurried after her, pushed open the door, and stepped inside the building.

But I did not get far. For I collided with someone rushing out. We bumped shoulders and both gave a startled yelp. The hall was especially dim, and I could barely see in front of my face.

"Heavens," said the woman.

Which is when I pounced, seizing the villain by the arm. She cried out in distress. Tried to pull away. But my grip was viselike.

"The game is up, Miss Always!" I hollered, dragging her through the front door and out onto the street. "What have your hideous hooded henchmen done with Rebecca? Where is she?"

When the sun hit our faces, I was able to look my captive in the eye. And it was rather a shock. For standing before me, in a dull brown dress, looking thoroughly shaken, was Miss Carnage. She was touching her substantial nose a great deal and seemed awfully startled. I let go of her instantly.

"Ivy, what on earth are you doing?" she said, her voice quivering.

"I could ask you the same question," was my reply. I looked past her, through the open door. "Did you pass a woman wearing a gray coat?"

"I saw no one," said Miss Carnage. "Ivy, why did you attack me? What is going on?"

"But you *must* have seen her," I said firmly. "She came into the building not a minute ago."

"Well . . . perhaps she went out through a back door."

I hurried inside again, past a staircase, to the very rear. Sure enough, there was a back door. And it was wide open. When I came back outside, Miss Carnage was still in a most agitated state.

"Well, Ivy," she said, brushing down her dress, "what have you to say for yourself? I'm stunned and shocked by your behavior."

I looked back at the building. Above the front door was a faded sign that read BUZZBY'S STAGE EMPORIUM—FOR ALL YOUR THEATRICAL NEEDS. Something did not feel right.

"Miss Carnage, what business have you in this place? They provide costumes and makeup for the theater, do they not?"

"I would not know. My dentist has an office on the top floor." She touched the side of her right cheek. "I have been in tremendous pain since last night."

I could see no signage on the building signaling a dentist's office. But before I could ask, Miss Carnage said, "Doctor Moonstone has only just moved here from Waterloo, and I was relieved that he would see me without an appointment." She flinched. "He said my molars are in a shocking state."

Which made perfect sense. Except for . . .

"Your voice," I said. "When we were in the hall and I could not see your face—I was so certain it was Miss Always who spoke."

"The writer?" The anxiety faded from her face and she burst into a fit of laughter. "A great many people sound alike, Ivy." Then she put her hands gently on my shoulders. "Do I *look* like Miss Always?"

"Not a bit, dear. Miss Always is plain but unremarkable. You, on the other hand, have that magnificent nose, a chin of staggering proportions, a plump belly, and the sort of teeth that would make a donkey blush."

Miss Carnage's arms dropped from my shoulders. "Yes . . . well . . ."

"But I cannot imagine what Miss Always was doing here," I said, looking back at the grim building. "I think I will visit

Buzzby's Stage Emporium and see what I can discover."

Without asking, the librarian turned me around, linked her arm in mine, and began walking with me away from the building.

"It worries me greatly that you are wandering the streets, following this woman," said Miss Carnage gravely. "How is it that you know Miss Always?"

"We met on a ship and became bosom friends," I heard myself say. "If we were better acquainted, I would tell you that Miss Always is a bloodthirsty gatekeeper with a talent for plunging daggers into hearts. Instead, I will simply tell you that Miss Always is a danger to society."

Miss Carnage was dazzled by my discretion. "Very wise, Ivy."

Lovely creature!

We turned the corner and headed back up the long avenue. Pausing at the Admiralty Bank, Miss Carnage explained that she had an appointment there.

"Ivy, promise me you will be more careful," she said firmly. "I will be a hive of nerves if I think you are roaming London chasing this dangerous writer."

From behind me, I heard a screech so unpleasant it could only come from one place.

"I do believe that strange woman just called out your name," said Miss Carnage.

I turned and wasn't utterly surprised to see Mother Snagsby stomping toward me with a look of thunder upon her face.

"That is Mother Snagsby. She frets terribly when I wander away."

"Do take care, Ivy. I must dash."

Miss Carnage headed off briskly in the opposite direction. She seemed in a frightful rush, whizzing past the bank (which was odd) and disappearing around the corner—just as Mother Snagsby was within striking distance.

My mother was huffing and puffing with all the enthusiasm of a steam train. Expressed her delight in finding me by cursing like a pirate. Then seized me by the arm and dragged me lovingly back to the dressmaker.

There was no supper that night. Even Mrs. Dickens was forbidden from visiting me with a merciful plate of pumpkin and cabbage. Mother Snagsby was appalled by my conduct. She said running from the dressmaker's shop like a bank robber was not the conduct of a gentleman's daughter. All the way home in the carriage she had quizzed me about why I had run off.

I felt it was best to make no mention of Miss Always.

Adding to my troubles was the fact that Mother Snagsby had inspected the viewing parlor and now knew that I had not dusted it. I had never seen her so angry. Her nostrils flared. Her magnificent mole twitched up a storm. For my crimes I was sent immediately to bed. The door was locked behind me.

Not even slightly tired, I lit a candle to ward off the darkness. This was not done because I felt spooked about seeing Miss Always. Or because I was troubled about what devious scheme she was brewing. Not a bit!

"Ivy . . ."

The voice was faint. But clear.

I jumped from the bed and hurried to the door. "Mrs. Dickens?"

Silence.

"Perhaps you do not wish to unlock the door lest Mother

Snagsby box your ears," I went on. "Perfectly understandable. But if there is any way you could slide a few raw potatoes under the door, I would be very—"

"Ivy . . ."

No, the voice was not coming from out in the hallway. It sounded nearby and far away, all at once. I hurried across the room, drew back the curtains, and looked down on Thackeray Street. Gas lamps lined the street, their honey-colored light

arresting the darkness. A carriage rolled by. Followed by a night constable in no great hurry.

"Ivy . . ."

It was maddening! Where was it coming from? A ghost, perhaps? So busy was I trying to solve this mystery that I had not noticed the warmth upon my skin. Nor the throbbing against my chest. Nor the way the pulsing beats of the stone began to quicken.

The candle blew out without warning. The room was entombed in a drapery of shadows.

But it did not last. For a glorious silvery light bloomed from under my nightdress. In the short time it took me to retrieve the necklace, the Clock Diamond's glow filled the bedroom, hitting the walls like a winter sun.

I dropped to the floor, sitting cross-legged, and stared into it. As the light started to dim inside the stone, I found her. Huddled in the corner of a bare room. Ghastly yellow walls. White floor. Her blond hair limp and stuck to her face.

"Ivy, don't come," whispered Rebecca Butterfield.

I wanted to cry out. No, I just wanted to cry.

"Rebecca," I whispered. "Rebecca, can you hear me?"

The girl seemed to be looking straight through the stone, right at me. Her skin gave off the faintest of glows. "Forget what you saw." Her breaths were shallow, her eyes vacant. She looked dreadfully tired. "Don't come for me, Ivy. They will be waiting."

"Who will be waiting, dear?" My voice was hoarse and wretched. "Rebecca, where are you? Tell me where you are!"

"You wore the stone, Ivy. You wore the stone and lived."

Rebecca's gaze shifted suddenly.

"Tell me where they are keeping you," I cried, as loud as I dared.

Her head dropped. Her eyes closed.

"Don't come for me."

Then the yellow of her room was swallowed by a hungry black mist. It churned and swirled, and when it parted, the Clock Diamond offered the night sky with a blanket of stars high above London.

She was gone.

8

The viewing parlor was the best room in the house. It had thick white carpet, oak chairs arranged in rows, a church organ in the corner. A wooden platform for the coffin with large brass candleholders on either side. Red velvet curtains covered the windows, while the wall opposite contained a vast mural featuring glorious clouds, ascending angels, and cherubs holding a long scroll with the words SNAGSBY'S DISCOUNT FUNERALS blazed across it in gold. All very tasteful.

"Working hard, young lady?" bellowed Mother Snagsby from upstairs.

"Wearing my fingers to the bone, dear," I called back.

Nearly a week had passed since I had seen Rebecca in the stone—and each day had been agony. I was desperate to escape from Mother Snagsby's gaze and visit the library. Get my hands on that manuscript. But the Snagsbys had been working me like a slave. I'd read poems at seven sickbeds (four had died while I was fast asleep, but as my mind was occupied on more important matters, this no longer seemed odd). Rebecca had *spoken*. Told me not to come. To forget what I had seen.

Impossible!

While I wasn't completely sure whether she could see or hear me, she certainly knew I was there. The Clock Diamond had never done that before. Miss Frost had made no mention of its having such powers. Beastly questions flared in my mind.

I needed Ambrose Crabtree's book. Yes, Miss Carnage had warned me that meddling with it might be perilous. But I wasn't the type to melt in the crucible of danger. Not for a moment!

"Do not forget to polish the casket!" screeched Mother Snagsby.

She had ordered me into the viewing parlor at first light

with strict instructions that I was not to leave until the room was shining like a new penny. There was a viewing in two hours, and Mother Snagsby's men (two perfectly pleasant buffoons) had already put the coffin in place.

I sighed as I ambled up the aisle between rows of wooden chairs. In a few hours they would be filled with grieving relatives. Gathered here for Mr. Talbot—who had choked on a carrot, fallen backwards out of a window, and landed in a heap.

It was an open coffin. I stepped up onto the platform. Looked down at poor Mr. Talbot. But he wasn't there. Someone else was. She had a halo of white hair and a blood-soaked nightdress. In other circumstances, I might have gasped and looked terribly shocked. But not today. Not even when the bloated creature's eyes shot open. And a dark cackle emerged from her lips.

"What have you done with Mr. Talbot, you blubbery abomination?" I said sternly.

"He took a walk," sang the Duchess of Trinity.

The devious fatso floated out of the coffin, spun around several times, giving off a spray of starlight, then came down in front of me.

"Hello, child," she purred.

"Go away," I said. "And give back Mr. Talbot! Where is he?"

The ghost smiled wickedly. Dark ribbons of smoke coiled from her nose, weaving into the air. They twisted around one another like rope and arranged themselves into the shape of an arrow. It pointed to the back wall. I turned around. There was Mr. Talbot in his best suit, propped up in a chair by the organ.

"Return him this instant, you hideous ghoul!"

"Dull child." With a flick of the Duchess's ghostly finger, Mr. Talbot stood up, his bones creaking and snapping in a ghastly manner. Then the Duchess nodded her head, and the corpse began to take staggering, halting steps up the aisle toward us. His arms were limp at his sides. His head snapped back and forth with alarming frequency. He stepped up onto the platform, his joints cracking like whips.

Mr. Talbot's stiff fingers gripped the edge of the coffin. But as he began to lift his brittle body into the casket, two snapped off and dropped to the floor. Which was deliciously shocking. When the corpse took his rightful place, his head resting against the satin cushion, I scooped up the digits. Placed Mr. Talbot's hands by his sides. And arranged the fingers as best I could.

The ghost still hovered before me.

"How do you like being a daughter, child? Is it all that you hoped it would be?"

"Go away."

"Alas, I cannot," came the dead woman's reply. "For I come on a most urgent matter and must ask you for a *small* favor."

Now it was my turn to laugh. "You're as batty as you are fiendish," I declared. "After what you did to Rebecca, I wouldn't help you if you were the last ghost in all of England."

"That poor girl was never my target," said the Duchess.

"No, it was Matilda you wanted to kill. Just so you could punish Lady Elizabeth and wreak vengeance. What you did was wickedly cruel!"

"That is true enough," said the ghost. "My actions were unforgivable."

I cannot say why it was such a shock to hear the Duchess admit her guilt. But it was.

"You wish to help Rebecca, do you not?" she said.

Well, of course I did! "Do you know where she is?" I asked quickly.

"Prospa is the world you seek."

"Prospa?"

The ghost nodded.

"How do I find Rebecca? Where is she?"

"I am between worlds," declared the Duchess, "and know little of such things." Then her eyes closed. She licked her lips, her black tongue slipping out like a serpent. "But if there is a way to unearth the girl's *exact* location, I will try and find it."

Which was wonderfully promising.

She opened her eyes again. "However, I require something in return."

I was frowning now. "Do not think you can fool me again," I said sternly. "If this is another one of your wicked schemes, I will know it."

"You be the judge, child," sang the ghost. "I only have one living relative—my cousin, Victor Grimwig. He is gravely ill, though he will not admit it. Victor's savings are scant, and although he dearly wants a proper burial, it must be one that he can afford."

Was the Duchess asking me to help arrange a discount funeral for her cousin? She seemed to read the wonder upon my face.

"Yes, child, I am hoping that you will help arrange for Victor to have one of your delightful premeasured coffins."

"What are you up to, Duchess? You're a hateful sort of ghost, positively bursting with bad intentions. Why do you wish to help your cousin?"

The Duchess of Trinity shook her head mournfully, the glow of her skin dimming. "I am trapped in the gray lands, child, neither in one place nor the other. There is only one way I can move on—I must do some good in the world." She looked at me, her eyes two dark wells. "My life was wasted on vengeance and hatred, and now I am trying to do a good deed. Surely there is no harm in that?"

I stepped down off the platform. Made no reply.

"Will you help me bring peace to my dear cousin?" She moved swiftly, flying to my side. "And I will see what I can discover about poor Rebecca."

Before I could answer, the unmistakable pounding of Mother Snagsby's boots on the stairs filled the parlor. I looked around at the dusty room. She would be furious. Keep me in there all day until it was clean. Which would make getting to the library and stealing that manuscript rather difficult.

The ghost seemed to read my mind.

"Perhaps I can help," she purred.

The Duchess glided to the middle of the room and hovered there. She puckered her pale lips. Then she started to turn on the spot, like an enormous ballerina in a music box. And as she did so, clusters of dust began to lift off the surfaces of chairs and tabletops and windowsills, flying at top speed into her ghoulish mouth.

In a few moments every surface sparkled and shone. Then she flew at Mother Snagsby's mural and vanished into one of her heavenly clouds.

Only her voice lingered. "Think on it, child," it said. "I will return soon for an answer."

"Who were you talking to?" said Mother Snagsby from the doorway.

"Mr. Talbot," I replied, pointing to the coffin. "He's frightfully good company."

"Don't be absurd," said Mother Snagsby, striding into the parlor.

She made her way around the room, running her finger across each and every surface. She frowned, a web of lines crowded around her eyes.

"Well?" I said brightly.

"It is . . . clean," came the faint reply. "Thoroughly clean."

I pushed the dusting rag into Mother Snagsby's hand and headed for the door. "You're welcome, dear."

Things began rather wonderfully. As I climbed the library steps, my mind fixed on the challenge ahead, I saw Miss Carnage off to one side, standing by a large pillar. She had her back to me, her head lowered. Which was perfect. I could slip inside undetected. But as I reached the doors, I glanced one final time at the librarian—and I saw a small figure dart away from her, disappearing around the side of the building.

Miss Carnage looked slightly unsettled when she turned and found me gawking at her.

"That was just a boy from the post office," she said quickly. "I am sending a rather important telegram to India."

Oh. *Now* I understood. The dreary librarian had a sweetheart in India. An officer in the British army. Miss Carnage had not told me a great deal about him, but from what I gathered he was frightfully neglectful.

"I find that the future weighs heavily, Ivy," she said, threading her arm in mine and walking with me into the busy library. "I have asked my *friend* to declare his intentions one way or the other, for I feel we have been courting long enough."

"I applaud you, Miss Carnage," I said, patting her arm. "If this brute thinks he can do better than you—which is highly likely—then it's best that you know now, so that you might find someone slightly less dashing."

But my words of inspiration did little to lift her spirits.

"Now I shall have to wait for his reply," she said, stepping behind the front desk—which was exactly where I did *not* want her to be. "Waiting is not easy, as I am rather impatient."

"I know just how you feel, dear. I once waited for my luck to change. Took eleven minutes. As you might imagine, I was *furious*."

After my triumph in the viewing parlor, I had managed to convince Mother Snagsby to let me visit the library. I *may* have told her that I had several overdue books that were certain to attract heavy fines. Mother Snagsby never met a penny she didn't love. I was to return the books and be back before lunch.

Which meant I had to get straight to the point.

"Miss Carnage, I confess that I have heard a troubling rumor."

"Oh?" said the librarian.

I looked through the glass petition into the office behind. As it was Monday and Mr. Ledger was out having tea with his mother, it was wonderfully empty. I leaned in for good effect. "I have heard whispers that the catalog has been tampered with."

The librarian gasped. Looked with alarm and horror at the large cabinet full of tiny drawers on the far side of the room—each containing hundreds of alphabetically arranged index cards identifying the location of each and every book in the grand library.

"Apparently all of the cards have been shuffled," I went on. "A search for *Gulliver's Travels* will send you to German history. It's utterly shocking."

"Heavens," said Miss Carnage, clutching her throat. "Excuse me, Ivy. I must see to this immediately."

The good woman hurried away. And so did I.

Finding the vault beneath the library was stupendously easy. Miss Carnage's detailed instructions could not have been more helpful if she had actually been *trying* to lead me there. I passed swiftly into the back office. Opened the bottom drawer. Found the key lying there beneath a pile of papers.

With lightning speed, I crossed the room, went down a short hall. The narrow stairs were rather rickety, but I was beneath the library in no time at all.

It was terribly gloomy down there. A long, dark chamber where even the shadows seemed to have shadows. Luckily, there was just enough light washing down from the stairway to locate a candle and a box of matches.

Armed with a decent source of light, I made my way toward the back. The crypt was a wonderland of crates and boxes and filing cabinets. Stone walls. Low arched ceiling. The musty smell of moldy paper and dampness.

To say I found the old printing press with ease would be an understatement. The large metal contraption wasn't even covered. And beneath it was a small green safe, visible to anyone who happened to pass by. It was all very disappointing.

I placed the key in the lock and turned it. Grabbed the rusted silver handle and pulled the thick metal door. It opened with a squeak. The contents of the safe were cast in darkness, so I pushed the candle forward.

What emerged in the flicking orange glow was a pile of five or six books, and beneath them a parcel tied with string. I set the candle down. Pulled out the books. *A Field Guide to Revolution*; *The Secret History of Cheese*; *Training Rabbits for Warfare*; *How to Hypnotize Your Elders* . . . not *exactly* the collection of dark and menacing tomes I had expected. And no sign of Ambrose Crabapple's manuscript.

I looked back at the vault. Pulled out the parcel tied with string. Unwrapped it. Bound inside a plain brown folder was a stack of parchment, covered in handwritten scrawl. And on the front, in spidery black ink:

Lifting the Veil

The Truth About Hidden Worlds and How to Get There

by Ambrose Crabtree

A great well of joy rose up inside of me. Here was hope, pure and simple. Rebecca was within reach. She would be saved! I tucked the manuscript beneath my apron and blew out the candle.

9

Nightfall could not come swiftly enough. After all, I had work to do. I ate my supper in record time (the roasted duck was a great disappointment; the onions, a triumph) and announced that I was exhausted after all that beastly dusting and wished to retire to bed. Mother Snagsby seemed to find this deeply suspicious, but Ezra excused me from the table and told me to get a good night's sleep.

"Do not forget," he added, with a twinkle in his eyes, "tomorrow Mrs. Roach and her daughters are coming to tea, and I know how much you are looking forward to that."

Actually, I *had* forgotten. Still, it was a thrilling thought! I hurried from the room. Tomorrow I would make new friends. And tonight I would find a way to reach an old one.

It had certainly been a day of high adventure. When I got home from the library, I had placed the manuscript under my mattress. Which is where I retrieved it from now, and I sat on the bed with the parchment in front of me. The pages were numbered, though not bound. The date on the front was 1834. Strangely, the parchment did not look yellowed or faded with age. I put this down to the fact that it had been locked away in the dark safe for decades.

With tremendous eagerness, I thumbed through the pages. Ambrose Crabtree had a fondness for words, and it appeared that he had written a great deal of nonsense. The first five chapters touched on subjects like time travel, immortality, and the nature of dreams.

Despair was beginning to set in just as I arrived at the final chapter, "Lifting the Veil." Again, there was a lot of waffle, which I skimmed over at top speed. Only stopping when I hit upon the following:

That there are other worlds, nestled beside our own, is a fact few are aware of. Yet they exist. If you are reading these pages, then there is every chance you know this already. I will also assume that you would be perfectly willing to defy the laws of time and space and journey to one or more of these hidden realms.

Alas, dear reader, I must inform you that it is quite impossible. You are wasting your time, and I bid you farewell.

Which was terribly unexpected! Also, frightfully rude. I turned the next page and it was blank. As was the one after that. Except for the fact that it was covered in scratch marks. I squinted. Held the page close to my face. Turned it over and whatnot. Only when I grabbed the candle from the bedside and held it under the parchment did the magic of it become clear. As the page began to brown from the heat, Ambrose Crabtree's hidden handwriting blossomed into view.

This is what I read.

Good, as you have arrived, I will assume you are a true seeker. Now let us get down to business. When one wishes to find a hidden world, one does not attempt to travel there. For there is no need to journey at all. Once the veil is lifted, you will find that this hidden world is much closer than you think. In fact, it is all around. All you must do is find the door and walk through it.

That was all very interesting, but I was still none the wiser about how I might lift this monstrously inconvenient veil and find Rebecca. I hoped against hope that the final paragraphs would hold the key.

Lifting the veil is impossible for most, as the necessary tools are rarely found in any single human being. First, one needs an ability to see what others cannot. Ghosts, for example. Second, one cannot find a hidden world if one does not know which world one is seeking. Third, and most importantly, one must have a connection to the world they seek in order for it to be revealed.

Extraordinary! It was as if Ambrose Crabtree was speaking directly to me. What a delightful coincidence! I satisfied every one of his three conditions—I could see ghosts, I knew exactly what hidden world I was seeking to find, and I had a direct connection to Prospa, for my dear friend Rebecca was being kept prisoner there.

Now all I needed was a way in. My heart thumped furiously as I read the final passage. It was a list.

The rules are very simple.

1. The veil must be lifted at night, preferably on a half-moon, although entry is possible under any moon for gifted travelers.

2. Concentration is the key.

3. Fix your gaze upon a single point.

4. Focus on what connects you to the world beyond the world.

5. Focus until everything around that single point begins to fall away.

6. Strong emotion is the hand that lifts the veil.

7. When you travel, it will feel as if your body has crossed into this other world, but it has not. Only your soul journeys across unseen borders, and you cannot be harmed.

8. Once the veil has lifted, do not stay longer than thirty minutes.

9. Go bravely.

I dropped the parchment and rushed to the window, drawing back the curtain. The sky was black and empty. If there was a moon, I couldn't see it from my vantage point. Which is why I fished out the Clock Diamond from under my nightdress—it showed a full moon. Terribly inconvenient! To lift the veil, I needed a *half*-moon. Although Ambrose Crabapple did say that for gifted travelers, entry was possible under any moon. . . .

Time to get to work. I hid the manuscript in a drawer beneath my undergarments. Took a wooden chair from against the wall and set it in the middle of the room. Sat upon it and focused on the picture above the dresser—it was another of Mother Snagsby's portraits of her daughter Gretel. She looked to be about eighteen, laughing madly as she stood in a gloriously flowering garden. Gretel had a full face, blushing cheeks, dark hair, pleasant smile.

It was slightly odd to me that someone as ancient as Mother Snagsby had a daughter so young—but perhaps she only looked like a weather-beaten coconut due to questionable skincare. Or a witch's curse.

Remembering all that I had read, I fixed my eyes on the

painting and kept them trained there. Then, in the wonderlands of my mind, I found Rebecca, pictured her in that yellow room, looking so fragile and wounded. And saw the pain in her eyes.

"I am coming, dear," I whispered.

For an age, nothing happened. I had been gazing into the portrait of Gretel for so long it was now something of a blur. But I kept Rebecca in mind. And Prospa. Kept staring. Until the walls around me seemed to ripple and bend. I felt a burning in my chest as the Clock Diamond came to life. A faint buzzing filled the room. Then the painting began to melt, sliding from the canvas as if it were porridge.

From the corners of my vision I could see the dressers and curtains and doors dissolving, like the world was falling away. The painting was now nothing more than a gold frame, and through it, I saw a single tree blooming. It was stark white, with bare, twisted limbs, and it seemed to have a lantern within it, for it glowed hauntingly.

Behind it, the ground began to shake and crack. Then a great forest of pale trees rose up. The buzzing grew louder, tickling my ears. And the heat of the stone burned my chest, throwing pulsing amber light into my face. I watched in wonder as—

I heard a key turn sharply in the lock. Then the handle twisting.

When the door to my bedroom flew open, the walls of my room flew up around me. The painting of Gretel bled quickly across the canvas, filling itself in. The buzzing ceased. The Clock Diamond dimmed. The veil had fallen.

"What in heavens is going on, young lady?" Mother Snagsby stalked into the bedroom and stood above me. "Explain yourself!"

"Explain what, dear?"

"That wretched noise," she spat, looking about with great suspicion, "and the light coming from underneath your door." She dropped down and looked under the bed. Got up again and searched the wardrobe. "It looked as if you had a dozen streetlamps in here."

I got up. "As you can see, Mother Snagsby, there are no streetlamps. As for the noise you heard, that was just me. I spent a few months in an ashram last summer—met a wonderful yogi who taught me how to chant. Delightful fellow. Spoke in tongues. Only ate birdseed."

"The Snagsbys do not *chant*. Stop it this instant."

"If you say so, dear."

When Mother Snagsby had departed, with strict instructions that I go to bed and stay there, I returned to the center of the room. Sat down. Stared at the portrait of Gretel. Thought of Rebecca. I could hear Mother Snagsby pacing up and down the hall outside. But I gazed and gazed into the painting until my eyes watered. Tried to block out the old goat's footsteps. Waited for the portrait to melt. For the walls to drop. For the woodlands to rise before me. But the world did not fall away. Though I cannot say the same for my spirits.

"What are you up to?"

"Not a thing," was my reply.

Mother Snagsby's battered face was a mask of mistrust. She was still smarting about last night. Certain that I was up to something dastardly.

"It seems to me," she declared, getting up from the breakfast table, "that you are forever on the brink of some calamity. You *cannot* be trusted."

The nerve! How could she accuse me of being deceitful,

simply because I was keeping things from her? Last night had been far more upsetting for me than it was for Mother Snagsby. While I was still bitterly disappointed that I had been unable to reach Rebecca, I was comforted by the fact that *something* had happened. But I feared that my bedroom was not the best location, given the noise and the glowing of the stone.

I would have to find somewhere else for my next attempt. In the meantime, I was feeling rather giddy about the day ahead.

"I have a good mind to cancel Mrs. Roach's visit," said Mother Snagsby sternly.

"That would be a great shame, dear," I said, putting down my napkin. "I'm practically positive that I would take the news rather badly—probably refuse to visit the deathbeds of your many valuable customers."

Mother Snagsby bristled in a glorious fashion. But she was beaten, and she knew it. "They may come for a *brief* visit, but it will be a very modest affair. Tuesday is market day, and Mrs. Dickens has more important things to do than wait upon us all afternoon."

"That will not be necessary," I said, getting up. "As you said,

Mrs. Dickens will be at the market, so *I* will be seeing to all the preparations."

Mother Snagsby looked startled. "You?"

"I have everything planned. First I will run you a bath, then I will clean the upstairs drawing room, then I will prepare some delicious treats for our visitors."

For a few enchanting moments, Mother Snagsby seemed lost for words. Then the cold glint sparkled in her eyes. "I bathe in the *evenings*."

Of course I knew that. For I was the one who fetched bucketloads of hot water to fill her tub. "Yes, dear, but as we are having guests today and you are looking particularly haggard, I have decided that a long, hot bath is the very least you deserve."

The old woman huffed. "Is that so?"

But I sensed a moment of weakness and lunged. "You do so much, Mother Snagsby," I said, looking wonderfully earnest, "working your horrid fingers to the bone. Isn't it a daughter's duty to take care of her mother?"

As I suspected, this had a winning effect.

Mother Snagsby looked at me with the sort of admiration she usually reserved for quality bacon. "I am pleased to hear it, young lady."

"Do hurry along!" barked Mother Snagsby as I entered the bathroom carrying the final bucket of hot water. "This bath is like ice!"

Which was complete nonsense. The water was perfectly warm. But that was the problem with Mother Snagsby—she had a fondness for complaint. And I understood why. It was all on account of that recipe book she kept hidden in the pocket of her dress. The one that she never, *ever* cooked from.

"This should make things better," I said, pouring the hot water into the bath.

"I suppose it will have to do," came Mother Snagsby's stiff reply.

Poor creature. The truth was, she hadn't the courage to cook from that treasured book of delicious dishes, fearing that she would be unable to make those recipes taste like her mother or grandmother used to make. Naturally, she was crestfallen.

Incapable of re-creating the flavors of her childhood. And that was why she was such an insufferable fathead.

But I was about to change all of that. All I needed was her recipe book. Which was concealed somewhere in the dress hanging on the back of the bathroom door. Right where Mother Snagsby could see it from her position in the tub.

"Now I must insist that you relax, Mother Snagsby," I said, putting down the bucket. "Close your eyes. Have a sleep."

"Impossible," snapped Mother Snagsby. "Sleep does not come easily to me, never has."

That was true enough. The poor creature spent half the night pacing the halls.

"Then you are in luck, dear," I said, fishing a small bunch of mint leaves from my apron. "For I have an excellent remedy for insomnia. You will sleep like a baby in its mother's arms."

"Will I indeed?"

I sprinkled the peppermint leaves into the bath.

"Breathe deeply, dear," I instructed. "The peppermint is stupendously soothing."

She closed her eyes, resting her head on the back of the bathtub.

"Now begin counting backwards from ten," I said, stepping behind her and picking up the empty bucket. "Nature will take care of the rest."

"That's it?" she sniffed. "A few mint leaves and some counting—*that's* your miraculous remedy?"

"Some of my patients report a slight stinging sensation before the delights of a deep sleep wash over them, but it will soon pass."

Mother Snagsby's eyes shot open. "Stinging? What's going to sting?"

I swung the bucket at the back of her head. It seemed the right moment. Mother Snagsby's head flew forward, then flopped back just as quickly. I thrust my hand behind her neck and eased her lumpy skull gently against the edge of the bath— for I have all the natural instincts of a guardian angel.

With Mother Snagsby out cold, I dashed across the bathroom and thrust my hand into the pockets of her dress. A winning smile creased my lips as I pulled out a rather drab book. On the front, in faded print, were the words *Augusta Snagsby's Family Recipes*. Wonderful! And on the side, a thick brass lock denying entry. Heartbreaking!

But I was confident that with a butter knife I could force it open.

"You will thank me for this, dear," I told the unconscious grumbler as I closed the door carefully behind me and set off at top speed for the kitchen. And as I went, I could only marvel at my own tender heart. For never has a bucket to the head been delivered with such loving kindness.

10

"How infuriating!"

I slipped the butter knife under the clasp and tried to pry the lock open. For the third time. No luck. During my years at the orphanage I had forced my way into the odd journal or two (in the interests of friendship and whatnot), and usually the locks gave way easily. But not this one. It was apparently unbreakable.

"Very strange indeed," I said, my heart positively plump with pity for Mother Snagsby. "Who locks a recipe book? The poor cow's off her rocker."

How else could I explain the fact that Mother Snagsby's

treasured book was locked up like a prison cell? I was certain there was heartbreak at the bottom of this monstrous puzzle. But I didn't have time to figure it out. I had guests to feed—and no recipe book to cook from! I recalled that Mother Snagsby was rather fond of Mrs. Dickens's almond cake—and I had helped her bake one only a few weeks before.

My baking skills were rather limited, but I intended to combine the ingredients with all the talent of an alchemist. Even though it wasn't one of Mother Snagbsy's family recipes, she would be deeply impressed by my efforts—filled to the brim with love and gratitude.

I made a quick list of the necessary items, then hurried into the pantry. The sugar and eggs were easy to find. The flour was not. For the jar was empty. Which was beastly. I couldn't be certain how long my sleeping remedy would work on Mother Snagsby—but I very much doubted there was time to run to the store. What to do?

"Ezra!" I said aloud.

Ezra had a small bag of flour in his workshop. I had seen it tucked away behind a stack of wood and boxes. No idea why the old coot would want or need flour, but as it perfectly suited my needs, I was glad of it. But there was a problem. Ezra would want to know *why* I needed the flour.

An ingenious and highly complex plan was quickly hatched. I dashed out to the workshop. Peeked through the small window. Ezra was hunched over a thick plank of oak, working at it with a chisel, his back to the door. Perfect. I tiptoed inside, making hardly a sound—for I have all the natural instincts of a church mouse. Ezra began to hum as he worked on the oak plank, and as he did, I quietly moved aside a box or two and some discarded wood, and scooped up the small sack marked FLOUR. Then I took off toward the kitchen.

The logs were crackling in the stove. The butter and sugar, ready for measuring. The eggs expertly separated. So far it was a glorious success. Until I remembered what was missing.

I looked about the kitchen, my heart sinking like a dropped anchor. How was it possible that the one ingredient I had overlooked in an almond cake was the *almonds*? I searched the larder three times, looking in every nook and cranny. Not an almond in sight. Sighing loudly, I gazed out the kitchen window. Which was terrifically fortunate. As my eyes fell upon the almond tree in the back garden.

If I felt slightly idiotic, it soon passed. After all, the tree was in a far corner near the gate, and the only person who paid it any attention was Ezra, who sometimes snoozed beneath its faded pink blossoms. I was soon out there collecting fallen almonds, which were scattered among the grass like pebbles.

So busy was I with the task that I didn't see her. All I heard was a branch snap. I looked up just as the girl leaped out from behind the tree. My hands flew to my mouth in shockingly timid display, the almonds tumbling from my apron.

She had golden-blond hair. A long white dress. And she stood before me, beaming radiantly. "Forgive me," said Estelle Dumbleby, her smile dimming. "I have startled you."

"It's my own fault, dear. What else is a tree for, other than jumping out from behind like a crazed lunatic?"

Estelle blushed and looked at the almonds pooled at my feet. She crouched down and began handing them back to me. "I would have come the front way," she said softly, "but I was anxious not to be seen." She peered up at me. "I should have waited until you were running an errand or walking to the library, but I simply *had* to know if you were able to discover anything about my brother and his connection to the Snagsbys."

"Well, of course I have," I heard myself say. "Been waist-deep in the Snagsbys' most private business."

"How brave you are," said Estelle, standing. "And what have you discovered?"

"That your brother Sebastian didn't know the Snagsbys at all. The dreary old coots have never heard of him. So you're barking up the wrong tree there, dear."

Estelle was frowning violently. "It would seem that my own inquiries have been rather more successful than yours, for my brother had business at this house. I know it for a fact."

"Highly doubtful. My inquiries were frightfully thorough."

"In the year before Sebastian vanished, he was rather ill—nothing life threatening, but his lungs were badly infected and he was bedridden for many months. My mother employed a nurse to care for him, and this young woman and my brother formed a foolish attachment." Her voice dropped and her eyes shifted about. "They fell in love."

"What has that to do with the Snagsbys?"

"Everything." Estelle looked past me to the house, her eyes traveling to the upper windows. "The nurse of whom I speak lived here, Ivy."

That was most unexpected. Estelle seemed pleased to have startled me.

"Perhaps now you will understand why I am so sure the Snagsbys are involved," she said.

"Was the nurse a lodger?"

Estelle fixed her eyes upon mine. "I believe so."

"I wish I could help, dear," I said, suddenly mindful of the time. "But I have a great deal on my plate at the present moment, and it would seem you are very capable of solving this mystery on your own."

"Please, Ivy, do not desert me," came the pitiful reply. "The truth about my brother lies somewhere in that house, and only you can find it."

Estelle's lips were trembling delightfully. Tears welled and dropped, flowing down her cheeks in a majestic display of heartbreak. While Mother Snagsby had made it very clear that the subject of Sebastian Dumbleby was closed, could I really reject this poor creature?

"Come to my home this Thursday for tea," said Estelle, handing me a card with her address on it. "If by then you have managed to find out anything that might assist my search, then I would be most grateful." She smiled warmly. "But if not, my great-uncle and I will have the consolation of your wonderful company."

She adored me! "Of course I will come," I said. "As for the nurse, let me see what I can find out."

Estelle kissed my cheek, and we parted ways beneath the almond blossoms.

While the cake was baking, I slipped upstairs and returned the recipe book to the pocket of Mother Snagsby's dress. The old goat was snoring with abandon, which was a blessing. Then I changed into my blue dress with the white sash. Fixed my hair. Dusted the drawing room and set out the good china for my guests.

By the time I returned to the kitchen, the cake was ready. I placed it atop the table and applied the vanilla icing. Then set about nestling each almond in a fetching circular pattern starting from the outside. The job was half completed when I heard Mother Snagsby's loud groan.

"My head hurts," she wailed.

"Perfectly normal at your age," I called back. "I'd be worried if your head *wasn't* throbbing like you'd been hit in the head with a bucket. Stay where you are, and I'll bring your robe."

With lightning speed—for I possess all the natural instincts of a recently fired cannonball—I finished placing the almonds and hid the cake in a cupboard by the hearth. Didn't want to risk Mother Snagsby spotting it and ruining the surprise.

"Where on earth have you been?" growled Mother Snagsby as I slipped her robe on. "I have been soaking in this tub for an eternity."

It was true. Her skin looked positively pickled.

"Terribly sorry, dear," I said, taking her dress off the hook. "But I was stupendously busy getting the house in order for our guests."

Mother Snagsby snatched the dress from my hands. "A likely story."

Her hand plunged into the pocket of her dress, and I saw a slight wave of relief cross her beady eyes when she felt her recipe book.

We stepped out into the hall and walked toward Mother Snagsby's bedroom, as I detailed all of my activities (leaving out certain moments that might cause her to erupt like a volcano). "I have dusted the drawing room, set out the cups and plates for tea, and prepared a tasty treat."

We paused in the doorway to her room. Mother Snagsby glanced at the clock on the wall.

"Mrs. Roach is not due for half an hour, so there is plenty of time for you to wax the banister. Wear your apron so your dress isn't spoiled."

Then she closed the door in my face.

11

"I do hope tea will be served promptly," declared Mrs. Roach, sniffing the air as if she was in a stable. "We were just at a lunch thrown by Lady Eckhart to celebrate my birthday. The journey across town was merciless and I am terribly parched, as are my girls."

"That's right, Mother," said Bernadette Roach with a nod of her head. "We are in desperate need of refreshments. Are we not, sister?"

"Most definitely," said Philomena Roach.

The sisters were perched on the edge of the sofa beside their mother, who was as wide as she was tall (which was *very* tall) and had the great fortune of resembling a cowbell. Her girls were about my age and perfectly ordinary in every way—blond hair worn in ringlets, small brown eyes, inoffensive noses.

"Hurry along with the tea," said Mother Snagsby, waving me toward the door, "and bring the refreshments for our guests."

"Not right now, dear," I said, wedging myself between the Roach sisters with heartbreaking delicacy. "I thought we might engage in some pleasant small talk first. You will find me *fascinating*, and I promise to look as if I feel the same about you. That way, we might get to know one another and become bosom friends."

Mrs. Roach regarded me with all the fondness of an ax murderer. "My girls are very selective when it comes to the company they keep. It is a great risk, taking a child off the streets—one never knows what one is going to get."

"It must be beastly, not knowing where you came from," offered Bernadette, shifting away from me. "You might belong to anyone. *Anyone* at all."

Philomena shuddered at the thought.

"Fetch the tea," said Mother Snagsby, and her voice allowed no room to disobey.

"Yes, Mother Snagsby."

Mrs. Dickens and I mounted the stairs—me carrying the cake plate, Mrs. Dickens the tea tray. The housekeeper stopped at the top to catch her breath.

"Are they nice girls, then?" she asked.

"Monstrous. But it's clear that they have taken rather a shine to me, which is terribly helpful, as I am told they host the most wonderful parties, full of thrilling entertainments."

Mrs. Dickens smiled kindly at me. "Some folks take a while to warm up to strangers."

I patted her on the head. "I have a birthday surprise for Mrs. Roach that is sure to win her affection. And one bite of my almond cake will have Mother Snagsby and those girls eating out of the palm of my hand."

"What sort of cake is that?" said Mother Snagsby when I put the plate down on the side table.

"Almond."

She murmured her approval. "It doesn't look *completely* inedible."

Bernadette eyed the cake greedily. And I distinctly saw Philomena lick her lips.

But Mrs. Roach was less enthusiastic. "I despise almonds. The nut of peasants, my late mother used to say."

"Was your mother something of a half-wit?" I fished out the candles and placed them by the cake. "I only ask because it's a known fact that almonds are the finest nuts in the world. Queen Victoria munches on them morning, noon, and night."

"What a dreadful thing to say!" snapped Mother Snagsby.

"My mother was a woman of great accomplishment," declared Mrs. Roach haughtily. "She spoke seven languages, studied art in Rome, was made an honorary professor in Greek mythology, *and* could recite the entire works of Shakespeare line for line."

I smiled sympathetically. "The poor cow must have been exhausted."

The entire Roach family seemed to clutch their chests and gasp as one.

"Who's for tea?" chimed Mrs. Dickens loudly. "Ivy, you fetch the cups and I will pour."

I did as she asked. And felt it was the perfect moment to make pleasant chitchat.

"Mrs. Roach," I said, holding a cup and saucer while Mrs. Dickens filled it with piping-hot tea, "your entertainments are the talk of London. Everywhere I go, I hear people exclaiming that Mrs. Roach is a—"

"Lemon!" growled Mrs. Roach.

"Well, you're slightly sour, dear, but I won't fret about it. As I was saying, if I were to be invited to one of your wonderful—"

"My tea, you fool!" she hissed. "I want *lemon* in my tea."

I released a playful giggle. "I didn't mean to imply that you are an unpleasant shrew with a vinegary nature. It was just a slip of the tongue. A joke between friends."

"Idiotic child," muttered Mother Snagsby.

With the tea poured, I dropped a slice of lemon in the cup and handed it to Mrs. Roach.

"As you recently celebrated a birthday," I said, starting to place the candles around the cake, "I thought it only fitting to mark the occasion with a few candles."

Mrs. Roach's stern expression softened. Just slightly. "How kind."

"A cake so fine needs to be presented properly," said Mrs. Dickens. She placed the plate on a silver trolley and wheeled it before Mrs. Roach and her daughters.

"We must all sing a round of 'Happy Birthday,'" I said, retrieving a box of matches from the mantle.

Mrs. Dickens brought over a stack of serving plates. "Where on earth did you get the flour, lass? I only just brought a pound home from the market, as there wasn't a speck left in the pantry."

I took out a match and struck it, the head sparking into life. "Ezra keeps some in the workshop," I said, igniting the first candle, then using it to light the rest. "He practically insisted that I take it."

"Flour in the workshop?" said Mrs. Dickens doubtfully.

At which point, Mother Snagsby leaped up from her seat and ran at me. She may have also cried out, "Stop! Stop!"

Which was rather odd.

"What on earth?" huffed Mrs. Roach.

I was placing the last candle in the cake when Mother Snagsby lunged, grabbing my arm with tremendous force. This caused the lit candle to drop from my hand and fall onto the cake. That really shouldn't have been a problem. Except that it was.

For the cake did something rather unexpected. It exploded. In hot chunks. Bursting into the air and flying about the room like missiles. Pieces splattered against the wall. Others, the windows and the door. Dark ash fell about the room like rain. But the real damage was done to the Roaches.

Cake detonated all over them. Mostly on their heads. Mrs. Roach had a chunk up her nose and one in her left ear. Bernadette's eyes and forehead were smothered in icing and almonds. Philomena had largely vanished behind a mask of red-hot cake.

And they were all shrieking and hollering as if something dreadful had just happened.

"Have you no sense?" barked Mother Snagsby as a generous lump of icing slipped from her gigantic mole. "That was not flour you *stole* from Ezra's workshop, it was gunpowder!"

"Well, that explains things," I said brightly.

"Gunpowder?" squawked Bernadette.

"My girls could have been killed!" cried Mrs. Roach. "*I* could have been killed!"

And poor Philomena began rocking back and forth, mumbling something about a bomb strike and urging us all to hurry to the nearest bunker.

"My skin is on fire!" bawled Mrs. Roach. "I will be scarred for life!"

Mrs. Dickens and Mother Snagsby were doing their best to clean up the guests with napkins and water. But I knew that something else was required.

So I bolted from the room. Stormed into the kitchen. Grabbed the necessary items. Then bounded back upstairs.

"Fear not," I declared, bursting into the drawing room, "I have a most excellent remedy for cake burns."

As I approached her, Mrs. Roach began to recoil. There wasn't time to apply the treatment with a brush. Which is why I cracked the egg on her forehead.

"Young lady!" thundered Mother Snagsby.

With the egg slithering down her face, Mrs. Roach squealed like a pig in a butcher shop. I plucked off most of the shell—being a stupendously considerate sort of girl—and began gently rubbing the yolk around her nose and ear.

"I am dreaming!" cried Mrs. Roach. "This must be a hideous dream! It must!"

"It only feels like a dream because the egg is so soothing, dear," I said tenderly. "This remedy is a balm that will ease the redness and leave no trace of a mark."

"Get off my mother!" roared Bernadette, pulling me away.

"Do not fret, girls," I said, picking up the four remaining eggs. "I have plenty for you as well."

This clearly excited Philomena, because she jumped up and began running from the room. Followed swiftly by her sister. Fortunately, I reached the door before they did, slamming it shut.

"You will thank me for this, girls," I announced in my most calming voice. "In certain parts of Japan, an egg to the face is a sign of great respect."

"Put down those eggs this instant!" ordered Mother Snagsby.

"Ivy, you mustn't," said Mrs. Dickens.

"Quite wrong, Mrs. Dickens, for I *must*."

The girls were now running about the room, pulling cake from their hair and crying like lunatics—and desperately searching for a way out. I had little choice but to chase after them, hurtling the eggs from a distance. One smashed directly on Bernadette's right cheek. She screamed and cursed my ancestors. Another hit Philomena square in the face. She wailed with gratitude. Even dropped to her knees.

"Don't be shy," I told them. "Rub the remedy in vigorously."

"Get away from us!" screeched Bernadette.

"Run, children!" shouted Mrs. Roach, leaping to her feet and making a dash for the door.

By that point I was on the other side of the drawing room with just one egg left. Bernadette pulled Philomena to her feet, and they ran toward their mother just as she threw the door open.

"That child is a devil!" Mrs. Roach bawled as she bolted down the hallway, a girl clutched in each hand. "Snagsby's Economic Funerals has buried the last of us, you mark my words!"

"Thank you so much for coming!" I called after them. "I will keep an eye out for my invitation to your next glorious party!"

The drawing room was in rather a shocking state.

Mother Snagsby was sitting in an armchair with her head in her hands. Mrs. Dickens was looking about the room in wonder. And Mrs. Roach and her two daughters charged down the stairs and ran screaming from the house. Which was *most* undignified.

12

There was no supper again that night. Mrs. Dickens was forbidden from bringing me so much as a breadcrumb. I was in exile. A figure of unutterable shame and disappointment. A daughter so beastly, Mother Snagsby said she could not bear to *look* at me.

Besides the glorious explosion, the only bright spot had been the tantalizing question of why Ezra had had gunpowder in his workshop. And why it was marked FLOUR. Tragically, it was all very innocent. The gunpowder was a relic from his hunting days. And he told me he kept it in an old flour sack because he hadn't anywhere else to put it. So, no great mystery there.

My spirits were alarmingly low. Despair had taken hold. Nothing was going as I had planned. And looming beneath the entire calamity, like a pit of tar in my stomach, was poor Rebecca.

But how could I be sure that what the stone had shown me was true? Perhaps it was a trick. One of Miss Always's wicked schemes. A plan to lure me to Prospa to see if I was the Dual— the girl who would finally cure her world of the Shadow, the plague that had killed millions. Then Miss Always would use me to control the kingdom. That is what Miss Frost believed. And even though she had lied to me about Rebecca being dead, I did not doubt her on that matter.

I scooped the necklace from under my nightgown and stared into the Clock Diamond. Willing it to show me another vision. A clue to *exactly* where Rebecca was being kept. But all it offered was the night sky over London, starless and bleak. There was only one way to reach her.

But I could not risk lifting the veil. The infernal buzzing and the glaring light from the stone were the problems. Mother Snagsby had nearly caught me last time, and as she already thought I was a horrid sort of girl, I didn't dare try it again. Not in the house, at any rate.

Which meant I had to get out. But how? Even though Mother Snagsby had stopped pacing the hall outside an hour ago, the door was locked, and the only two keys were with her and Mrs. Dickens. And the window had been nailed shut ever since I had climbed out of it early one morning in an attempt to reach the kitchen door. (I had been on the point of near starvation, not having eaten a morsel since dinner.) Sliding down the drainpipe had proved rather difficult. It was raining and I had lost my grip, plummeting toward the hard ground. Fortunately, a passing milk woman broke my fall.

But she made a great fuss as her pails of milk spilled across the cobblestones. Mother Snagsby had come flying out, her nightcap fluttering furiously. She was quick to blame me for the mishap. Felt the need to declare that I wasn't a blood relative and that she would have no objection should the milk woman wish to clobber me with her wooden yoke.

The window had been nailed shut ever since. So finding a way out was a monstrous challenge, even for me. I paced the bedroom until I grew tired. Although I had a great many talents, I hadn't a clue how to get out of a locked room.

Defeated, I dropped down onto the bed and let out a bewildered sigh. But it was quickly replaced by a frown. For the blanket at the end of the bed had begun to rise. Lifting up as if someone or something was under it. Naturally, I scrambled to the other end of the bed.

By then the blanket was hovering above the mattress, all aglow. It was clear that something mountainous was concealed beneath it, and I quickly surmised that there was only one ball of luminous blubber that could be responsible for such a display. Then the blanket fell in a heap, slipping through her as if she were not there.

"What an *interesting* day you've had, child," sang the dead Duchess.

"Mind your business, you fiendish fatso."

The ghost laughed, her nostrils smoking like a furnace. "If it is any consolation, never have a mother and her two daughters been more deserving of an exploding cake."

I ignored her, pouting magnificently and folding my arms.

She moved slowly toward me, leaving a trail of starlight in her wake. "Didn't I help you with your mother on my last visit? She was most impressed by your dusting—you know she was."

Yes, it was true. But that had been before this afternoon's tea.

The Duchess of Trinity licked her lips, her black tongue slithering like an eel. "Will you help me? Will you arrange a discount funeral for my dear cousin Victor?"

I climbed off the bed. "That all depends. What can you tell me about Rebecca?"

"I *do* have some news that might interest you, but first I must have your promise that you will help me."

"The last time you asked for my *help*, it was a clever plot to kill Matilda. Why should I trust you this time?"

The Duchess nodded her head. "I will be honest, child. You will probably discover that Victor wrote a pamphlet about me, following my death, in which he pointed out my many faults."

I was frowning with gusto.

"Now most girls your age would think that was the perfect motivation for vengeance." She thrust her plump and largely transparent finger at my chest. "I know *you* will see that I admired Victor for his unflinching honesty. He cared nothing for my title and treated me as an equal. You understand, do you not?"

Well, of course I did. "Your cousin was the only person who had the courage to tell you what a miserable, miserly, monstrous old bat you really are. And you loved him for it."

"How wise you are, child."

"It comes easily, dear. For I have all the natural wisdom of a potbellied yogi. Or at the very least, a spotted owl."

The light inside the Duchess bloomed, brightening the dim bedroom. "But say nothing about our communication to my cousin when you approach him about the coffin," she warned. "It might set him against the idea if he knew it came from me."

"Yes, yes, he won't suspect a thing," I said impatiently. "Now tell me about Rebecca. What have you learned? Have you seen her? Where is she being held?"

"Prospa House," came the reply. "Your friend is in Prospa House."

Progress at last! "How will I find this place?"

There was no reply. The Duchess just hovered before me,

looking rather thoughtful. Perhaps she was thinking. Then she said, "You have no business there, child."

"Rebecca is my friend. There is no more important business, it seems to me." My gaze hardened. "How do I find Prospa House?"

"You know how," purred the Duchess.

And of course I did. But I couldn't accomplish anything locked in my bedroom.

A faint smile crossed the ghost's pallid lips. Without a word she began to close in on herself until she was nothing more than a ball of light, white smoke lifting from it like a smoldering coal. The ball flew swiftly across the room and stopped before the door handle. Then the Duchess's plump finger emerged from inside the ghostly sphere and darted at the keyhole. The finger molded itself into a key and slipped into the lock. I heard a crisp *click*.

Then the Duchess was gone.

I was already at the door when I heard her ghostly refrain.

"You have no business there, child."

I turned the handle and slipped out into the hall.

London in the wee hours was painfully quiet. The silence was occasionally broken by a passing carriage. Or the odd dog barking. The sky was black and final. Not a star to be found. Gas lamps did their best to throw splashes of light about the place.

My stomach was a tangle. My mind a whirlwind. I had expected that being away from the house would make lifting the veil and reaching Prospa as easy as falling from a log. But it had not. I had stopped several times and employed the techniques set out in Ambrose Crabtree's manuscript. At first I stared into a streetlamp, which nearly sent me blind. Next I chose to focus on a discarded carriage at the end of a narrow alley. Again, no luck.

So lost was I in thoughts of Rebecca and reaching her that I wandered rather far from home. Gone were the neat rows of terraces. In their place were large buildings of dark brick with barred windows. My pace never faltered—I didn't know where I was headed, but I pushed on. Unable or unwilling to stop. As if a beacon was flaring in the distance. I couldn't see it, yet it felt as if I was following its signal. Rebecca's haunted face was reaching to the farthest corners of my mind. And I repeated the words "Prospa House" again and again.

Turning left, I walked the length of a footpath. Stopped. Looked up—the sign said WINSLOW STREET. I sighed. The hour was late, and it was probably time to head home before my escape was discovered. But I only took a few steps before I stopped again.

My attention was captured by a cavernous space between a shoe factory and a boardinghouse. Even in the faint lamplight I could see that the building had been torn down or had burned. Great piles of bricks lay about like stacks of coal. It was a ruin. All that remained was a part of the front wall. A hole where a window used to be. And the front door with the frame around it.

I crossed the street to take a closer look. The door was set back from the footpath, and on the crumbling wall beside it was a brass plaque, tarnished and worn by age. My eyes moved back to the door, standing proud among the remnants of the building that had once held it up. I thought of my lost friend. And it was happening before I even knew it.

A familiar buzzing charged the night air. Under my dress, the Clock Diamond awoke, hot against my skin. The buildings on either side of the lot began to bend and ripple. Then they melted away, dropping silently. The ground shook until my teeth began to chatter. All the while I watched the door. Even when a great white wall breached the ground and pushed up, lifting toward the heavens.

This new building seemed to stretch, like it had just woken up, spreading out left and right. It was a beast, tall and wide. Walls flew up and out. Vast windows filled in with glass. Ribbed columns rose along the front. The front door colored itself a glossy black. A gold knocker, shaped like a half-moon, pushed out with ease. The tarnished plaque began to glow and glisten as if it had just been polished. Then a path of silvery stone blossomed beneath my feet. A hedge grew up on either side of me, rising to my shoulders. The leaves on the bushes glowed bloodred.

I walked toward the door. Stopped before it. The plaque read PROSPA HOUSE. My heart lurched. My mouth dried. I was here! I glanced up at the building, trying to take it all in. The windows were cast in darkness. Save for one on the third floor where a candle burned. A shadow swept suddenly across it. Then the light went out.

I reached for the handle, praying the front door would not

be locked. But as my hand closed around it, I felt . . . nothing. My hand was bunched in a fist, having passed straight through the silver knob. Most peculiar! Suddenly I heard the rumble of voices as two men came around the side of the building. Their heads were shorn and both were dressed in ghastly orange coats and black boots. They had a perfect view of the front door, where I was standing like a lump. But they appeared not to see me!

I recalled Ambrose Crabtree's rules—did he not mention that when a person crossed between worlds, only their soul took the journey? Perhaps this meant I was a kind of spirit, unable to open doors and whatnot. Which would be a great help in sneaking about the place, but could make rescuing Rebecca rather difficult.

Then the door began to flicker, like a candle in the wind, fading one moment, then whole and solid the next. Between each flicker I would catch a glimpse through the door—but instead of finding a hallway or a room behind it, all I could see were piles of bricks. Fearing that time was against me, I lunged for the handle again.

"What's going on here, then?"

As I spun around, I felt a great *swoosh* of air as Prospa House fell away behind me. The stone path dissolved into the ground in seconds, and the neat red hedge melted like snow. Once again I was on the grim and unremarkable Winslow Street. And a rather portly night constable was coming toward me, wearing a look of profound suspicion.

"It's four in the morning. What are you doing wandering around Stockwell all by yourself?"

He was short. Double chin. Eyes set wide apart. Ginger whiskers only added to the catastrophe.

"What business is it of yours?" I demanded to know.

To have reached Prospa and have it ripped away was the cruelest of blows.

The constable seemed slightly startled. "Well . . . it's my job, that's what, and you should be at home tucked up in bed. You better come with me, missy."

"It's a sad state of affairs when a twelve-year-old girl can't roam the streets in the dead of night without being harassed by a constable," I declared with a huff. "My instinct is to grab your baton and teach you a thing or two about manners. But as it's late,

I'll let you off with a firm slap on the wrist and a general warning."

I slapped his pasty wrist with great commitment and then, with the constable still looking utterly stupefied, I ran like the wind without glancing back.

13 *
*

"I locked that door, I'm sure of it," muttered Mrs. Dickens, spooning a generous helping of porridge into my bowl. "Your mother was madder than a hungry bear after that cake calamity, and she told me to lock your bedroom door and check it again before I turned in for the night."

When Mrs. Dickens had come to wake me up, she was rather startled to find my bedroom door already unlocked. Once I had crept back into the house, I had no way of locking the door behind me. Naturally, I called to the Duchess of Trinity, requesting that she come back and lock it. But she hadn't.

"Mrs. Dickens, you mustn't be too hard on yourself," I said, adding a pinch of cinnamon to my porridge and shoveling a dainty helping into my mouth. "You are as old as the sun, and your brain is practically pickled from all of that whiskey you drink."

"I take a wee sip every now and then, nothing more." The housekeeper looked suitably crestfallen. "My mind's always been sharp as a tack."

"And now you can barely remember your name. It's monstrously sad."

"Mrs. Snagsby would throw me out on the street if she knew," said Mrs. Dickens, returning the pot of porridge to the stove. "I've never seen her so angry, not in all my years at this house."

"How was I to know there was gunpowder in the flour sack?" I declared. "It was a *small* mistake—a few flesh wounds, the odd facial scar. Nothing to fret about." A great wave of sorrow rose up and swallowed me. I looked at the housekeeper, and something in her kindly eyes made me say, "Mrs. Dickens, why doesn't Mother Snagsby like me?"

"What a thing to ask!" She sat down beside me. "Lass, you mustn't take it to heart, though I admit she's a stern sort of woman. That's just her way." I saw her eyes lift to a small portrait of Gretel sitting above the hearth. "Give her time, and she will warm to you."

"She must miss her terribly," I said, pointing to the picture.

"You are right," said Mrs. Dickens faintly. "It's as if she doesn't remember how to be happy without Miss Gretel around."

"How long has she been in Paris?"

The housekeeper got up suddenly and busied herself wiping the table. "Well, that's a hard one. . . . I'm not a great one for numbers."

I put down the spoon and wiped my mouth. "Mrs. Dickens, is there something you're not telling me?"

"If you have time to sit around talking," snapped a cold voice, "then you have time to sweep the front steps."

We both turned as Mother Snagsby stalked into the kitchen.

"After that, you can help Mrs. Dickens set the drawing room to rights," she instructed. "It is still in a shocking state after the fiasco yesterday."

I was positively grim faced. "About that, dear. I want you to know that I feel *partly* responsible for what—"

"Save your breath, young lady," she snarled. "Complete your chores and keep your mouth closed. That is all I require of you."

Then she turned her back and walked out. Which might have been rather soul destroying, if not for the brilliant idea that blossomed inside my head. I took my bowl to the sink, all the while unraveling the mystery of Gretel Snagsby.

She wasn't in Paris at finishing school. No, she was somewhere far more thrilling. The girl had fallen in love with a young man and had run away to be with him. And who was this dashing, yet sickly, young suitor? None other than the missing brother of Estelle Dumbleby, that's who! Estelle had told me that Sebastian had been ill and that he had formed an attachment to his nursemaid. A nursemaid who lived at the Snagsbys' home. That girl was Gretel Snagsby!

Their love was of a most secret kind, owing to the fact that Gretel was a mere coffin maker's daughter and Sebastian was a genuine aristocrat. Therefore, the young lovers decided to head for the hills and live out their days in exile. Hidden from view, but wondrously together.

And as I grabbed the broom and set off for the front steps, I felt something like my old self again. How could I not? For now I had *two* missions. To save Rebecca. And to reunite Mother Snagsby with her runaway daughter.

"But why must you take my keys, lass?"

"I have to go out on urgent business, and I know what a strain it will be dragging yourself up and down the stairs to let me back in."

The solution to my first—and most pressing—mission came to me while I was wiping cream and icing from the walls in the drawing room. Although my adventure the night before hadn't been a complete success, I had at least managed to reach Prospa House.

So it was terribly important that I be able to escape my bedroom and try again. But I could hardly rely on the Duchess. Which was why I had to get my hands on the great bunch of keys dangling from Mrs. Dickens's belt.

"Your mother left strict instructions that you weren't to leave the house," said Mrs. Dickens (who was being shockingly difficult).

"Mother Snagsby is meeting with her accountant and will be gone all afternoon," was my perfectly reasonable reply. "Besides, Mr. Blackhorn's service is tomorrow, and we haven't enough candles."

"But I bought a dozen last week."

"You poor, overworked windbag—that was *three* weeks ago," I said, sitting her down on the couch. "Is it any wonder you forgot to lock my bedroom door last night?"

"I haven't felt myself these past few days."

"Of course you haven't. Your brain is faulty, your breath is criminal, and your nerves are shattered." With heartbreaking tenderness I pushed her against the armrest and untied the keys fixed to her belt. "I must insist, Mrs. Dickens, that you let me take these, and I will return them as soon as I get back. Honestly, dear, you know it makes sense."

Although the housekeeper had begun to sniffle, wondering aloud what would become of her, she had the good sense to agree with me.

I chose a locksmith in one of the less reputable parts of town. That way, there was no chance that Mrs. Dickens or the Snagsbys would discover that I was having the key to my bedroom door copied. The locksmith was a gruff-looking fellow, but he asked few questions and said to come back at two o'clock. The cost would be two shillings. Fortunately, Mrs. Dickens had given me five shillings to buy more candles.

Which meant a tidy profit for me. But as I had come by the money dishonestly (the candles Mrs. Dickens had purchased last week were hidden in a drawer in the viewing parlor), I felt the only proper thing to do with the remaining three shillings was to spend it on cake and hot chocolate.

With a few hours to spare, I went in search of a suitable teahouse. It was while I was roaming the busy streets that I had a most peculiar feeling. People were rushing past me, this way and that, yet all the while I sensed someone or something shadowing my every step. I spun around. No sign of anyone even slightly nefarious.

I darted to the left, vanishing into the shadows of a narrow lane. From this vantage point, wedged between a tavern and a tripe shop, I could watch the passersby. If there was a villain hot on my heels, he would soon be revealed.

But no one devious or underhanded caught my attention. Just a gaggle of perfectly ordinary folk going about their business. Including Miss Carnage. Which was a remarkable coincidence! She passed by. Stopped. Walked back and stared into the darkened alley where I was safely concealed. Turned and looked in the other direction. There was a hardness to her gaze that I had never seen before. A kind of grim determination. Perhaps she had eaten some bad fruit.

I felt the moment was right to step out of the shadows.

"Ivy!" exclaimed Miss Carnage, adjusting her thick spectacles. "How unexpected! What on earth are you doing in this part of town?"

"What are *you* doing in this part of town?"

Miss Carnage smiled tightly. "I am seeking out books," she explained. "A man in the next street has a collection on South American history that he hopes might be of some interest to the London library."

Which made perfect sense. A librarian's life is full of such adventures.

"I've had the strangest feeling I was being followed," I said next. "Then you appear as if out of thin air. Which is violently interesting."

The librarian blushed. "I must make a confession, Ivy. I first spotted you from across the road, and I was rather worried that you were on the trail of the unpleasant Miss Always again. So I decided to follow you and make sure that you were safe. Are you terribly cross with me?"

For the briefest of moments I had doubted her. But now I felt terribly foolish.

"I'm here on most important business," I announced. "I would tell you all about it, but I'm afraid you would faint from the shock."

"Is it . . ." Miss Carnage moved awfully close to me. "Is it to do with your friend who is far away?"

Miss Carnage was stupendously clever!

"Yes, dear, in a way."

"I do wish you would go to the authorities, Ivy. I am very

worried for your friend—and for *you*. Most worried, indeed."

"Fear not, Miss Carnage," I said, slapping her arm gallantly, "I have the matter in hand."

The librarian folded her arms over her plump belly. She looked wonderfully grave. "Yesterday I had reason to open the library vault and . . . and I was shocked to discover that Ambrose Crabtree's manuscript was missing. Ivy, please do not feel that I am accusing you of any crime, but I must ask if—"

"If I stole it and started tampering with the laws of time and space? Never, dear. Not for all the tea in China."

Miss Carnage was still frowning. "I am very pleased to hear it, as I regret ever telling you about that dreadful book." Her gaze narrowed. "May I ask—have you had any luck locating your friend?"

"I . . . I have yet to reach Rebecca." For some reason I did not wish to say anymore.

"But you have tried?" said Miss Carnage carefully.

I nodded my head.

"Perhaps not hard enough," she said, rather abruptly. But her face quickly softened, and once again she was her old self.

"What I mean is, if there is some urgency to her situation, then you must do everything that you can—within reason, of course. Perhaps you would let me be of some assistance?"

"Heavens no," I replied. "My plate is rather full at the moment, but you would be of no help at all, being a bookworm and whatnot."

Miss Carnage nodded her head. Smiled faintly. "Yes, you are probably right."

Falling asleep wasn't the plan. The *plan* was to wait until the house grew dark. Until Mother Snagsby stopped pacing the halls. Then, with my new key, I would unlock the bedroom door, sneak out of the house, and head back to Winslow Street in search of Prospa House.

But as I sat in bed and counted the minutes, sleep came to claim me. And it was sleep of the deepest kind. I am certain that I would not have awakened until morning, were it not for the Clock Diamond. It came to life in the still night, glowing like a lighthouse and growing hot against my skin. I woke with a start. Quickly came to my senses.

The house was utterly quiet—no sound of Mother Snagsby pacing about outside. The battered clock told me it was just past one in the morning. As I fished the necklace out from under my nightdress, the word "Rebecca" rushed to my lips.

I prayed that she would be there.

The night sky above London bloomed, then faded inside the mystical stone, a yellow room taking its place. In it, an iron bed. Bare white floor. A chair against the wall. A girl curled up in it, wearing an ivory nightdress. Her face paler than before, dulled and slightly hazy, though the room around her was crisp enough. This time Rebecca wasn't looking at me. Her gaze was distant.

"Rebecca," I whispered. "Rebecca, it's me, Ivy. Can you hear me, dear? Can you see me?"

The girl began to rock back and forth, her hair falling over her eyes.

"Are you in Prospa House?" I asked urgently. "Nod your head if that is where you are."

She made no reply.

"I will be back there as soon as I can, and I will bring you home."

Rebecca lifted her eyes. Just for a second. Looked right through the stone. Then her head dropped, and she was shaking.

"Talk to me, dear. Tell me exactly where you are so that I might find you."

Rebecca glanced up suddenly. But not at me. Her eyes glistened with fear. A shadow crossed her face. Then a brutish arm seized her wrist. She screamed, but the sound was muffled and faint. The chair toppled over as the girl was wrenched from view.

14

I had murder in my heart. Rage in my soul. And I was glad of it!

The walk to Stockwell had passed in a blur. I did not note the three-quarter moon. Or the rain falling lightly on the cobblestones. I cared little for the fact that I was walking about London in my nightdress. My feet bare.

Rebecca was in grave trouble. Frightful peril. She was being treated monstrously. Who knew where that brute was dragging her away to? Nowhere pleasant, I was sure of that! A great ocean of fury churned and crashed inside me. Never had I felt such blinding anger.

As I turned down Winslow Street, the air seemed to thicken around me. It began to buzz urgently and somehow slowly, though I continued to move with ease. The Clock Diamond was so hot against my chest I was certain it was blistering my skin. The stone's glow erupted from under my nightdress, an orb of orange and yellow, lighting the footpath before me. I must have looked positively ghostly. Luckily, there was no sign of that tomato-headed constable.

Rebecca was a constant in my thoughts. But I wasn't worried about reaching her, for as I prepared to cross the street, the lamppost beside me melted into the footpath. The road beneath my feet, with its damp cobblestones, dissolved like mud and sank into the darkness as thick blocks of silvery stone took its place. An empty carriage fell away. Number six of Ambrose Crabtree's rules promised that "Strong emotion lifts the veil." He was awfully clever, for a crackpot.

Before I even reached it, the shoe factory and the boardinghouse standing on either side of the empty lot began to ripple and bend and blur. Then they vanished as if the earth had opened its mouth and swallowed them up. The ground shook, the buzzing intensified, and I was not even slightly shocked when Prospa House rose before me, with its ribbed columns, high white walls, and countless windows. This time, pale woodlands grew up around it—trees like thousands of ghostly guards surrounding the building. The effect was rather chilling.

Not that I had anything to fear. As I had learned on my last visit, I was something of a ghost in this world. As I walked the path between the bloodred hedges, I looked up to see if any of the windows had a light burning. When I did, I glanced for the first time at the night sky. It was dark and empty, save for the three-quarter moon. I might have wondered whether it was the same moon I had seen above London just moments before—if not for the fact that *this* moon had an emerald hue.

All the windows were darkened. I walked around the side of the building. Glanced up again. The warm yolk of candlelight glowed from a window on the first floor. It was open; the curtains fluttered gently in the night air. Even better, there was a rather large white tree close by, allowing perfect access to the window from a monstrously helpful branch. What a stroke of great fortune!

I heard the muffled sound of voices, the stomping of feet. But it sounded as if they were coming from the other side of the building. I felt safe enough.

But how was I to climb a tree if I was little more than a ghost in this world? In a display of hot-blooded frustration, I hit the tree trunk with gusto and kicked it once or twice. Then gasped with delight. Reached out again and touched the trunk. It felt strangely warm beneath my hand. For whatever reason, I seemed to be more fully in Prospa on this visit.

I hitched up my nightdress and, gripping the trunk as if it were a rich aunt with no dependents, began my ascent. The tree was wonderfully knotted, so there were plenty of places to grasp. When it was within reach, I grabbed the lowest branch and moved from limb to limb, clambering up with ease.

When I was high enough, I crawled along a thick bough toward the window. Unfortunately, the branch stopped short of the window ledge. A certain amount of jumping would be required. I was now looking directly through the window and couldn't see anybody about. Perfect. I tastefully assumed a squatting position, took a deep breath, then leaped into the air with all the enthusiasm of an ill-tempered kangaroo.

My landing was slightly clumsy. I heard something snap as my left leg hit the narrow stone ledge. Luckily I am immune to such injuries, and the pain dissolved in no time. I gripped the sides of the window casing. Quickly found my footing. Slipped through the open window. The room was dark. Walls, a gloomy shade of purple. Door shut. A nearly spent candle sat on a low table.

I grabbed it to have a look around. An iron bed. Single chair against the wall. White floor. Apart from the wall color, it was just like the room I had seen Rebecca in. Which meant my friend must be close by. I strode toward the door with the kind of confidence only an invisible girl in a strange house can muster.

"No more," came a rasping voice. "Please, not another one."

I jumped. "Who's there?"

The voice had come from the corner of the room. Naturally, I hurried there, candle extended. "It's plain bad manners to skulk about in the shadows. Show yourself this instant!"

"Not another one," said the voice again. "I haven't . . . I haven't the strength."

The candle's flame threw golden shadows upon the wall. It took a moment or two to find him. For he was huddled in the corner, sitting on the floor. I crouched down. Lifted the candle to get a better look. But the light made him flinch, his hands flying over his eyes. The man's skin was terribly pale, almost transparent. It was as if you could see *through* it, to the purple wall behind. Which was most peculiar.

And just as with Rebecca in the stone, the poor man seemed to give off a faint glow. Not enough to brighten the gloomy corner of the room, but more like the last embers of a fading light burning within him.

"Please . . . no more."

"I'm not here to hurt you, dear. I have come in search of my friend—her name is Rebecca Butterfield. Do you know where I might find her?"

"You aren't one of them?"

"One of *who*?"

The man slowly lowered his hands. Lifted his head. Opened

his eyes. He had sunken cheeks. Gray whiskers. A vacant stare. Still, there was no doubt. It was him.

"Mr. Blackhorn?"

Tears pooled in his eyes as they roamed my face. I cannot say if he recognized me or not. My thoughts were a tempest. How could I be face-to-face with Mr. Blackhorn? The same Mr. Blackhorn to whom I had read a charming bedside poem. The same Mr. Blackhorn whose wife had a delightfully unruly wig. The same Mr. Blackhorn who was to be buried by the Snagsbys tomorrow afternoon!

"What happened to you, dear?" I said urgently. "How on earth did you get here?"

I heard the jangle of keys just moments before the door flew open. Acted with lightning speed, I quickly blew out the candle and rolled under the bed. A set of black boots stalked into the shadowy chamber and crossed to the window.

"Justice Hallow must be awful fond of you, Mr. Blackhorn." The woman had a voice of the deep and booming variety. "None of the others get their room aired out every night."

I heard the window being closed and took the opportunity

to slide out and hide behind the door. From there I got a good look at the intruder. Her hair was dark and shorn close to her skull. Her face, battle scarred and boorish. She wore a stiff white dress with a high neck and the same revolting orange coat I had seen on those two men during my first visit. A dagger hung from her belt.

"Bed for you," she said, crossing the room. When the frail man stumbled as he tried to stand, she lifted him as if he were an infant and carried him to the bed. "You've got work again tomorrow, so rest up."

Mr. Blackmore began to whimper and sob. Which was heartbreaking. But I could not forget my mission. Nor could I forget number eight of Ambrose Crabtree's rules: "Do not stay longer than thirty minutes." Time was against me.

With the bald barracuda occupied tucking Mr. Blackhorn into bed, I shot out from behind the door and tiptoed from the room. Well, that was the plan. Alas, the unsightly creature seemed to have the instincts of a jungle cat. She spun around and was charging at me before I crossed the threshold.

Luckily, she had left her keys in the lock. So I slammed

the door shut and locked it. Naturally she did a great deal of thunderous banging. Quite a bit of yelling. Something about pulling me limb from limb and roasting me slowly on a spit.

By then I was already charging down the vast hall, her set of heavy copper keys clutched in my hand. It was my firm belief that *one* of them would unlock the door of Rebecca's room. All I had to do was find it.

As I ran, I noticed something remarkable about the wide hallway. While its walls, ceilings, and floors were white, each unmarked door was a different shade of purple—from the deepest, darkest hue at one end, to the faintest of lilacs at the other.

At the far end of the corridor, I found a grand staircase. As the building was seven or eight stories high, I decided to head up, not down, taking two steps at a time. The next level was another enormous hallway, dotted with unmarked doors. All in shades of blue. The floor above that, green.

Despite the tightness in my chest, I tore up the stairs again to the next floor. And stopped. Panting. Relieved. For it was another hall, filled with a great bank of doors on either side—in every shade of yellow. At last! Now all I had to do was try and recall the *exact* hue I had seen in the vision of Rebecca's room. Then I would find my friend.

I ran down the hall, past the deeper shades, only stopping when the golds began to soften. From there, I felt the safest thing to do was bang on all the doors, calling Rebecca's name. And I would have too (it was a perfectly good plan), if not for the Clock Diamond. It began to flare under my nightdress. I scooped it out, and when I looked within the stone it was wondrously, marvelously yellow. Surely it *must* be the shade I had seen in Rebecca's room?

I ran past the last two dozen doors. Found a perfect match in mere seconds. Tucked away the Clock Diamond and tried to open the door. Naturally, it was locked.

"Rebecca!" I called, banging on the door. "Are you in there, dear?"

I didn't wait for a reply. Just lifted the great bundle of keys and began trying each one.

"You are no doubt stunned that I have found you," I went on. "Much of the credit must go to a kindly wizard I met at

Covent Garden market by the name of Ambrose Crabtree. For the princely sum of three lemon tarts and a poodle, he taught me a frightfully mystical technique called Lifting the Veil—and it would seem I'm rather good at it."

"Ivy—"

"And I had little trouble breaking into this beastly house, thanks to an open window and a handy tree—the Pockets are prone to such timely strokes of good fortune. I have a distant cousin by the name of Jack who had the most thrilling luck with a handful of beans."

"I knew you would come, Ivy."

Rebecca! I heard movement from the other side of the door, and I was certain that my friend was pressed against it. Only a piece of wood separated us now.

"Of course I have come," I said, trying another three keys with rapid speed. "I know you have been suffering horribly, dear, but that is over now. We will be back in London in no time."

"You have done just as they hoped," said Rebecca, her voice so faint I had to strain to hear it. "They wanted me to draw you here . . . but I *tried* to warn you, Ivy. Why did you not listen?"

"Was I supposed to leave you in this place?" I said, pulling out another key and replacing it with the next.

"Yes, that is just what you must do." Rebecca's voice found new strength. "Oh, Ivy, you must go—no good can come of this."

"*Every* good can come of this. You belong at home with your family. They will be beside themselves with joy at Butterfield Park when you return."

"Stop it!" The harshness in her words stung me. "You don't understand! It is too late for any of that."

Silence. I could hear her breathing through the door. Or perhaps I imagined it.

"Rebecca, what are they doing to you? What is happening in this house?"

"The end of hope," she replied, "for it cannot survive here. I have accepted my fate, Ivy, and now you must too. If you come again, it will only make things worse for me. Leave Prospa and do not come back."

"I am not leaving without you."

"You *must*, for if they find you they will—"

"There she is!" Then a loud whistle.

I turned, the keys tumbling from my hand. Coming toward me was the hulking beast I had locked in Mr. Blackhorn's room downstairs, and beside her, a rather enormous man with the same buzzed haircut and orange coat.

"I may have to delay your rescue, dear," I called out with tremendous calm.

Rebecca pounded on the door. "Run, Ivy! Get far away!"

But I didn't. "Fear not, Rebecca. Number seven in Ambrose Crabtree's list of rules states that only my soul has crossed into Prospa and I cannot be harmed. I am safely back in London, even as we speak. So you see, nothing at all to worry about."

Which made it something of a shock when the two burly guards grabbed me by the arms and threw me against the wall.

The female ruffian gawked at me. Then gasped. "It's *her*."

"She's awake," trumpeted her male counterpart. "Justice Hallow will give us medals for this."

"Unhand me this instant, or I shall administer the cruelest of thrashings to you both!"

In response, they began dragging me down the hallway.

I did the reasonable thing—screamed, tried my best to bite them viciously, kicked with tremendous enthusiasm. My captors barely flinched. We had just reached the stairwell when I stomped on the woman's boot. It helped. The mean-spirited cow bellowed and released her grip on my arm. Which I quickly put to good use, pocking her pigeon-brained sidekick in the left eyeball. He let out a cry that would shock a midwife and stumbled back.

I took off like a light, racing back toward Rebecca's room. Scooped up the keys and began another feeble round of roulette, hoping against hope that I would find the right key and free her.

"Hold tight, dear!" I called out.

"Go, Ivy! Go this instant!"

"Stuff and nonsense. I cannot leave you here, and I won't."

My head flew back. How could it not? The female guard had grabbed me by the hair and yanked me with force. The keys were snatched from my hand. I struggled valiantly, but in no time I was once again being dragged down the hall.

"Justice Hallow can deal with you now," said the brute, snickering coldly.

"Don't let them take you, Ivy," cried Rebecca. "Whatever you do, don't let them take you!"

"It seems I haven't a choice in the matter, dear!" I called back.

"Ivy, you control it!" she shouted. "You got here, and you can leave the same way."

"Shut your mouth, Butterfield, if you know what's good for you!" snarled the lady baboon.

"But how?" I cried.

"You lifted the veil . . ." My friend's voice was growing weak. "You lifted it, now bring it down. Bring it down, Ivy."

We were at the stairs by then, and they were frog-marching me down the first flight. That's when I let my arms slacken. My legs turn to jelly. I wasn't really sure what I was doing; I just knew that I had London in my mind. And Rebecca in my heart. So I let it all go.

I heard one of the guards cry out. Something like, "Hold her, you fool!"

"I'm trying," came the anxious reply.

The stairs began to buckle, rising and falling, like an ocean tide. Then my captor's arms—indeed their whole bodies— simply melted away. As Prospa House began to fall, I fell with it. And it wasn't even slightly terrifying.

I closed my eyes, arms out, and plummeted along with

the building. But my landing was of the featherbed variety. All at once I felt solid ground beneath me. I think I rolled once or twice. My nightdress was damp, and I was lying on the wet cobblestones of Winslow Street. Everything was just as I had left it. I got to my feet. Stood there in a daze.

Rebecca had been so close. Just a door between us. But I had failed to bring her home. And Mr. Blackhorn . . . what of him? The sound of his heartbroken sobs rang in my ears. What on earth was happening to them in Prospa House? Were they not meant to heal those dying of the Shadow (the beastly plague that had killed millions in Prospa)? And why did Rebecca not want to be rescued? It was all so unfair. And confusing. And sad.

As I stepped up onto the footpath, my eyes began to mist. It was just the wind. Nothing more. I took one final look at the dark void where Prospa House had been just moments before, wiped the tears from my face, and headed for home.

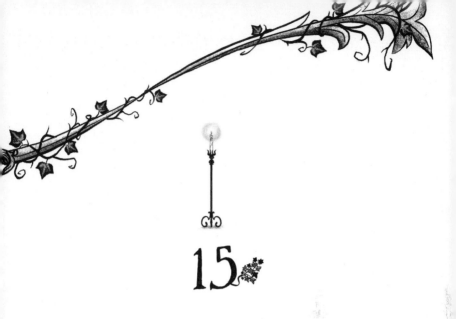

15

"Y our reading was very moving, Ivy."

"Was it?"

Ezra nodded his head (complete with wobbly jowls) and ushered me to a seat by the shuttered window. "But perhaps you might ask your friend at the library for something more *uplifting* next time. Now you rest a spell while Mother Snagsby and I see to business."

Mrs. Rushmore's liver was diseased. The doctor gave her a week. Perhaps two. She didn't want to trouble her family with funeral arrangements and whatnot, so she had called on the Snagsbys. The poem had gone down very well. It was Scottish, I think—about death coming in the night when you least expect it and how we are all doomed in the end. Mrs. Rushmore had wailed like a fire alarm.

I am ashamed to say I didn't read with tremendous feeling. My thoughts were crowded with the events of the previous night. Rebecca. The dark deeds of Prospa House. And what of Mr. Blackhorn? How did *he* get there? And how was it that those bullish guards seemed to recognize me? "She's awake." That was what one of them had said. What on earth did any of it mean? Oh, it was a tangled web!

"Here." Mother Snagsby was holding out a glass of warm milk.

"I'm not thirsty."

"Of course you are," she replied firmly. "Mrs. Rushmore has a great many questions, and I haven't time to argue."

I took the milk. And offered something in return. "I've been wondering about Mr. Blackhorn."

"What of him?"

"Do you recall anything strange about his passing? Anything unusual or out of the ordinary?"

"Such as?"

I knew I must be magnificently cagey to avoid arousing suspicion.

"Well, who can say? Perhaps he made mention of a pressing engagement in a faraway place. Or perhaps he was slightly less dead than you thought?" I gave Mother Snagsby my most understanding gaze. "Is that possible, dear? For yes, nod once. If no, continue to stare at me with withering antipathy."

"Mr. Blackhorn's funeral is this afternoon at two," she said calmly, "and I assure you, young lady, we do not bury the *living* at Snagsby's Economic Funerals." She pointed to the glass. "Drink it and button your lips."

Mother Snagsby was soon hunched over Mrs. Rushmore's bed, whispering about what type of wood she might prefer for the coffin. Meanwhile, Ezra was measuring the poor old woman for length. They were a harmless pair. Shriveled as year-old raisins, but harmless.

I drank down the milk. A muddle of tangled thoughts stretched to the farthest reaches of my mind. And as I wrestled with them, something warm and utterly comforting crept over me. Like a hot-water bottle on a winter's night. Or a generous hug. It reached up and gently pulled me down. It was too delicious to resist. So I didn't.

When Ezra woke me up, the stone felt warm against my skin. Mrs. Rushmore was now covered by a sheet. Mother Snagsby said it was a blessing. The poor lady had died suddenly and was at peace.

Miss Carnage had seen right through me.

"You are not yourself, Ivy, there is no point denying it." She pulled up a chair and sat down beside me. "I insist you tell me what is troubling you. After all, if you cannot tell a bosom—" She stopped suddenly. Blinked a great deal.

"Bathroom trouble, dear?"

The librarian laughed rather enthusiastically. "Goodness no. As I was saying, if you cannot confide in a *sympathetic* friend, who can you confide in?"

I had left the house before Mr. Blackhorn's viewing began. Mother Snagsby was busy making sure everything was ready— flowers, organ music, sandwiches and tea afterwards—so I was able to slip away undetected. Not that I didn't have a perfectly good excuse to visit the library. Ezra had requested that I seek out more *uplifting* poetry. But I couldn't pretend that that was the real reason. I hadn't been able to look at Mrs. Blackhorn when she arrived, dressed in black and sobbing madly. Even her tremendous wig, which was wonderfully crooked, did nothing to lift my spirits.

"It's terribly complicated," I heard myself tell Miss Carnage.

"Has something happened, Ivy?" Miss Carnage had her hand on my hand. She was squeezing it most sympathetically. "Have you had news of your friend?"

I nodded. "I was able to reach her."

The librarian gasped. "You did?"

"It all happened so quickly—I went back to Winslow Street, not sure why, but it just felt right, and the next thing I knew, there I was. Finding her room wasn't easy. There were so many shades of yellow, and then those guards recognized me and it all ended rather badly."

"They recognized you?"

"I think so. Oh, I don't know."

Miss Carnage looked awfully perplexed, but she soon snapped out of it. "You told me that your friend was somewhere far away—but Winslow Street is in London."

"That was just where I departed from."

"How are you back so soon?" asked the curious librarian.

"Could only stay thirty minutes," I said with a shrug. "It's one of the rules—though I have my doubts about several of the others."

"One of the rules?" Miss Carnage gasped again, only this time her hand flew to her shockingly large chin and she stared at me in dismay. "It was *you* who stole Ambrose Crabtree's manuscript from the vault, was it not? Oh, Ivy, I am bitterly disappointed—you lied to me!"

"Highly doubtful. I'm violently honest, as a general rule."

"Even after I warned you not to . . ." The flustered creature stood up. Sat back down again. "You must return it this instant and promise never to meddle with such things again."

"Return what, dear?"

"The manuscript that was stolen."

"Stolen?"

Miss Carnage nodded vigorously. "Stolen by you!"

"Stolen by you? Well, I'm sure you had your reasons, let's say no more about it."

I was practically positive the subject was closed. Miss Carnage felt differently. She took me by the hand into the back office. Shut the door. Sat me down at her desk and said, "That book has great power and is not to be trifled with. If Ambrose Crabtree's rules are not followed to the letter, they could lead to certain death."

The nerve! "Miss Carnage, while I am perfectly innocent of any crime, I can say with some confidence that if I *had* stolen the manuscript, I would find the instructions terribly easy to follow."

Miss Carnage pushed her spectacles up her bent nose. "I see."

"And as for those silly rules, I can only suspect Mr. Crabtree was drunk on rum cake when he wrote them. Some are stupendously wrong—so I've heard."

"Go on," said Miss Carnage, leaning forward.

"Number seven says that when a person crosses, only their soul takes the journey and they cannot be harmed. Well, I have it on good authority that a person can be thrown about and pulled by the hair in a most unpleasant manner."

The librarian paled. "Heavens."

"I want so much to help her, but Rebecca said . . ." My voice had dropped to a whisper, and I found myself looking at Miss Carnage most earnestly. "She said I should never come back.

197

That it would only make things worse for her. I must confess, dear, I am not entirely sure what I should do. I cannot leave her in that hideous place, but I couldn't bear the thought that I was inflicting more suffering upon her by going back."

"You poor girl," said Miss Carnage with such tenderness. "We will not dwell on the manuscript's whereabouts, but you are very right to heed your friend's plea and stay away." She cleared her throat. "After all, you have done everything that can be asked of a friend. Who could blame you for giving up? I am sure Rebecca will understand."

Despite the fact that softhearted Miss Carnage was trying to reassure me, it had quite the opposite effect. How could I think for one moment that it was better to leave Rebecca to her fate? It would be unforgivable!

"I'm sorry, Miss Carnage, but my friend needs me, and I won't give up on her."

The librarian smiled faintly. "How brave you are, Ivy."

The Dumblebys' house was splendid.

Estelle greeted me at the door as if we were old friends, then ushered me upstairs to meet her uncle. The old man rarely left his private chambers and was terribly frail.

"I am so pleased you were able to come," said Estelle as we climbed the majestic staircase with its cast-iron banister. "I was worried you would not be able to get away."

"There is a viewing this morning," I explained helpfully. "Then Mother Snagsby is to meet with a grieving widow who wants her husband stuffed and mounted on the wall. So I am quite free."

"That is excellent news," said Estelle with a warm smile. "I am sorry our friendship has to be such a secret, but if there were any other way . . ."

"Think nothing of it, dear. I'm gifted at skullduggery."

Baron Dumbleby was a marvelous creature. Short arms. Legs like mushroom stalks. Face like a pickled artichoke. His tongue darted in and out with tremendous frequency. Which was a treat. And he was rather bent over. As I was well used to conversing with aristocrats, I greeted him warmly, then remarked that he looked rather like a footrest.

His butler glared at me as if I had said something improper.

But the Baron chuckled softly. "I have never been what you

might call towering, and these days my back has a mind of its own."

"I do hope you like cake, Ivy," said Estelle as the tea trolley was wheeled in by a maid they called Bertha. "We have strawberry cream and vanilla cake."

"I will have a slice of both, and don't be shy on the portions. I'm utterly famished."

While Estelle busied herself at the trolley, I helped Baron Dumbleby take a seat by the fire, putting a pillow at his back in a devastating display of goodwill. The poor creature grimaced as he sat down.

"Does your back hurt terribly?" I asked.

"I'm afraid so," said the Baron softly.

"I have an excellent remedy. All I require is a cup of lard, a length of string, two wooden spoons, and a trapdoor."

The Baron laughed playfully. Can't imagine what about.

I noticed the minute portrait of a rather handsome young man on the side table. He had brown hair, intelligent eyes, and a shy smile. And he bore a striking resemblance to Estelle.

When the tea was laid out, and the maid and butler had departed, we engaged in pleasant small talk until the Baron asked Estelle to fetch his glasses from the dressing room.

"Of course, Uncle," she said.

When she was gone, the Baron turned to me and said, "I am so very glad Estelle has made a new friend. She doesn't spend enough time with girls her own age. My niece carries such sadness around that it breaks an old man's heart. Her mother's passing was a great shock and, of course, Sebastian . . ."

"Oh, yes, I know just how she feels. I recently lost a dear friend, though I am trying my very hardest to bring her back again. But as for Sebastian, I wouldn't worry about him."

"Do you know something of my nephew?"

"Only that he was a rather sickly fellow, who fell head over heels for his nurse." I took a large bite of strawberry cream cake.

"I suppose Estelle told you the sorry tale," said Baron Dumbleby, picking up the miniature portrait. "Was he not a fine-looking fellow?"

"Monstrously fetching."

"Sebastian was a shy young man, kept mostly to himself— but this girl seemed to bring him alive. They formed rather a close bond."

"That would never have lasted." Estelle had returned with her uncle's spectacles. She dropped it in the old man's lap rather abruptly. "Before *she* came along, my brother was devoted to us. He was to take over the Dumbleby coal mines and see that we prospered as we had when my father was alive. But he lost all interest in such things when he met that girl."

While I was utterly certain that the mystery girl who had captured Sebastian's heart was Gretel Snagsby, I decided to do a little digging before I revealed my shocking discovery.

"What did she look like?" I asked casually.

"Dark hair and common features," said Estelle, sitting down on the plump couch next to me and hugging a silk cushion. "Her eyes were large and blue, and I'm certain she used them to mesmerize my brother, though I cannot imagine what he saw in her."

Gretel had dark hair, and her eyes were blue—though I cannot say they looked especially large or mesmerizing in Mother Snagsby's many portraits. But it must be her!

"Hold on to your bloomers, dears," I declared, shoveling the last bite of cake into my gullet, "for I am about to solve the mystery of Sebastian and his one true love."

Estelle gasped. Practically lunged at me. "You know what happened to my brother?"

"Not at all," I said brightly. "But I *can* reveal the identity of the young lady who won his heart."

Baron Dumbleby looked rather startled.

"You can?" said Estelle.

"Why do you look so uneasy, dear?" I asked. "Does the news not please you?"

"I am just disappointed, as we already know about Anastasia Radcliff."

I was frowning. "Who is Anastasia Radcliff?"

"The very girl we have just been talking about," came Estelle's impatient reply.

Which was most unexpected!

"My mother had advertised for a nurse, and Anastasia was the first to apply, spinning a tale about how she was new to London and had no family connections. My mother was a kindhearted soul. She took pity on the girl."

"Anastasia had such a sweet nature, it was impossible not to be charmed by her," added Baron Dumbleby.

This made Estelle stare daggers at her old uncle.

"Her references were good, and Mother had no reason to suspect her." Then Estelle turned her narrowed eyes upon me. "She came *highly* recommended by a close friend of our former housekeeper's—a most trustworthy woman, who worked as a cook for your parents."

"Oh?" I said.

"Mrs. Gloria Dickens," said Estelle. "You know her, I suppose?"

"Never heard of her, dear. The current cook is a short man from the Congo with eleven fingers and an enormous spice rack."

"Really?" Estelle's smile wasn't especially pleasant. "I have it on good authority that Mrs. Dickens still works for the Snagsbys."

"Who can say?" I slapped the girl on the knee. "One cook is much the same as the next, don't you think?"

"Anastasia claimed she was a lodger at your house, though your parents denied ever having met her—which is why I am certain they know the *real* story." Estelle picked up her teacup and sipped it delicately. "My mother spied the girl slipping love notes to my brother, though the proof was never found. Miss Radcliff was dismissed that very afternoon, and my brother disappeared three days later. As far as we can tell, no one has seen them since."

"Surely she and your brother ran away together?" I said with certainty.

Estelle shook her head, and tears began to pool in her eyes. "Sebastian would never do such a thing. My mother ordered him to break it off, and he said that he would."

"Then what do you suppose happened?"

"It's really very simple," whispered Estelle. "Anastasia Radcliff murdered him."

Mrs. Dickens was attacking the drawing-room rug with great enthusiasm when I entered the back garden.

I picked up a paddle from the chair and joined her by the almond tree. The housekeeper stopped beating the carpet for a moment and wiped her damp brow. "Where have you been, lass?"

"Here and there," I said. "Let me help."

I drew back my arm and began thrashing the carpet as if it were a wayward son who had just lost the family estate, and quite possibly his pants, in a rather thrilling game of checkers. Between poundings,

I broached the subject that was uppermost in my mind.

"What do you know of a girl called Anastasia Radcliff?"

Mrs. Dickens responded with a coughing fit. Then she said, "Who's that, then?"

"You tell me, dear." I gave the carpet another whack or two. "After all, you recommended her for a job as a nurse to Sebastian Dumbleby."

"Did I now?" She chuckled, but I wasn't convinced. "Well, as you pointed out, my mind's not what it used to be."

"Stuff and nonsense. I also believe Anastasia was a lodger in this house until she and Sebastian mysteriously disappeared."

"What a story!" But I could see the flicker of panic dancing in the housekeeper's eyes. "Who's been filling your head with such things?"

"Sebastian's sister. She's convinced that Anastasia Radcliff was a most wicked sort of girl. A girl who killed the man she was supposed to love and then ran away, never to be seen again."

"That girl wouldn't harm a fly!" declared Mrs. Dickens with great force. "She loved Sebastian more than her own life, and he felt the same way about her."

I wanted to kiss the chunky fool. How easily I had outwitted her! "I thought you had never heard of Anastasia Radcliff?"

Mrs. Dickens looked crestfallen. "It was a long time ago," she said, wiping her brow again and taking a seat. "What you are asking goes awful deep and way back. Some things are beyond understanding. . . . I don't reckon I understand them myself."

"Perhaps I should speak to Mother Snagsby about it," I said next.

The housekeeper leaped up. "You *mustn't*."

"Why? Why mustn't I?" Something urgent, a deep kind of unease, had stirred inside me. I couldn't explain it, as this little drama had nothing to do with me, but it was there. "Who was Anastasia Radcliff, Mrs. Dickens? And why are you so terrified to talk about her?"

"Perhaps I can enlighten you," came a voice from behind us.

"Lord have mercy," muttered Mrs. Dickens.

Mother Snagsby was standing by the back gate, a stone's throw from the almond tree. She had her eyes trained on me. They were cold but calm.

"It seems you are searching for answers. I believe I can be of assistance." She swept past us and headed toward the house. "Please join me in my office."

16

"Sit."

I did. Immediately.

Mother Snagsby was seated behind her large desk, hunched over like Quasimodo's less attractive older sister.

"You are quite the detective, Ivy. I am most impressed."

She had never called me Ivy before. It was always "young lady." Progress at last!

"Even after I made my feelings about the Dumblebys quite clear, you continued to pursue the matter," she said next. "I'm quite sure you visited their home today. At the very least, you have talked with them at length and seem wedded to their cause."

"Estelle just wants to know what happened to her brother. People do not vanish into thin air."

"Unless they wish to." Mother Snagsby puckered her lips as if she was going to whistle. "Just because Miss Dumbleby doesn't know what happened to her brother does not mean that he has been the victim of some unpleasant crime. Do you understand?"

"Not even a little."

Mother Snagsby sighed, and there was sadness in it. "You are right to suppose that the girl who went to work at the Dumblebys' came from this house, and you are also right to suppose that she and Sebastian formed the deepest of bonds." The old goat laid her hands flat on her desk. "But you are quite wrong to assume she was a lodger."

My frown was immediate. "Then what was she?"

"My daughter."

I confess this made me slightly bug-eyed. "You have *two* daughters?"

"I . . . I have one daughter." Mother Snagsby glanced fleetingly at the portrait of Gretel above the fireplace. (The girl looked to be about thirteen, dark hair loose around her shoulders, a cat curled up in her lap.) "Gretel wanted more than anything to do *good* in the world, and she wasn't satisfied with sitting around taking tea and planning parties, as other young girls might—she longed to be of use."

"That's awfully noble," I said.

"I suppose it is." Mother Snagsby didn't sound convinced. "She had foolish ideas about working as a nursemaid—naturally, I forbade it. No daughter of mine was going to work in service, delivering babies or mopping fevered brows." She smiled faintly. "When Gretel turned eighteen and came of age, she went behind my back and convinced Mrs. Dickens to help her find a position, which is how she came to work for the Dumblebys. I knew nothing of it for quite some months."

"Did you not wonder where she was all day?"

"My daughter was rather clever, and I was rather busy," said Mother Snagsby with some pride. "She told me she was reading to an invalid cousin across town, and as she was that sort of girl, I believed her."

"Then who is Anastasia Radcliff?"

"I should think that was perfectly obvious—Gretel gave a different name to avoid detection."

Which made perfect sense. But not completely.

"When Sebastian's family began looking for him, why did you not tell them the truth about who Anastasia really was? Surely that would have put their minds at ease."

"I did not wish to mire the Snagsby name in scandal. What good would have come of it?"

That really only left one question. And it was of the most important variety.

"What happened to Gretel and Sebastian?"

"The young man's family disapproved most strongly of the match, as did I." Mother Snagsby closed her eyes briefly. "They were from two different worlds and had no business being together. As you might imagine, young love is hard to snuff out, and they fled in the night without leaving so much as a note." She huffed, which seemed to signify that our conversation was over. "And now you know everything."

I found myself looking with astonishment at Mother Snagsby. "Don't you wonder where they are?"

"What would be the use? I trust they are content with their choices and . . . and that they have found peace."

"It must be a thrill to know that Gretel is with her one true love."

Mother Snagsby rubbed her brow. "Yes, it is a great comfort."

Then she mumbled something about pressing business matters, and shooed me from the room.

The girl arrived unannounced on Friday morning. Which was horrendously impolite. But also perfectly timed.

"You are alone?"

"Utterly," I said, offering her Ezra's favorite chair by the bookcase. It was positioned at an angle, facing away from the mantel—which suited my needs.

"I do apologize," said Estelle, taking off her hat, "but as I was in the neighborhood visiting friends, I thought I would drop by and see if you were at home. I was rather worried that I had scared you off yesterday. My great-uncle gave me a thorough scolding when you left."

"You did seem slightly crackers," I said, plopping down on a seat opposite her.

Estelle kept glancing at the door. "Your parents are out?"

"Yes, thank heavens." Ezra was at the blacksmith having his tools sharpened, Mother Snagsby was running errands in town, and Mrs. Dickens had the morning off.

"And your cook from the Congo?"

"Drowned in a bucket of glue," I told her. "Happened last night. We're utterly heartbroken, as he left no instructions for lunch."

The faintest of smirks appeared on her face, but it quickly faded. "I confess, I was hoping to speak with you again about Sebastian."

"Actually, dear, after a great deal of deduction, snooping, and tomfoolery, I have made a most thrilling discovery on that front."

The girl was now perched on the very edge of her seat, her

cheeks aglow. "What is it, Ivy? Oh, please tell me!"

"Anastasia Radcliff is not the villain you suppose her to be. In fact, Anastasia Radcliff is not even her name."

"That doesn't surprise me at all," said the girl coldly. "My mother spent a great deal of money tracing her background and could find no family connections in all of England. When a girl wishes to hide her shameful past and win a rich husband, it stands to reason she would use an alias."

"Actually, your brother fell in love with a kindhearted girl who only wanted to do good in the world."

"Kindhearted?" Estelle's frown was most fetching. "After what she did to my brother, I am shocked that you would say such a thing, Ivy."

"But I do not believe your brother is dead."

"Oh, but he is—Mother could feel it in her bones, and I feel it too."

"And what if you are wrong?"

"I would be glad of it," said the girl fiercely. "Only one person can tell us what happened to Sebastian, but she simply refuses. Stubborn fool!"

"I do not understand," I said, looking gloriously baffled. "Who refuses?"

Estelle tried to sigh with embarrassment. The results were questionable. "What I mean is, Anastasia ran away so that she would never have to reveal what she had done."

"In a moment, perhaps two, you are going to feel like a monumental idiot," I said tenderly. The time had arrived, and I stood up. "The fact is, your brother fell in love with a girl from a fine family. A girl who changed her name so that she could tend to your brother without her mother knowing it." I pointed triumphantly at the mantle behind Estelle. "And that girl is . . . Gretel Snagsby!"

"Gretel *Snagsby*?"

Estelle twisted in her chair to look at the portrait of Gretel above the fireplace.

"You cannot mean her?" she said, pointing rather dismissively at the painting.

"I expect the years have dulled your memory, as you were just a small girl at the time. Or perhaps you are naturally dim-witted when it comes to faces." I hurried over and waved my hand up at the portrait majestically. "She might appear a little younger than you recall, but you must admit, this is Anastasia Radcliff."

The infuriating girl reached for her hat and stood up. "You are quite wrong, Ivy. That is *not* the girl who took my brother away."

17

Mother Snagsby prowled the house again that night, walking past my bedroom door at least a thousand times as she stalked the halls. Did she *never* sleep? I was waiting for an opportune moment to steal away to Winslow Street and journey once again to Prospa House.

I had stared and stared into the Clock Diamond, willing it to show me another vision of Rebecca. Just so that I might know that she was all right. That she hadn't met some grisly fate on my account. But the stone offered only a sparkling night sky.

Following our conversation in her office, I hoped that

Mother Snagsby and I had turned a corner. She had taken me into her confidence, told me all about her runaway daughter.

But if Gretel was really Anastasia, why did Estelle not recognize her in the painting? It made no sense! Yet I did not dare question Mother Snagbsy about it—she hardly looked my way over dinner. Offered little more than a severe word or two about the state of my apron. Everything was just as it had always been.

I heard Mother Snagsby moving past the door, her footsteps fading. Then silence. At last she had retired to bed. Then the click of her shoes as she turned and headed back again.

The old woman would tire in time. She *had* to. Until then, I would stay awake. Frightfully bright-eyed and alert. And when the moment was right, away I would go. At least, that was the plan. But my eyes grew heavy. My head dropped to my chest. I only closed them for a moment. Perhaps two. But alas, the battle was lost. At least for tonight.

The Snagsbys sent me off to Hackney with their blessing. In a carriage, no less.

"Tell Mr. Grimwig that we offer an additional five percent if he's likely to expire in the next seven days," said Ezra as I took off my apron and put on my bonnet. "That's a very generous offer, and no funeral home will do better."

"Yes, dear, I'll give him all the grisly details."

I had told the Snagsbys that a dear friend from Paris had written to me about her cousin, Victor Grimwig, who was gravely ill and in imminent need of a pine box and a hole in the ground. Mother Snagsby quizzed me on Mr. Grimwig's particulars—of which I knew very little, so naturally I made up something fascinating—and decided he sounded like just the sort of customer she liked.

"Though I fail to see why we cannot come with you," she declared as the coach pulled up outside.

"Mr. Grimwig must not suspect that we are after his business. He's a suspicious sort of character who rarely parts with his money." I smiled knowingly. "If you two grim fossils turn up, he will wonder how you knew of his illness and turn you away. Allow *me* to lay the groundwork, and when it is time to measure him up, you can come back with me."

Mother Snagsby grunted. "We never turn down a customer

at Snagsby's Economic Funerals, so I expect you to represent us well and bring home a sale."

Despite the generous helping of troubles currently piled upon my plate, I had not forgotten my promise to the Duchess of Trinity. Yes, she was a hideous, murderous, double-crossing ghoul. But a small voice in my head told me that the Duchess might be of some further use to me. And I knew for certain that this wasn't another one of her wicked schemes. For how could there be any danger in a discount coffin?

"What's this about then?"

Victor Grimwig was a great disappointment. Average height. Thin face. Largely bald, save for two fuzzy gray tufts above his ears. He was neatly dressed. Fond of black. And not terribly pleased to see me.

"As part of a Snagsby's Economic Funerals Saturday bonanza, we are offering one lucky resident of Hackney a stupendous discount on a high-quality coffin," I announced. "And *you*, Mr. Grimwig, are that lucky resident!"

Which was only a lie in the sense that it wasn't at all true.

"I don't want a discount coffin," said Mr. Grimwig, "thank you very much."

"You're terribly welcome and isn't it marvelous?" I felt the moment was right to push past him and enter the small, but neat, sitting room. There were two cats on the windowsill and another by the fire. I sat down on a faded armchair beside a potted fern and got down to business. "Would you prefer oak or something in maple?"

Victor stood in the doorway and coughed rather violently. "For what?"

"Your coffin, of course." I smoothed out my apron. "Honestly, dear, keep up."

Victor coughed again. "I can assure you that I am in fine health and have no need for any of your coffins."

"Stuff and nonsense. Half of our customers claim to be in fine health and just minutes later are dead as a fence post."

"I have a cold, that's all," he said.

"A cold is the beginning of practically every fatal disease, surely you know that?"

Victor paled slightly. Closed the front door and sat down. A ginger cat on the windowsill jumped down and sat in his lap.

"It's nothing to worry about, that's what Dr. Benson said."

"Dr. Benson?" I snorted magnificently. "Dr. Benson told my godfather he had a mild case of hay fever—the poor man had a sneezing fit that *very* afternoon that took his head clear off. It shot right through the dining-room window and killed his horse."

"I think it's you that needs a doctor," said Victor with a raspy chuckle. "I might have a cold, but you're off your rocker, you are."

"You are losing him, child."

It was *her*. I looked about the room frantically. But I couldn't see a ghoulish ball of light or a ghostly apparition in the bright sitting room. Then I glanced to my left, and sure enough, there was the Duchess of Trinity in the potted fern. She was about the size of my thumb, and looked rather like a water drop on one of the leaves closest to my head.

"I have the matter in hand," I whispered.

"What's that you said?" Mr. Grimwig looked mildly concerned.

"Your flair for invention has broken the spell," said the Duchess sternly. "The way to his heart is through his cats, but you must act quickly, child."

"Very well," I whispered, "now kindly shut your pie hole and let me get on with it."

Mr. Grimwig's forehead was etched with a scowl. "Did you just tell me to shut my pie hole?"

"Not you, dear. The gasbag in the fern."

"I will have to ask you to leave." Mr. Grimwig put the cat to one side and stood up. Straightened his tie. "Does your mother know you're out wandering the streets trying to sell coffins?"

"Yes, dear, it was her idea." I crossed the cozy room and knelt down beside the black cat lying in front of the fire. I stroked the beast most tenderly. "I adore most animals as a general rule, but these lazy fur balls are definitely my favorite. I can see that you take excellent care of them."

"I try my best."

"It must worry you *terribly* knowing that after you are gone, they will be thrown in a sack and drowned in the river."

"Never! Not my boys!"

"Yes, dear, I'm afraid so. Unless you have family who will take them in?"

Mr. Grimwig hesitated. "Well . . . no, I don't suppose I do."

"Haven't you any relatives?"

"Well, I had a cousin, but she's gone now."

"You must miss her a great deal."

He laughed drily. "She loved money and little besides. There are turnips with more charity than that *Duchess*."

"Slanderous fool!" bellowed the Duchess. Then she must have remembered the gray lands, for her voice lost its fury. "Oh, but such *courage*, to point out what a horrible creature I was and smear my name. Bravo, Cousin Victor!"

"Mr. Grimwig, if you die without planning your funeral, the city will use your savings to pay for a coffin and plot. But if you

took up our generous offer, and purchased a *discount* funeral, you would save a great many pounds. Pounds that could be left for the care and well-being of your cats."

Judging by the way his nose was scrunched, he appeared to be deep in thought. "There's some sense in that, I suppose."

"I knew you were much wiser than you looked." I jumped up. "My associates and I will come next week to measure you up, collect payment, and whatnot." I slapped his arm in the way all businessmen do when cementing a deal. "When the Snagsbys call, it would help a great deal if you had taken to your bed. Moan and groan. Dribble to your heart's content. If you could wet the bed, that would be thrilling. At Snagsby's Economic Funerals, those close to death can save an additional five percent."

"But I feel perfectly—"

"Remember the cats, dear," I said sagely. "The less you spend on your funeral, the more you have for them."

The delightful man nodded his head. "True enough."

The Duchess of Trinity's glow was alarmingly bright and filled the cabin with ripples of blue light.

"You have done well, child," she said, hovering above the seat opposite me as the carriage carried me back to Paddington. "I am in your debt."

"Yes, yes, I'm overflowing with good deeds. Now tell me what is happening to Rebecca at Prospa House."

"I do not know the mysteries of the universe, child. One hears the faintest of whispers, the merest fragment passing on the wind . . . I only know that when the girl put on the necklace, her fate was sealed and her destiny tethered to this *other* world."

"How did Mr. Blackhorn end up there?"

"Perhaps he took a wrong turn."

I folded my arms. "Are you not sorry for what you did to Rebecca? Because if you aren't, then our deal is off."

"I am crushed, child!" wailed the Duchess. "While I knew the stone was an instrument of death, I knew nothing of its *other* powers."

"And that's supposed to excuse you?" I snapped. "Because of you, Rebecca didn't reach her mother, which is all she ever wanted." The anger had drained from my voice, and all that remained was sorrow. "Duchess, please help me. How do I bring her home?"

She sighed, and it sounded like a lion's growl. "I do not

know, child—and I am sorry for that. But if it is answers you seek, may I make a suggestion?"

I nodded my head. "Go on."

"You've noticed that every Sunday, your parents leave the house on private business."

"It's hardly a secret. They go to Bayswater to visit Ezra's sister."

The Duchess was suddenly upon me, floating an inch from my face.

"Follow them," she whispered.

Then she vanished through the roof of the carriage.

The Snagsbys set off on foot, as they did every Sunday, and walked to the train station. There they purchased two tickets and boarded a train. But not to Bayswater. Instead, as I sat in third class, one carriage behind them, we rolled out of London and headed south, toward Sussex.

The Snagsbys got off at Arundel. Walked through the village without stopping. Over a small stone bridge. Along the only road leading out of town. I was magnificent. More shadow than girl. Slipping behind trees if Ezra stopped to wipe his forehead.

Leaping into tall grass when Mother Snagsby turned her head even slightly. All the while staying wondrously undetected.

I expected them to turn at each farmhouse we passed, certain *one* of those must be their destination. They didn't. Instead, they mounted a low hill and paused in a meadow, beyond which I could see a church steeple. Mother Snagsby and Ezra set to work, picking a large bunch of wildflowers between them. Then the ancient couple, backs bent, entered the solitary churchyard.

A low stone fence surrounded the vicarage, and I climbed it. Crossed the rather unkempt yard. Mounted the next fence and found myself not ten feet from where the Snagsbys had stopped. We were in a graveyard. I was hidden behind a crypt with a glorious marble angel guarding the door. The Snagsbys stood before a white headstone. I was too far away to read what was inscribed on it.

There was an urn with some wilted flowers at the far end. Ezra pulled them out. Fetched some water from a nearby pump. Then filled the urn with the wildflowers they had picked. As he did this, Mother Snagsby retrieved a cloth from her bag and a bottle of something or other and began scrubbing the gravestone.

I cannot say exactly how much time passed. When their

jobs were completed, the old couple sat down on either side of the grave. No words passed between them. At one point Mother Snagsby's rounded shoulders began to shake. Just a little. I believe she might have been weeping. When they were done, Ezra kissed his hand and pressed it to the headstone. But Mother Snagsby did not. Instead, she leaned forward and laid her cheek against the stone. Keeping it there for the longest time.

Then they collected their things and walked slowly from the churchyard.

When they were almost at the bottom of the hill, I bounded between the tombs and was upon the grave in question. The white headstone sparkled in the morning sun as if it was brand-new. But it wasn't. The date carved in the stone told the tale— it was more than thirty years old. And as I read the record of who lay in the ground beneath my feet, I could hear my heart hammer in my chest. For it changed everything.

GRETEL MARGARET SNAGSBY

BELOVED DAUGHTER

DIED, AGE SIX

18

I came upon him as I was making my escape.

"Ezra?"

When I had arrived home from Sussex, the Snagsbys were still out—they were picking from a new selection of coffin handles and fittings across town and had left word with Mrs. Dickens that they would not be back until late afternoon. When they finally returned, I said nothing about what I had seen that day. Nor did I quiz Mrs. Dickens. I simply hadn't the words.

Mother Snagsby looked awfully tired. Barely touched her

dinner. And retired early to bed. For once, she did not walk the halls.

Which was why I used my key to unlock my bedroom door and slip out. My destination was Winslow Street. But really, it was Prospa House. And Rebecca. But as I passed the hall, I saw a candle burning in the sitting room. Ezra was in his favorite chair, a nightcap upon his head, staring out at the dark night.

I entered the room. How could I not?

"Ezra?" I said again.

He looked up at me, his eyes clouding over. He scratched his whiskers and seemed rather puzzled. I understood his confusion.

"The lock on my bedroom door must be faulty," I said, sitting on a wooden chair beside the window. "I was in need of light refreshment and was on my way down to the kitchen when I saw the candle burning in here."

Ezra nodded. "Seems neither of us is in the mood for sleep."

What I said next was both the only thing that made any sense and the one thing I hadn't the right to say. But all else was stuff and nonsense.

"I followed you today. I saw where you went. I know who is buried there."

"Yes," said Ezra.

"You *knew*?"

"Wasn't hard to see you skulking about behind us."

"But why did you not try to stop me from seeing where you were going?"

Ezra shrugged. "A secret can be a heavy thing to carry."

"Does Mother Snagsby know?"

"I don't think so," said Ezra, meeting my gaze. "I'd be awful grateful if we kept it that way, Ivy."

"Of course."

In the half-light, I saw glimpses of Gretel's portrait above the mantle. The one of her reading a book by candlelight. A pretty girl of fourteen or fifteen. An age Gretel Snagsby had never reached.

Ezra seemed to read my mind. "We waited a long time for our Gretel to come along, and when she did, it's fair to say she was a breath of fresh air and we were never the same again. She had just turned six when scarlet fever took hold. . . . It was quick and cruel—she was gone in eight days."

"I'm awfully sorry."

Ezra nodded again. "You're probably wondering about the paintings."

Now it was my turn to nod.

"Mother Snagsby lost her mind," I said thoughtfully, "and you were kind enough to go along with it."

But Ezra shook his head. "Those paintings are how she *kept* her mind. They made the sadness and the weight easier to carry."

"Of course," I said at last.

"We visit her grave every week, we know well enough that she's gone, but when we glance up at her picture, there is *life*, Ivy, and we let ourselves imagine that she is just across the ocean, enjoying her life in Paris."

"What baffles me is why Mother Snagsby would have me believe that Gretel ran away with Sebastian Dumbleby."

This was the first moment I had seen any hesitation in Ezra's face. He rubbed his jowls. "Well . . . I suppose it was less painful to pretend she had a daughter who ran away for love, than one whose little body hadn't the strength to go on."

I could accept that. But it demanded a follow-up question.

"So who is Anastasia Radcliff?"

"Just a girl who lived with us for a time," said Ezra, and even in the softness of his words, I heard new sadness. "She had run away from an unhappy home and turned up on our doorstep, looking for lodgings. We gave her a place to stay and never asked too much—I won't deny that her resemblance to our Gretel had a part to play in that."

"It was a second chance," I said rather boldly.

"Yes," whispered the old man.

"What happened to Anastasia, dear?"

"You might say she followed her heart." He sighed faintly and offered me the smallest of smiles. "It's late, Ivy. Off to bed with you."

I had a few other questions. But the old man turned his gaze back to the darkened window, and although he still sat right across from me, Ezra Snagsby had drifted away and was somewhere else entirely.

I had never purchased a bullfrog before. But as I wasn't very knowledgeable about frogs, giving five pence to the grubby boy next door for procuring the beast seemed a small price to pay. The reason for this slimy purchase was really very simple: Mother Snagsby needed cheering up.

She barely said a word at breakfast, munching on her beloved bacon and poring over a stack of bills. Mrs. Dickens was busy cleaning the attic (which was in a frightful state). I was to walk into town and buy a few yards of cream satin for the three coffins Ezra was finishing up. It was business as usual. But how could it be, now that I knew the truth?

"You have errands to run," Mother Snagsby said as I took her by the hand and led her outside, "and I have letters to write." She squinted in the warm morning sun. "What is so important, and why could you not tell me inside?"

I looked over her face intently, at the thick layer of powder papering over the ravages of time. The crow's-feet making tracks around her eyes. And the colossal mole on her upper lip. And then I thought of Gretel. And my heart melted for the irritable dingbat.

While I could do nothing about all that she had lost, I could certainly fix *one* of her other burdens. With that in mind, I walked her to Mrs. Dickens's vegetable patch near the back fence.

"Just what are you up to?" she snapped as I opened the gate and beckoned for her to join me by a row of carrots. I had my basket of ingredients hidden within reach, behind the cabbages.

"I am about to share one of my most highly anticipated natural remedies," I answered. "It is my gift to you, and you shall have it forevermore."

"If it's anything like your sleeping remedy, I want nothing of it," she snarled. "I had a headache for three days!"

She turned to leave. Which was out of the question. As such, I felt the kindest course of action was to put my boot behind her ankle and push her over. I am pleased to report that Mother Snagsby fell softly into the soil. The wind was *barely* knocked out of her. For I possess a light touch—having all the natural instincts of a butterfly. Or at the very least, a well-intentioned fruit bat.

"Good god, what are you doing?" She screeched like a crow (the grateful siren song of nervous excitement). Tried desperately to heave herself up—I suspect, to kiss my forehead.

"Relax, dear," I said dropping down behind her and pinning her arms with my knees.

"Let me up, young lady!" she thundered. "Ezra! Ezra, come quick, the girl has taken leave of her senses!"

"Ezra is collecting wood from the mill," I told her as I pulled the rope from my pocket and, with tremendous affection, tied her wrists to the fence posts.

"You cannot . . . it's a crime! Untie me this instant!"

I was now free to retrieve my basket of goodies. I opened it and pulled out the tin of tea leaves, then the butter knife and the jar of treacle.

Mother Snagsby's fury vanished behind a rather frightful grin. "Are we to have a picnic?" she said hopefully. "Excellent idea. Now you untie me, and we shall sit here in the garden and enjoy our refreshments. It will be such fun! Hurry, petal, remove mother's restraints and we can get started!"

I giggled and patted her flushed cheek. "Silly creature."

Just at that moment, the bullfrog croaked rather loudly from within the basket.

Mother Snagsby's head shot up. "What was that?"

"Indigestion," I said, smiling kindly. "Perfectly natural at your age, so do not be embarrassed."

I took a handful of tea leaves and pooled them in my hand. Then I poured a large helping of treacle over it. Mixed it together into a sticky paste. All the while Mother Snagsby thrashed about, kicking her legs and trying to pull off the restraints.

"This is the foundation," I explained helpfully. "I will apply it first and then move on to the secret ingredient."

"Apply it where?" snarled Mother Snagsby, pausing for breath.

"That monster on your face, dear." I used the butter knife to spread the gooey paste all over the haggard old woman's mole. "Do not misunderstand, a mole that large is gloriously interesting—I'm sure I could hang my hat on it. But I am confident that if we could remove this one stupendous blemish, there's a perfectly dull funeral director just waiting to burst out."

"You dreadful girl! I will skin you alive! Don't you *dare* do it—I demand you untie me!"

I reached back into the basket. "It is time for the secret ingredient."

Which was when I pulled out the bullfrog. He was of average

size. Yellow and green. Big mouth. Enormous neck. Croaked a few times in protest.

There was a small amount of unpleasantness when Mother Snagsby saw the frog. Threats about sending me to work in a glue factory. Tying me to a lamppost and praying for lightning.

"A bullfrog excretes all sorts of useful chemicals when terrified." While I didn't like explaining my remedies as a general rule, I felt it only fair to reassure the sobbing creature, as she had now started calling for the gates of hell to open and swallow me up. "Chemicals that will eat right through the barnacle on your face. Are you not stunned?"

"Stunned? *Stunned?* If you dare to put that slimy beast anywhere near me, I will see you hang!"

She seemed to be expressing a slight hint of reluctance in moving forward with the treatment. The paste had begun to dry in the sun and was of a perfect consistency. The bullfrog was sure to stick, with just a little pressure.

"When this is over, we will hug like long-lost sisters and discuss a suitably luxurious reward."

"Do not do it, young lady," she growled. "I will lock you in your room for a thousand days and nights. I will see to it that your life is one long list of chores!"

"Hush, dear. You're spoiling the moment."

I gave a warm smile of encouragement, then stuck the bullfrog to her face.

19

Ezra tested the lock and made a few adjustments.

"There," he said, pointing with his screwdriver. "Good as new."

"I don't see why you had to change it," I said rather sullenly.

It was my own fault, of course. I had told Ezra that the lock to my bedroom was faulty when I had come upon him the previous night. And now there would be no journey to Prospa until I figured out a new escape route.

"Mother Snagsby insisted," said Ezra, picking up his toolbox from the floor, "and I'm not inclined to argue with her today."

"She seems upset," I said, plopping down on the bed. "Have you two quarreled?"

A faint smile rose up. "I think she's bothered about that business with the bullfrog this morning."

Oh, *that*. The bullfrog had been a terrible disappointment. I had decided to read to Mother Snagsby while we waited for the remedy to melt away her mountainous love spot. And I had selected the next thrilling installment of simply the best novel ever written: *The Devilish Debutante*.

So engrossed was I in the tale—Evangeline had just pushed her fiancé out of a hayloft so she could marry her sister's one true love—that I did not notice that the paste had begun to give. It was a great shock when the bullfrog dug its flailing back legs into Mother Snagsby's chin and leaped to freedom.

I chased the dishonorable creature, of course. But it vanished behind a row of parsnips. When I returned to Mother Snagsby, she had managed to untether one of her restraints with her forefinger and thumb. She jumped up and charged toward the house, pulling me by the ear behind her. Outrageous!

Ezra took the new key from the lock and slipped it in his

pocket. "Don't worry yourself, Ivy. A good night's sleep, and Mother Snagsby will see things differently."

"Perhaps you might remind her that Mr. Grimwig is to be measured for his coffin tomorrow afternoon—and that it is all thanks to me."

Ezra nodded his head and looked at me in a kindly fashion. Then shuffled off, just as Mrs. Dickens burst through the door carrying a tray with my dinner upon it. Cold chicken and a glass of cider. That was all Mother Snagsby had allowed.

"You eat this," said Mrs. Dickens, putting the tray upon the chest of drawers, "and in a spell, I will see if I can't rustle up some pudding for desert." She sat down on the chair and sighed. "Mrs. Snagsby's been running me ragged all afternoon."

"Probably my fault, dear."

The housekeeper giggled. "Did you really glue a frog to her face?"

"If you know a better way to treat large moles, I would love to hear it."

Mrs. Dickens giggled again.

"I was just trying to do a good turn."

"I believe you, lass, but Mrs. Snagsby takes a long while to warm to people, and a bullfrog is not the way to do it! Her life's been mighty hard and—"

The housekeeper stopped.

"It's all right. I know all about Gretel."

Mrs. Dickens gasped. "Who told you?"

"A friend. I can understand that Mother Snagsby has suffered a great loss, that she suffers *still*, but I only wish she had told me herself."

"These are complicated matters."

I nodded my head. "I also know about Anastasia and how she came to live here."

Again the housekeeper looked positively startled. "What do you know *exactly*?"

"That she fled an unhappy home, and that the Snagsbys came to love her. And that she ran away with Sebastian Dumbleby and has not been seen since."

"That girl was head over heels in love, she was. Even when they weren't together, she would write Sebastian long letters. . . . I've never seen a girl so giddy with love."

"What I don't understand is—why it was such a great secret?"

"Anastasia was the answer to a lot of silent prayers, it seems to me," said Mrs. Dickens, getting to her feet with a groan, "for she seemed to drop clear from the heavens. Talking about her brings back the sorrow, I suppose. It would be fair to say she became a second daughter."

My mind flew to Mother Snagsby with her cheek pressed to Gretel's headstone. "I don't suppose she has the heart for a third."

The housekeeper hurried over and kissed my forehead. "Eat your supper, lass, and I'll see about that pudding."

"I'm here to see Estelle."

"Was she expecting you?"

"Not exactly . . . but we are always dropping in on each other unannounced."

I had come about the letters. After Mrs. Dickens had mentioned that Anastasia was always writing notes to Sebastian, I recalled Estelle making a similar comment. Which gave me a brilliant idea. Two, actually. The first was that if Sebastian loved Anastasia as much as I had been told, he was unlikely to discard her letters. Which meant they might be hidden somewhere ingenious in his private quarters. And as I was a gifted finder, I was certain to unearth them.

The second brilliant idea was this: those letters might very well spell out *where* the young lovebirds planned to begin their new life together. So while returning to Prospa and saving Rebecca was proving monstrously difficult, I could at least reunite Mother Snagsby with the girl who had mended (then broken) her heavy heart.

Now all I needed to do was get inside the grand house so I could begin my search.

"Miss Dumbleby is not at home," said the butler firmly. "Good day, miss."

The door shut before I could protest.

Not willing to give up, I decided to try gaining entry through the kitchen, which was *sure* to be open. Unfortunately, a frightfully glum lump was sitting right in front of the door, shelling peas. It was Bertha. Estelle's maid.

"Do not mind me, dear," I said, trying to squeeze past her. "I just need to pop inside for an hour or two."

Bertha recognized me from my last visit and brightened. "Are you here to see Miss Dumbleby? I can fetch her, if you like."

"Isn't she out?"

"Um . . ." Bertha looked confused for a moment. (I sensed this happened quite often.) "Course she is, I'd forget me own head if it wasn't stuck on."

"Just between you and me, I have secret business here." I lowered my voice for added effect. "I am on the brink of discovering the whereabouts of the sweethearts who first fell in love under this very roof."

"Master Sebastian and Miss Radcliff?"

I nodded. "Did you work here then?"

"No, miss, but my ma did."

I decided to plead my case once more. "The house I live in has seen a great deal of sorrow, and I know, I just *know*, that if I could discover where Anastasia and Sebastian have gone, I could make some of what is wrong right again. At least a little."

Bertha put down her bowl of peas and stood up. But she

did not turn and go into the house. Instead, she came down the stairs and said, "Follow me."

She led me to the stables as if we were two thieves in the night.

"They aren't together," she whispered, pulling me into a feeding stall.

"Who aren't?"

"Master Sebastian and Miss Radcliff," came the surprising reply.

"How do you know?"

"I don't, not for sure, but my ma swore it was true."

"How did *she* know?"

"It was nearly a year after Mr. Dumbleby had vanished, and Ma answered the door to a young woman who was searching for Anastasia. She asked to speak with Miss Estelle's mother, Lady Vivian."

Oh. Was *that* all? It must have been Mother Snagsby or Mrs. Dickens. But wait—why would they still be looking for Anastasia one year after she vanished? After all, they knew she and Sebastian had run away together.

"Did this woman get a meeting with Lady Vivian?"

"She wouldn't see her," said Bertha.

Now I was frowning. "But none of this proves anything about Sebastian and Anastasia. Why do you believe they are not together?"

"Because the lady who came calling said that she had been on Anastasia's trail for months and that the young woman had returned to London just a few days before." The maid bit her bottom lip. "There's more besides. This woman believed that Anastasia had already called at the house to speak with Lady Vivian on a most important matter."

I gasped and did not regret it for a moment. "And did she?"

Bertha shook her head. "My ma spoke with Lady Vivian, and Lady Vivian said Anastasia hadn't darkened her door since the day she was dismissed."

"Why, *why* would Anastasia come back to London alone?" And if she had come back, I was certain she would seek refuge with the Snagsbys, not the Dumblebys. And why had Estelle never mentioned this strange visitor? Perhaps she did not know!

"Ma never saw any sign of Anastasia, but her mind was made up—she believed every word that redheaded stranger said."

It was those last few words that did it. Caused the tiny lumps to rise on my skin. The chill up my spine. "Did this stranger have a name?" I said slowly.

"Yes . . . no . . . oh, it's on the tip of my tongue." The maid slapped her forehead. "I'm always getting muddled, I am. I'd forget my head if it wasn't—"

"Yes, dear, but luckily, it *is* stuck on." I tried to sound calm and not the least bit agitated. "Are you sure you cannot remember her name? It might be rather important."

Bertha blushed and looked down at her feet. "I'd have to check with Ma," she said bashfully. "She remembers everything about her, from her freckles to her black dress. Ma said she was a pretty thing, but she dressed like an undertaker."

I could stand it no longer. "Was her name Miss Frost?"

Bertha brightened like a burning building. "However did you know?"

20

"So when I pass, let my kin rejoice from floor to rafter;

And know that I have come home, to the sweet hereafter."

"Lovely, Ivy," said Ezra quietly, "just lovely."

Victor Grimwig's bedroom was small, but rather cheery. Soft afternoon sun drifted in through the picture window. A chest of drawers and a fine armchair sat along the back wall. A jug and basin on the side table. Victor lay in a single bed with the blankets pulled up to his chin, his three cats lying around him like cushions. He was putting on a marvelous show.

"Mr. Grimwig, may I ask what your malady is?" said Mother

Snagsby, drawing the curtains and bringing a cheerless gloom to the bedroom. "Your color is remarkably healthy."

"He has an incurable head cold," I said quickly. "Isn't that right, dear?"

Mr. Grimwig coughed violently. "Oh, yes, very true."

"Well done," I whispered. "If you could throw in the occasional exhausted shudder, I think that extra discount would be guaranteed."

"I've taken a sleeping tonic," he replied in hushed tones, "to make it more convincing and such."

"Forgive me, Mr. Grimwig," said Mother Snagsby as she retrieved a sample board from her bag with a series of brass, gold, and silver handles fixed to it. "Has your doctor given you any idea how much time you have left with us?"

"Not long at all," I said with suitable regret. "Mr. Grimwig's doctor believes he will snuff it within the week. Hopefully sooner."

"I see." Mother Snagsby handed the board to Ezra and then asked Mr. Grimwig if he would mind if she heated some milk.

"Don't see why not, though I'm not thirsty myself."

As Mother Snagsby walked briskly from the room, Ezra ran through a list of options regarding Mr. Grimwig's coffin. In response, Mr. Grimwig selected the very cheapest fittings money could buy.

"Didn't I tell you things would work out splendidly?" I said, fluffing his pillows with great care.

"Now, Ivy, you let Mr. Grimwig rest," said Ezra, taking the tape measure from around his neck. He pointed to the chair against the wall, "Mother Snagsby and I will finish things up."

I looked back at the door to ensure the old goat had not yet returned.

"Ezra, how well do you know Miss Frost?"

After my conversation with Bertha, I could not get the tomato-headed governess out of my mind. Some great mischief was afoot if Miss Frost was involved! But I had been denied any opportunity to confront the Snagsbys with what I had learned— the carriage was already waiting to take us to Mr. Grimwig's when I arrived back from Estelle's house.

"Miss Frost?" The tape measure slackened in his hands. "Well, she is an acquaintance of sorts. . . . We don't know her well at all."

"I don't think that's true, dear."

Ezra shuffled around the bed and led me away from Mr. Grimwig. "What makes you say such a thing, Ivy?"

"Because I'm practically certain you know her far better than you will admit. I found a brush in my room filled with red hair, and I recently learned that Miss Frost was looking for Anastasia Radcliff a full year after she vanished. And I'm awfully curious about why she would be interested in a girl who was a lodger at your house."

Ezra looked to Mr. Grimwig. Then at the doorway. Then back at me. "When we get home, come and see me in the workshop." He scratched at his whiskers, and for once I found the gentle wobble of his cheeks rather horrid. "We can talk then, and I'll try and explain a thing or two."

The heavy footsteps of Mother Snagsby broke the spell. She bustled in, clutching a glass of milk, and directed me to sit in the chair and stay out of mischief.

"Here," she said, holding out the milk.

I sighed. Why on earth did she insist that I drink that dreary milk? It was the same every time. Milk, then sleep. Milk does that to people, I supposed. But I did not wish to sleep. I needed my wits about me, as I planned to lift the veil that very night and bring Rebecca home. I would break the glass and jump out my bedroom window if I had to. Whatever it took to save my friend.

"I'm not thirsty."

"Of course you are," came the firm reply. "Take it."

Compounding my misery, the Clock Diamond simply refused to cooperate. What use was it to have a mystical stone around my neck if it wasn't any help in thoroughly mystical matters?

I took the glass of milk. "Very well, though I don't see *why*."

Mother Snagsby watched me take two mouthfuls. Then, satisfied, she went back to Victor's bedside to discuss the delicate issue of payment. I did not finish the rest. It was true that I wasn't in the least thirsty. But something else—a grim tightening in my stomach—told me not to drink it. Which was silly. Still, with Mother Snagsby trying to wake Mr. Grimwig (he had nodded off) and Ezra finishing up his measurements, I poured the remaining milk into Mr. Grimwig's left slipper.

It didn't take long for the warmth to wash over me, but it

was lighter than before. I willed my eyes to stay open. And they did . . . for a time. Then the room began to blur. The last thing I saw was Mother Snagsby walking toward me.

My mouth was dry. My head ached. Where was I? Oh, yes, Mr. Grimwig. I rubbed my temples, opened my eyes. Then closed them. As my vision cleared, I looked across the small chamber. Ezra and Mother Snagsby were on either side of the bed. Huddled around Mr. Grimwig, who was sound asleep. They were talking to each other—or was it to Mr. Grimwig? I could not make out what they were saying. Besides, that wasn't what had captured my attention.

I reached to my chest. Felt for it rather frantically. Which was foolish. I knew perfectly well that it wasn't there. How could it be? For Ezra was gently lifting Mr. Grimwig's head from the pillow, and Mother Snagsby was fixing the Clock Diamond around his neck.

21

"Save yourself, Mr. Grimwig!" I cried, leaping up. "They mean to steal your soul!"

The room trembled with an insistent buzzing. The Clock Diamond began pulsing a brilliant white as it came to life.

Mr. Grimwig's eyes flew open. "My *what*?"

Mother Snagsby gasped. Ezra stumbled back. And poor Mr. Grimwig jumped from the bed, sending cats flying and the necklace tumbling to the ground. Luckily for him, the clasp had not closed.

Mother Snagsby had her eyes on the necklace pooled on the

ground at her feet. I sprinted across the room and scooped it up.

The Clock Diamond began to dim in my hand.

"What's that, then?" said Mr. Grimwig, pointing at the necklace. "I demand to know what's going on!"

"It's really very simple," I declared, "for now it all makes sense—the warm milk, the falling asleep for no apparent reason, the stone feeling warm against my skin."

"Be careful what you say," warned Mother Snagsby, indicating Mr. Grimwig.

"Why should he not know what sort of monsters you are?" I was shouting, and it felt awfully good. "You are in cahoots with Miss Frost, are you not? That is why she sent me to you— so that you could get your hands on the Clock Diamond and use it to kill, just like you did with Mr. Blackhorn."

"He made the deal willingly," said Mother Snagsby, and there was steel in her gaze. "He was on the brink of death, and we offered him a chance to escape his fate and live on."

"He is not living!" I yelled. "He is suffering, you cold-blooded devil! Just as Rebecca is suffering because of that stone's wicked promise." I shifted my gaze to Ezra. "How could you? How could you do this work?"

The old man sat down on the bed, head bent. "Miss Frost put the stone in our care some twenty years ago. . . . She trusted us to use it only on those whose life here was at an end." He looked up at me, and there was pleading in his eyes. "We offered them hope, Ivy."

"There is no hope in Prospa House—that is what Rebecca said, and I have seen it for myself."

"You think you're very clever, don't you?" said Mother Snagsby. "Poring over that foolish manuscript and meddling where you had no business. If I hadn't roamed the halls every night, limiting your ability to *travel*, you and the stone would have been lost to Prospa weeks ago."

"We are just trying to help in our own way," said Ezra gently. "That's all, just help."

"Must we explain ourselves?" snapped Mother Snagsby, her lumpy nostrils flaring. "Surely even *she* can see that if one soul from this world, a soul that is near death, can save a great many in Prospa, then it is worth the price."

"You seem very sure of yourself," I said.

"I am sure, young lady," she declared proudly.

"It won't bring Gretel back." It was a cruel thing to say. But I could not resist.

Mother Snagsby appeared stunned. Or was it wounded? She turned to Ezra, who looked at his feet and said nothing.

"I followed you last Sunday," I said, by way of an explanation.

"You had no right!" Then the ferocity in her eyes faltered, as if she had just recalled a moment of unspeakable sadness. "My little girl . . ." She shook her head vigorously. "If there was any way, *any* chance, that she could have been cured or that she might have lived on somewhere else, even for a short time, then I would have taken it, no matter the cost."

"I never wanted a coffin in the first place," said Mr. Grimwig, looking most upset. "I'm as healthy as a horse, I am."

Mother Snagsby had her arms behind her back now. She stepped toward me. "Time is all that matters," she said softly. "Time is worth a *small* amount of suffering, don't you think?"

"You have been lying to me this whole time, haven't you?"

I said. "You never wanted a new daughter—it was just about the stone."

Neither of them answered. They didn't have to.

I shrugged. "It's probably for the best. As parents go, you're rather murderous and insane."

Mother Snagsby lunged for my hand, knocking the Clock Diamond to the ground. We both leaped for it, becoming horribly entangled.

"Give it to me!" she hissed.

"It's *mine*, you humpbacked jackal!" I shouted back.

I grabbed it first, but Mother Snagsby struck like a snake and snatched it from my grasp. In a bid to get it back, I seized her arm roughly—and the villain charged at me, tripping over my leg. As she did, the contents of her pocket went flying. Her recipe book shot out and hit the metal bedpost with a clank. The lock snapped open on impact, and a stack of loose pages fanned out like a deck of cards across the floor.

Mother Snagsby gasped.

I only glanced down for a moment or two, but it was enough to capture my interest. For they were not a collection of family recipes. Each page contained a small portrait in pencil and, beneath it, a name. The one closest to me was a rather stern-looking woman. She had white hair. Sad eyes. And at the bottom of the portrait, a name: KATHERINE JEPSON. Another was a man with tremendous muttonchops and a wrinkled brow. The name: NATHANIAL HUME.

"What are they?" I heard myself ask.

"None of your business," came Mother Snagsby's sharp reply as she began to pick them up.

With the instincts of a jewel thief, I struck while she was distracted, ripping the Clock Diamond from her hand. She barely reacted. I leaped back and slipped the stone into my pocket.

Ezra was collecting the miniature portraits alongside his wife. Which was when I saw the old man pick up a sketch of Mr. Blackhorn. And the truth of what I was seeing hit me. For it made sense. Horrid sense.

"These are drawings of your victims, aren't they?" I crouched down and picked up a handful, giving Mother Snagsby the wickedest of scowls. "These are the people you tricked with the stone—the souls you sent to suffer in Prospa like poor Mr. Blackhorn!"

She snatched the sketches from my hand. "They are brave and noble, every one of them, and I honor their courage and their sacrifice the only way I know how."

"You're all mad! Stark raving mad!" shouted Mr. Grimwig. "I'm fetching the constable. He can deal with the lot of you."

Then he scooped up as many of his cats as he could manage (two) and ran out onto the street in his nightshirt.

"We must go," said Mother Snagsby, "before he returns with the law."

Ezra took the sketches from his wife's hands and placed them carefully back in the book with the others he had collected. "I hope one day you might understand, Ivy . . . understand and forgive us."

Despite his obvious insanity, I was touched by the helplessness in his voice. I noticed that one of the portraits had been overlooked, lying near the bedpost. Out of some lingering affection for the old man, I hurried over and picked it up. I was just about to hand it to him when I glanced down at it. Mother Snagsby saw too and lunged.

But I was too quick. And besides, I had already seen enough.

The portrait was of a handsome young man. Brown hair. Bright eyes. Looked remarkably like his younger sister. I did not even have to read the name printed underneath to know. But there it was anyway, in Mother's Snagsby's neat handwriting . . . SEBASTIAN DUMBLEBY.

"You killed him?" I had begun to back away, toward the door. "You killed Sebastian Dumbleby with the Clock Diamond?"

It did not seem possible.

Ezra was shaking his head. "It's not at all what you think."

"Oh, but it is exactly what I think, for here is his picture!" I threw it on the ground. "Estelle believes that Anastasia killed her brother, but it was you. That was why Anastasia came back to see the Dumblebys after so much time had passed—she was still looking for Sebastian, just as they were. I'm right, aren't I?"

"Sebastian put on the necklace of his own free will," said the old man meekly.

"And why would he do that? Have you two told so many lies that you no longer recognize the truth?"

Mother Snagsby let out a scornful snicker. "You are the authority on lying, young lady, so I suppose you would know."

Which was an outrageous thing to say!

Ezra shuffled over and bent down to pick up Sebastian's sketch. But that's not what happened. The old man appeared to bend down. Then, when he was close enough, he pounced. Swung me around and pulled my arms behind my back. I struggled, but his grip was surprisingly firm for a fossil.

"We can talk at home," he whispered, "just like I promised."

"You will not tear down our life's work." Mother Snagsby's voice was bone-chillingly calm as she stalked toward me. "We have only just gotten the Clock Diamond back, and I am not about to lose it a second time."

She fished the necklace out of my pocket and clutched it greedily.

"Take her to the carriage," she ordered her husband.

Just at that moment, the black cat Mr. Grimwig had left

behind jumped from the bed and began to hiss at us.

Which was about the time I lifted my boot and brought it down on Ezra's foot. He howled and released his hold on me. Mother Snagsby ran to the side table and I gave chase, determined to get the necklace back. She picked up an empty jug and turned back, just as I felt Ezra grab me from behind.

"I wish there was another way, Ivy," he said.

Mother Snagsby threw the jug at my head. I ducked in a display of thrilling speed, and the missile hit Ezra instead. He plummeted to the ground, as you would expect. I was certain Mother Snagsby would cry out in anguish and run to him. But instead she picked up the sample board full of coffin handles. Then thundered toward me, the board above her head, her face a mask of rage.

Which is when I picked up the cat. "Sorry, dear," I whispered to it, "this is something of an emergency."

And then I threw it in the general vicinity of her face. The cat landed on her hair and proceeded to climb it.

"Get off me!" shrieked Mother Snagsby.

I wanted to retrieve the stone, but Ezra was already getting to his feet and Mother Snagsby was spinning around the bedroom like a top. Fearing capture and a grisly fate, I turned on my heels and took off. It was torture to leave the diamond in their clutches, but I bolted from the cottage and did not look back.

22

Dusk had settled over London. The last slivers of pink in the sky were yielding to darkness. I had been wandering for hours. Not lost, but lost all the same.

I thought of going to Estelle and telling her what I had learned about Sebastian. Poor Sebastian! A young man who had died before I was even born had somehow captured my sympathy. What had possessed the Snagsbys to use the Clock Diamond on him? What was to be gained? And how could I break the news to his sister?

Hyde Park was a ghost town when I got there. The people

had all gone home. Home to their warm fires and loving families. I sat down on a bench along Rotten Row. Certain I looked achingly forsaken by the light of the quarter moon.

"Well, Ivy," I sighed wistfully. "What are you going to do now?"

A piercing scream provided the answer. It breached the still night like a siren. A girl's cry. One of great distress. I peered across the vast stretch of parkland and could just make out the silhouette of a carriage on the thoroughfare. Not far from it, a struggle was taking place.

The girl cried out again.

It was impossible to tell how many people were involved, but it didn't matter—I was already racing toward the fray. As I got closer, I saw two burly men pulling a girl to the carriage door. She was putting up a tremendous fight. Her arms swung. Her legs kicked in defiance.

"Let me go, you beasts!" she hollered.

But the girl was quickly overpowered, thrown into the back of the carriage like a sack of potatoes.

I was nearly upon them by that point. "Stop, you monstrous brutes!"

The bigger of the two ruffians slammed the carriage door shut—the girl pounded on the darkened window and called for help. Then he fell in beside his partner in crime.

They began walking toward me.

"What have we here?" the shorter one said.

"Get her!" barked the tall one.

They charged at me. And I charged back. Landed a few decent punches. The odd kick that hit the appropriate target. Tragically, this seemed to amuse the brutes.

"She's got spirit," one of them said with a snigger.

It shames me to say that it took only one of them to restrain me. The hoodlum gripping my arm and the back of my neck frog-marched me toward the carriage. The door was opened, and I was lifted off the ground and flung into the back. The door locked behind me. Next, I heard the crack of the whip as the carriage took off at great speed, throwing me into the seat.

"Pocket?"

I glanced to my left, still violently out of breath, and took my first look at the girl I had tried to rescue. "What on *earth*?" was my response.

Matilda Butterfield wiped the tears from her eyes. "I'm not crying, Pocket, just be clear about that."

"Of course not, dear. Your face is merely releasing excess liquid. Happens to me on occasion."

The noise from the horses and carriage wheels was deafening. A furious symphony of roar and rumble. Matilda pounded on the carriage roof. "Stop the carriage this instant, you sons of dairymaids!"

The carriage turned left, then right, then right again. I pulled back the curtain and looked out. I no longer knew what part of London we were in. I just knew it wasn't a nice part of town. The buildings were grim. The people lurking about, even grimmer.

"I assume we've been kidnapped," said Matilda calmly.

I nodded. "Does seem that way."

With the curtain parted, soft moonlight pierced the darkened cabin. It was then that I noticed Matilda was dressed in a rather fetching pink silk gown. Her black hair arranged with flowers. She noticed me noticing.

"I was at a frightful ball with Mother and I decided to walk home, as it was only a few blocks from our townhouse." She pounded the window. "These spineless criminals grabbed me from the street and pulled me into the park."

"Have you seen them before?"

Matilda shook her head. Frowned. "Why are you in Hyde Park at this hour?"

"Oh, just a moonlit walk."

Matilda folded her arms as if she were cold. "What do you think they want with us, Pocket?"

I looked out of the window and saw dark London flying by. "Nothing splendid."

The room was small. No, the *cell* was small. For that's what it was. Dank and small. No windows. Bare floor. Dark stone walls with mildew bleeding down from the ceiling. The smell of damp and filth. The only light, a tallow candle atop a stool. A bed against the wall. A large and positively grim metal door the only point of entry.

The carriage had entered a lane and slowed, turning in through a pair of gates. We had been dragged from the carriage in a most undignified display and shoved through a door and into a long, dank corridor. It was impossible to know where we were.

Matilda had put up a brave fight. And I had been wonderfully vicious. There was a great deal of scratching and kicking. But it was all in vain. We were carried in. Pushed to the back of the cell. Held there as our ankles were shackled, tethered by a length of chain to the wall behind us.

"You cannot do this!" roared Matilda. "I am a Butterfield, you blockheads—have you any idea what my grandmother will do to you when she finds out what you've done?"

"She's got to find you first, ain't she?" said the tall one.

Which was shocking grammar. But largely true. The disagreeable hoodlums checked the shackles, making sure the padlocks were secure. They muttered something about a pint of beer, then began to leave. Which, strange as it may sound, terrified me more than if they had stayed.

"Do not leave us here!" shrieked Matilda. "Unlock these chains!"

They were at the door now. Soon to be gone.

Desperate for a morsel of information about our plight, I tried a less abusive approach. "I realize you poor fellows are probably the product of defective parenting," I said, oozing charm, "and therefore, can hardly be blamed for kidnapping us. But would you be so kind as to tell us where we are?"

The shorter of the two ruffians took pity. "Lashwood," he said.

The metal door swung shut. I heard the heavy bolt slide into place.

23

"But Lashwood is a madhouse," I said, feeling rather mystified. "Who would want to lock us in a madhouse? I'm not even *slightly* bonkers."

Everyone had heard of Lashwood. It was an insane asylum in Islington, of the most unpleasant variety. The worst in all of London, some said. Which begged the question—what was going on?

"This is a mistake!" shouted Matilda, stomping her foot. "Let us out! We do not belong here!" She turned to me, trying bravely to control her tears. "Do something, Pocket!"

Screams of anguish and madness could be heard through

the damp walls. A rat scurried across the floor at great speed.

"My options are rather limited at the present moment, dear," I said, tugging the chain around my ankle for effect. "We will simply have to wait for someone who isn't a kidnapping thug to come by, so we can straighten out this whole thing."

Matilda began to howl. Pull on her chain. Call for a constable. Demand fresh bloomers and a bubble bath. She only stopped when we heard the bolt on the door sliding back. Matilda and I exchanged anxious and hopeful looks as the door opened and a rather hefty woman in a grimy black-and-white dress came in with a bucket and ladle.

She stopped a few feet away from us and stuck a finger up her nose, foraging about with abandon.

"Water?" she said with little enthusiasm.

"Water?" bellowed Matilda. "Unlock us, you ghastly trollop!"

She looked at me. "Water?"

"Allow me to explain our situation. We are two perfectly upstanding girls who were wickedly taken from Hyde Park and locked in this horrid madhouse. You look like a softhearted sort, so would you be so kind as to ask one of the doctors to pay us a visit?"

"What's in it for me, then?"

Luckily, I was ready for such a question. "Are you a spinster, dear?"

She frowned. "What of it?"

"Well, I know a shoemaker in Bristol in search of a wife. He specifically asked for a nose picker of wide girth." I smiled encouragingly. "I would be glad to pass on your particulars *if* you would talk to the doctor about visiting us."

"I hate Bristol," she said.

"You have to help us!" roared Matilda.

"I hate Bristol," she said again. And with that she walked out and locked the door.

Hours passed. I cannot be certain how many. Matilda quieted down.

"Surely your mother will sound the alarm," I said hopefully.

"Of course she will," snapped Matilda. Her hair had begun to wilt, the flowers coming loose and scattering around our feet like snowdrops. "Mother will be beside herself when she discovers I have not come home. She will summon the British army, if that's what it takes."

Which was awfully encouraging.

"And Grandmother will have a fit!" she declared. "That's if her heart doesn't give out—after what happened with Rebecca, I don't think she could take another Butterfield disaster."

"Your cousin is alive," I heard myself say.

Matilda laughed. Yes, *laughed*. I couldn't blame her.

"What did you say?"

"I said, Rebecca is alive." I slid down the wall and sat on the cold floor. "It's a terrifically long story that doesn't yet have an ending—but the fact remains, I have seen her, and she lives."

"Maybe you do belong in here, Pocket. You're mad."

"The Clock Diamond does more than just kill," I said softly.

Matilda joined me on the floor, her knees tucked up inside her ball gown. "But *how*?"

"When she wore the Clock Diamond, her soul was taken to a place called Prospa. She is not happy there and suffers greatly, but I am doing my best to bring her back."

"Are you wearing it?" Matilda's eyes sparkled eagerly in the dim light. "Perhaps the necklace can help us get out of here. Have you got it, Pocket?"

I felt a stab of regret. Of longing. I shook my head.

"You're lying," hissed Matilda.

Before I could reply, the door opened with a torturous creak. Pale light from the corridor washed into the small cell. The doctor. It had to be the doctor!

I heard the clicking of a cane over the stone floor—like the ticks of a grandfather clock. And it chilled me to the bone. For it couldn't be. Could it? A bewildered frown was already settling on my face, just as Lady Elizabeth Butterfield walked into the dank chamber.

"Welcome," said the old bat.

Matilda and I leaped to our feet, our chains rattling in a ghastly symphony.

"You don't know how pleased I am to see you, dear!" I cried, showering Lady Elizabeth with my most grateful, yet stunned, expression. "We have had the most shocking ordeal. Kidnapped. Pushed about. Chained to a wall. Haven't we, Matilda?"

The girl did not reply. She only grinned.

"Matilda, is this true?" said Lady Elizabeth, peering at her granddaughter.

"Every word, Grandmother."

"Pleased to hear it," she huffed.

Which was odd. I felt I was missing something. Why were they talking in such a strange manner? It only made sense when Matilda bent down and removed the shackle from around her ankle with ease. After all, it had never been locked.

She kicked it away and took her place beside Lady Elizabeth.

By this stage I was shaking my head. "I don't understand."

Lady Elizabeth lifted her cane and pointed it at me. "You filled Rebecca's head with dangerous nonsense, and I am certain it led to her death. And you destroyed Matilda's birthday ball, making her the laughingstock of Suffolk. The Butterfield name is now mired in scandal and tragedy, and it is all because of you, Miss Pocket."

"Grandmother didn't think you were stupid enough to fall for our little trick," said Matilda brightly, "but I promised her that you were."

"We've had you followed for weeks," said Lady Elizabeth with delight.

"This whole night has been . . . ?" I didn't finish the sentence. It was too awful.

"This whole night has been the beginning," said Lady Elizabeth. "The beginning of retribution for your sins, Miss Pocket."

The old bat was just as I remembered her. Head like a walnut. Hands like talons. Bony as a skeleton. Full of fury. Miss Frost had warned me that Lady Elizabeth would direct her venom at me after Rebecca's death, but I had not taken her seriously.

"You cannot do this," I said. "A person cannot be committed to a madhouse without a doctor's say-so. I have read of such things in perfectly reputable novels."

Lady Elizabeth huffed. "Never read a novel that didn't make me want to shoot the author with a musket." She turned her wrinkled head toward the door. "Professor, come!"

I did not know it, but a figure had been listening in the corridor outside, waiting for his cue. He walked briskly into the cell and smiled rather gushingly at Lady Elizabeth.

"Professor Ploomgate is one of the most respected doctors in the country," said Lady Elizabeth. "And as I am a member of the board here at Lashwood and a rather *generous* benefactress, he agreed to assess your questionable mental state."

"How are you feeling, Ivy?" said Professor Ploomgate.

"Never better, dear," I said, as sanely as I knew how. "Apart from being the victim of a rather vengeful old bat and her hateful granddaughter."

"I see," said the Professor, with a meaningful nod of his head.

He was impossibly grim. Sour expression. Eyes of the green and bulging variety. A forehead so vast and furrowed, it was practically crying out for wallpaper. But as frightful as he appeared, he was a respected doctor and was certain to see through this wicked scheme.

"Do you speak with ghosts, Ivy?" he asked next.

"Only when absolutely necessary," was my winning reply.

"Very interesting."

"Now she thinks Rebecca is alive in some other world," Matilda added helpfully, "and just a short time ago, she told me she had visited there herself."

The Professor's bulging eyes threatened to pop clear out of their sockets. "The patient said she had traveled to another world?"

"Perhaps she has," said Matilda. "There is a necklace she possesses that is rather unusual."

"Claptrap!" barked Lady Elizabeth. She hit the Professor's

shoe with her cane. "Is this not proof enough that she's deranged?"

"Is this true, Ivy?" He stepped toward me. "Do you believe that you have left this world and reached another?"

The situation was getting rather out of hand.

"Look, Professor Plumcake," I said, "I think there has been—"

"Ploomgate," he said tersely. "My name is Professor *Ploomgate.*"

"Well, that's not your fault, dear. It's rather like your forehead—regrettable, but entirely out of your control. Now be a good man and unchain me."

"What did I tell you?" snapped Lady Elizabeth, hitting the Professor's shoe again. "Here is a girl of low rank, a *nobody*, who tells wild stories about herself as easily as she breathes. If that isn't a sign of mental disorder, I don't know what is!"

Professor Ploomgate lifted his head. Closed his eyes. Then opened them again and took a sharp intake of breath. "In my professional opinion, the girl is disturbed." He turned and patted old Walnut Head on the shoulder. "You were right to bring her here, Lady Elizabeth."

"She only wants to punish me," I said urgently. "This is about revenge, Professor, not the state of my mind. If you can't see that, dear, then *you're* the mental patient."

Perhaps this wasn't the best course of action. The professor walked from the cell, ignoring my loud protests.

"Come, Matilda, let us go," said Lady Elizabeth.

"Wait," said the girl.

She stepped close to me, and I could see the hunger in her eyes. "Where is it, Pocket?"

And I knew just what she meant. The horrid girl searched my neck. And the pockets of my apron. And my dress.

"What have you done with it?" she hissed.

"Rebecca is alive," I whispered, "and all you care about is the diamond that took her away. Shame on you, dear."

Something flashed over her face. It was fleeting. But it was there.

She stomped toward the door. "I will meet you in the carriage, Grandmother."

Lady Elizabeth scowled at me for the longest time. I slid down the wall and sat again. Staring at the opened door.

Longing to pass through it and be free.

"Does it soothe your guilt, Miss Pocket, to imagine that Rebecca has escaped death and lives on in some far-flung world?" she said curtly.

"Does it soothe your guilt to lock me up in this place?"

"Why should *I* feel guilt?"

I looked up at her without fear. "Why were you not kinder? Why did you not try and understand about the clocks, about the piece of her that was missing?"

"She looked in one piece to me," barked Lady Elizabeth.

But she knew *exactly* what I meant.

"The girl had lost her mother. Did she need to lose her common sense as well?" Lady Elizabeth's worn face hardened right before my eyes. "Rebecca needed a firm hand, not a soft touch."

"She needed *you*, dear. But instead of love, you showered her with disapproval."

"Get comfortable, Miss Pocket," said the old bat, lifting her cane once more and pointing it at me, "for you are going to be an inmate at Lashwood for a *very* long time."

24

There was music in the madhouse. It went on all night.
Courtesy of a woman humming, her voice echoing down the
empty corridor—no doubt some lunatic locked in another cell.
She had just the one tune. And as soon as she was finished, she
would start again.

Her pitch was perfect, but as that first night stretched on in
endless misery, and the tune kept repeating again and again, I
would gladly have smothered her with my apron.

There were other voices. Shrieks of lunacy. Wretched
sobbing. One fellow called for his mother every ten minutes.

Another swore like a pirate and made violent threats.

I spent most of my time trying to lift the veil. Hoping to make the bleak madhouse fall away and Prospa House rise up. But without the Clock Diamond, all I managed to conjure was a headache.

Being a girl of bright ideas, I then decided to call upon the Duchess of Trinity.

"I'd like to box your ears for *again* trying to use me for a horrid act of revenge," I said aloud. "But the thing is, I'm in rather a pickle, and I was wondering if you could drop in and offer some assistance."

Nothing. Not even a ghostly cackle.

As the cell was small and wretched, I passed the time in a variety of ways. Sitting was a great favorite. Walking about until I reached the end of my chain also figured prominently.

Professor Ploomgate had not visited again. The hefty woman in the grimy black-and-white dress would come with a bowl of gruel. A ladle of water. I did not change my clothes, for I had no others. I did not wash. I did not see the sky. Such was my new life.

Three days passed like this.

Someone new brought the gruel on day four. (Saturday, I think—though it was hard to keep track.) A boy of about nine or ten. Dark hair. Brown skin. Large hazel eyes. Interesting ears. He came in silently, carrying two buckets, and served me a helping of slop.

As we were only fed twice a day, I ate it as if it were Mrs. Dickens's finest porridge. When I had scraped the very dregs from the wooden bowl, I wiped my mouth on my sleeve and handed the bowl back to him.

Then the boy did something most extraordinary. He filled the bowl with another helping of gruel. As if that were not enough, he then pulled a piece of stale bread from his pocket and handed it to me!

"You wouldn't happen to have a few uncooked potatoes in there, would you?" I said, biting into the bread and savoring its crusty goodness.

He looked at me strangely. As if eating raw potatoes required an explanation.

"I'm a tiny bit dead," I said between mouthfuls, "and it's had rather a strange effect on my appetite."

"Blimey," he replied, clearly impressed. "I'll see what I can rustle up tomorrow."

"Have you worked in this ghastly place long?"

"Just started this week. Pay's terrible, but there's plenty to eat and I can sleep down in the cellar most nights."

"You sleep here?"

"When I have to."

"What's your name, dear?"

"Jago," was his answer. "If you're being official-like, I'm *Oliver* Jago, but it's a rotter of a name, so I chucked it."

I used the last of the bread to mop up the gruel. "I knew an Oliver once. An orphan, of course, with hideous eating habits." I shoved the bread into my mouth and chewed it feverishly. "He was always asking for *more*. Which is frightfully bad form."

A bell sounded from somewhere up above us, signaling the end of dinner.

Jago picked up the buckets. "See you tomorrow, I guess."

"Yes, dear. I'll be waiting."

The boy stopped and looked back at me.

"You're awful young. What you in for, then?"

"Revenge," was my answer.

He shrugged. "Good a reason as any."

I began to look forward to Jago's visits most eagerly. He took to calling me chatterbox. Can't think why. And he would always give me extra gruel and bread. Even the odd potato (lovely boy!). In the few minutes we had, Jago would tell me of life outside— about foraging around London for an extra penny or two. He never said anything about his family. I assumed because he didn't have one.

Being a shy sort of girl, I was reluctant to speak about myself. But slowly I came out of my shell (not unlike a sea turtle) and told him a few snippets from my wondrous adventures. He seemed awfully impressed.

As he was taking his leave one evening, the humming lady's endless melody rolled in like an afternoon breeze. A very *annoying* breeze.

"I'm to feed her next," he said eagerly. "She's right mad, she is."

"Doesn't she know any other tune?"

"Hums it for the baby," explained Jago. "'Sleep and Dream, My Sweet,' it's called."

I gasped. "Of course . . . it's a lullaby."

"Matron says she's been here for years."

"And she has a baby?"

"Not here, she don't."

"Jago, would you be a dear and ask Professor Ploomgate to stop by? I rather fear he has forgotten about me, and I'm awfully keen to get out of this beastly cell. You see, I'm not at all deranged."

The boy thought on it a moment, then said, "Sorry, chatterbox, they'd chuck me out on my ear if I made a racket about one of you lot."

That next morning, when Jago came with breakfast (more cold slop), he was called out into the corridor by an orderly barking instructions about cleaning the pots in the kitchen when he was done. I was sitting on the ground, scratching at the skin around the shackle on my right ankle. It was violently itchy. As was my hair. Fleas were a distinct possibility.

I heard the sound of footsteps. And voices. Perhaps Professor Ploomgate had come to see me! I was just getting to my feet when I saw the professor and a young woman walk briskly by. They were deep in conversation and did not glance my way.

The girl had shiny brown hair, worn up. A dazzling white dress. And a matching feather hat. And she looked remarkably like Estelle Dumbleby. But that was quite impossible. What would she be doing here? Then a thrilling thought burst into my mind—she had noticed I was missing and was on the hunt for me!

I ran at top speed toward the corridor. "Estelle, it's me, your dear friend!"

Three things happened quickly. First, the chain reached its end, the shackle digging into my ankle and stopping me cold. Second, the orderly charged into the small cell and put his calloused hand over my mouth. Third, Jago slammed the door shut.

After that, all I heard was the madwoman humming.

Matilda came on the thirteenth day.

I suspect she was there to gloat, with Lady Elizabeth's blessing. I could not imagine her dropping by without it. Matilda had on a yellow muslin dress. Her black hair flared with splashes of scarlet in the candlelight. She told the orderly to leave and close the door.

"Well, Pocket, how do you like your new home?" She did not get too close. "Grandmother hopes you are settling in nicely."

I patted down my hair as if it was not a greasy tangle. "It's really rather wonderful," I said brightly. "Haven't had this much time to myself since I spent that summer by the Hudson River in a locked box. And the food is remarkable."

"You are miserable, admit it."

"Stuff and nonsense. Look around, dear. I have this gloriously creepy cell, a constant stream of lunatics bellowing about their troubles. There are at least three ghosts wandering about the place dragging balls and chains—and that's not even the *best* part."

My smile was mischievous. As if I had a delicious secret.

Matilda was frowning. She didn't want to ask. Not for anything. But how could she not?

"What is the best part?" she demanded to know.

I cupped my ear for effect. And sure enough, among the shrieks and hollering, you could hear her pretty tune.

"It's just some lunatic humming," said Matilda, folding her arms.

"But don't you see? This is the perfect place to write my great Gothic novel—there is inspiration in the very mold on the walls, the rats at my feet, and the slop in my bowl."

"Nice try, Pocket," said Matilda with a sneer, "but you haven't any paper."

"I'm writing it in my head, dear. All the best novelists do these days."

"Sounds utterly mental—you deserve to be locked up." She paused. Seemed to be trying to find the right words. "Listen, Pocket, I'm not saying I believe a word of what you said the other day, but I want you to tell me about Rebecca. Tell me everything from the beginning, and do not stop until you were thrown into the carriage in Hyde Park."

"All right."

And that is just what I did. Leaving no detail out. When I was done, Matilda looked past me to the dank wall. Then down at the floor. Then the flea-ridden bed.

"Why should I believe you?" she asked at last.

It was an excellent point. I only had one answer.

"Because you know that a girl simply doesn't shrivel up and die when she puts on a necklace. The Clock Diamond can do wondrous and wicked things. But unless I get it back from the beastly pair of nincompoops who have it, I won't be able to reach Rebecca and bring her home."

"Grandmother wants you to rot in this place."

"And what do you want, dear?"

She frowned as if the idea had never occurred to her before. Then the malice returned to her pretty blue eyes. "Nice try, Pocket."

I missed the sky terribly. Sometimes it was all that I could think about. My cell had no windows, and the only way I could tell whether it was day or night was by the delivery of breakfast and dinner. So I would imagine it—a full moon and a scattering of stars. Or a sunrise over London, dappling the streets in ginger.

Sleep eluded me that night. So I lay there in the dark. The humming lady had gone mercifully quiet. I scratched at my arms to sooth the itching fleabites. Wondered about Matilda's visit. Wished I had said something more.

The bolt of my cell door suddenly slid back. It was quieter than usual. Slower too. I jumped to my feet. Clenched my fists as I prepared to do battle. Who was coming upon me in the dead of night?

Soft light bled into the room as the door opened. Followed by a short figure—the light pushed around him, but I could not see his face. He carried something in his arms.

"I've pummeled bigger men than you, shorty," I declared, "so be warned!"

The figure closed the door. Casting the cell in darkness again. I heard the rustle of clothes. Then the strike of a match. The flame found a candle held in his hand and its glow leaped all over his face.

I stepped forward. "What are you doing here? Dinner was over hours ago."

Jago was holding a dark cape. But seemed slightly lost for words.

"Oh, you delightful street urchin," I said, taking the cape and fixing it around my neck. "You have brought me this to warm me against the cold night." I yawned. "What time is it?"

"A bit after eight."

"It's been such a horrid day, and I expect I've been rather short with you since you helped that brute silence me."

"I'm right sorry about that," he said bashfully. "It's the job, that's all. If I didn't help, they might get to thinking I was doing special favors for you and such. Now listen—"

"Perfectly understandable. As I told you when that buffoon took his hand away from my mouth, I thought perhaps I had seen a dear friend of mine. But that couldn't be—"

"Won't you hush for a second, chatterbox? We haven't much time."

"Time for what?" I said rather sullenly.

"I'm fixing to get you out of this place."

I gasped with shock and delight. "When? Tonight?"

Jago crouched down, pulled out a set of keys, and proceeded to unlock the shackle at my ankle. With that, I was freed. He stood up and held out his grimy hand. And I took it.

CRUMBLE STREET

25

Twenty minutes. That's all we had. Twenty minutes to break out of this fortress. The keys that unlocked the side door and the back gate hung on a hook in the watchman's office. He used them to check all of the doors and gates every hour on the hour. The rest of the time, he dozed at his desk.

Jago had waited until he nodded off, then expertly lifted the keys. But in twenty minutes, when the clock in the watchman's office chimed nine o'clock, he would wake and reach for those keys. And when he discovered they were not there, he would sound the alarm.

"There won't be no second chances," said Jago as we slipped out into the corridor, "so keep close."

"Right behind you," I said softly.

A few candles burned on brackets along the dank hallway. We moved swiftly, the cries and taunts of lost souls making it hard to hear anything else. Luckily, Jago did.

We were at the end of the corridor when he stopped me. Stuck his nose around the corner, then shot back.

"It's Matron!" he hissed. "Blimey, we're done for."

"Jago, is that you?" called the matron sternly.

The poor boy turned pale (well, as pale as his skin would allow). Thinking with the kind of crafty quick-wittedness you might expect from a seasoned criminal, I rushed to the nearest cell door, drew back the bolt, and slipped inside.

Jago hastily closed the door behind me. Through the wall I heard the sound of Matron scolding him for wandering about the halls when he should be upstairs scrubbing pots.

Inside all was darkness. My eyes slowly adjusted to the light as I edged into the corner. It hadn't occurred to me that there might be some danger in choosing to hide in the cell of a mental patient. There hadn't been time.

As the darkness gradually ceded to shadows and shapes, I could just make out a bed against the far wall and a figure upon it. I could hear slow breathing and supposed the inmate was asleep. But a sudden shriek from a nearby cell changed that.

First, there was the rustle of a chain. A gasp. Then she started to hum. The rich melody of her voice seemed to slither through my ears and track about my body. There was something glorious and haunting in it.

"Mmmm mm mmmm mm," she hummed.

I stepped forward softly. As I did, the dark light around her seemed to lift, offering a faint glimpse. What a sight it was! Long matted hair covered her face like a curtain. She wore a nightgown that I was sure at one time had been white. Her feet were bare and black with soot. And she was hugging herself tightly. The music stopped suddenly. She lifted her head as a wolf might, and I heard her sniff the air.

I backed away, retreating to my corner. I wasn't scared, but something else. Something I could neither name nor understand.

"Hello, dear," I said softly.

She drew back, her chains rattling.

"I mean no harm," I whispered next. "I have been listening to you hum these past thirteen days, and when it wasn't driving me batty, it was perfectly lovely. You have tremendous pitch, for a lunatic."

"Mmmm mm mmmm mm," she began again.

Then the door opened swiftly, and Jago appeared. But the woman did not pause, and her melody covered our voices as I rushed toward him.

"That was close," said Jago. "Someone posh from the board's come by unexpected, and they're all in a flap. Come, we haven't much time."

"Good-bye," I whispered.

I stepped out into the corridor, and Jago bolted the door behind us.

Then we took off again down the passageway. Turned at the far end and ran until we reached a set of back stairs. Once there, Jago did a most unexpected thing. He took the keys and placed them in my hands.

A frown creased my forehead. "Are you not coming down with me?"

He ignored the question. "You go down these stairs and

follow the hall to the eastern door. Use this key to unlock it. From there it's a short dash across the yard to the back gate. Use *this* one to unlock that—then run for your life."

"But if I take the keys, you won't be able to put them back before the alarm is raised."

"It's too late for that now," said the boy. "I'll make a racket when I get upstairs and ring the bell myself. Then I'll point them in the wrong direction."

"But what if they find out what you've done?"

"I'm a smart one, chatterbox. They'll never know it's me."

"Why are you helping me?"

"'Cause you don't belong here."

I hugged the little ragamuffin and took off down the stairs.

My instructions were simple enough, and I followed them well. At the bottom of the stairs I found a long passageway with a door at the end. I took off at top speed, my eyes fixed on the path to freedom.

I was nearly halfway there when I came to a shuddering stop. A corridor peeled off to my left. The smart thing would have been to run right past it as fast as I could. But I heard the distinct echo of voices. I pulled up. Panting wildly.

A man was speaking. Then a woman bellowed over him. Her voice unmistakable.

"My granddaughter tells me that she is as impossibly cheerful as ever," snapped old Walnut Head. "Why is her spirit not broken? Are you running a resort or a madhouse, Professor Ploomgate?"

"We have deprived her of liberty, sunlight, nutrition," came the Professor's insipid reply. "I do not know what else we can do."

"Think of something, you lumbering jackass!"

With every moment, their voices and the click of Lady Elizabeth's cane grew louder. They were coming right toward me. The obvious solution was to run back—but where would that lead? Jago was about to raise the alarm and the halls would be swarming with orderlies, all on the lookout. The only option was to risk exposure and make a run for it.

With tremendous care, I took a peek. It was only the briefest of glimpses, but it was enough. The group consisted of Professor Ploomgate, Lady Elizabeth, and Matilda. They were perhaps thirty feet away. Lady Elizabeth and the Professor were deep in conversation and did not see me. But Matilda did. I was practically positive.

"Grandmother," said the pretty brat, "there's something you should know."

"What is it?" said the old bat gruffly.

The game was up. I prepared to run.

"My bracelet is missing, and I know I had it on when we arrived. We simply *must* go back and look for it. After all, if anyone in this beastly place was to find it, I would never see it again."

"I assure you," said Professor Ploomgate, "that my staff are of the highest morals and character."

"Claptrap!" huffed Lady Elizabeth. "Come, we will retrace our steps and see if it has fallen off somewhere along the way."

And with that, I heard them turn around and walk back the way they had come.

Just then the bell began to ring and I heard raised voices sounding the alarm.

I took off, racing toward the eastern door.

"We've got a runner!" came a frantic cry.

My hands shook as I found the right key and unlocked the heavy door. I charged outside, cold wind swirling around me. There were lamplights dotted around the high brick wall, and I soon spotted the way out. I could hear other footsteps pounding the ground as I ran.

The back gate had a large padlock connected to a thick chain.

"Check all the gates!" bellowed a guard.

I said a silent prayer that the key would work as I slipped it in. The padlock released with a glorious *click*. I pulled on the chain. Unlatched the gate. Practically leaped through it. And all the while, I was unable to comprehend why Matilda Butterfield had let me escape. It was astounding! Impossible!

A narrow lane hugged the wall surrounding Lashwood, and I ran along it until a side street came into view. I could hear frantic yelling on the other side of the wall, whistles being blown and boots thumping across the yard.

A single gaslight lit the next street. As I charged along the footpath, my cape flying out behind me, I could hear a carriage approaching. So I slowed, hugging the row of terraces to obscure myself. Waited for it to pass.

Then I felt it. A presence behind me. Terribly close. A hand gripped my arm. Without turning around, I pulled violently away. The carriage swept by, the sound thunderous, and I sprinted onto the road and lunged at it. Grabbing the rear bracket, I managed to hoist myself up, holding on for dear life.

As it sped away, I dared to look back. But I could see no sign of my attacker.

There was only one place I could think to go. One place I might seek refuge. So that is where I went.

After all, my options were limited. The Snagsbys' was out of the question, on the grounds that they were violent criminals. Miss Carnage was tragically out of reach, as I did not know where she lived. And the London library would surely be closed at this late hour. So that only left one option, and I felt that under the circumstances, it was a good one.

Unfortunately, not everyone agreed.

"Miss Estelle and the Baron have retired to bed."

It was the butler again. He looked me up and down with disapproval. Perhaps because I looked like a girl who had just escaped from a madhouse—matted hair, dirty clothes, stinking to high heaven.

"I have news for Miss Estelle. I would have come sooner, but I was rather preoccupied at Lashwood."

"As I said, Miss Estelle has retired to bed."

"It's all right, Lampton," came a bright voice.

Estelle appeared in all her loveliness. Almost as if she had been hiding behind the door. "Ivy is a dear friend and is always welcome."

I was terribly moved by her bright smile. How it would fade when I told her about Sebastian's fate.

As I walked in, I hit the butler on the shoulder and spoke from the corner of my mouth. "Have a mop and bucket brought in immediately. There is sure to be an ocean of tears."

When I entered the magnificent drawing room, Estelle took my cape and offered me a comfortable armchair.

"Ivy . . . ," said Estelle, frowning as she sat down opposite me. "I do not quite know how to say this, but you look rather disheveled. Where have you been?"

"In a madhouse, dear." I felt the truth was my best option. "It's a dreadfully long story, but I was the victim of a vengeful old bat with hatred in her heart."

Estelle gasped with great conviction. "Where were you imprisoned?"

"Lashwood. Actually, dear, I'm almost certain I saw you there."

"Me? What a strange thing to say."

"I'm sure it was just someone who *looked* like you, but the resemblance was stupendous."

A maid came in, and Estelle ordered tea and refreshments. Then she stood up.

"We must run you a bath and do something about your clothes. You wait here and have something to eat while I see to all the details."

"Do hurry, dear, for I have some rather grim news to report."

Estelle nodded and quickly walked from the drawing room. I sat back and took a long breath as I glanced around the sumptuous chamber. My friend would no doubt insist that I stay on with them. As a treasured friend and sister. It was sure to be a perfectly pleasant life.

Oh, but the Clock Diamond. And Rebecca. I could not forget my mission. At first light, I would return to the Snagsbys' and demand the necklace back. Failing that, I would find a way to steal it, before they could use it again on another unsuspecting victim. But for tonight, I would allow myself a brief window of rest and fine food.

I closed my eyes. But the sound of sobbing out in the hall brought me quickly to my feet. I hurried out and found a maid carrying a tray up the stairs, crying like a rainstorm. It was Bertha, who had been so helpful on my last visit.

"Whatever's the matter, dear?"

It turned out that her mother had taken ill. And all she wanted to do was rush home to care for her, but first she had to serve Baron Dumbleby his coffee and read to him until he nodded off.

"Here, give it to me," I said, taking the tray from her hands. "You go home to your mother, and I will take the coffee to the Baron. I practically live here now."

Bertha hurried away, wiping her eyes, and I made my way upstairs to the Baron's private quarters.

I found the little aristocrat in his bed, propped up by a small mountain of satin pillows, fast asleep. His teeth were in a jar beside the bed, and as he breathed in and out, his lips sank into his mouth, then shot out, flapping with abandon. It was delightful.

When I set the tray down, he roused. His head lifted from the pillow, then fell back again. Though still groggy, he seemed to recognize me. "Has she gone?"

"Who, dear?"

"Anastasia," he whispered. "I cannot bear to hear her. . . . She will not stop."

I frowned. The poor thing was still half asleep. "You are confused, Baron Dumbleby."

"She came back," said the old man, and his milky eyes stared intently into the darkness. "She came back to this house."

"Yes, I know all about that," I said, sitting on the bed beside him. "Do not ask me how—Bertha swore me to secrecy and I'm a girl of my word."

Baron Dumbleby looked startled. "You know about Anastasia?"

"Oh yes."

His trembling hand reached for mine. "We only wanted the truth about Sebastian—you understand, don't you? We had no choice. . . ."

"No choice about what, dear?"

"A year had passed without a word," said the Baron, "and then she turned up and told us such a tale—she was delirious."

"Who? Anastasia?"

"That's right." Estelle had come into the bedroom chamber. She stood with her back to the fire, a blue nightdress in her arms. "Anastasia told my mother that she and Sebastian had been married and that my brother was dead. My mother turned her away at the door."

My mind was a fog. I was tired and hungry. It was hard to make sense of what I was being told. "Anastasia told your mother that Sebastian was dead?"

Estelle nodded curtly and threw the nightdress aside.

"But if you knew . . ." I stood up and let Baron Dumbleby's hand slip from mine. "Why did you pretend that your mother had not set eyes on Anastasia since she dismissed her?"

"Because Anastasia is a liar!" hissed Estelle. "My mother searched the whole of England and could not find any record of a marriage between them." She looked at me with something like hatred. "I remember her sitting down on the stairs in the hall and telling my mother a story so absurd only a lunatic would believe a word of it."

"McCloud was our very best maid," declared the Baron, making no sense at all.

"Hush, Uncle," said Estelle firmly, walking toward the bed.

The Baron chuckled. "Her name was McGrath, of course, but from the first moment Lady Vivian clapped eyes on her and saw that birthmark under her eye, shaped just like a cloud, it had to be McCloud!"

Something did not add up. I gazed at Estelle. "You said that when Anastasia came back, your mother turned her away at the door. . . . Yet just now you said she was sitting on the stairs in the hall telling her tale."

"What does it matter?" came the terse reply. "She sat on the stairs and spun a ridiculous story about being from some faraway world, cursed by a terrible plague."

I gasped.

"She wanted my mother to believe that when she was forced to return to this *other* world, Sebastian had followed after her, even though he knew it would cost him his life." Estelle laughed coldly. "They were the ravings of a lunatic."

Could it be? Was Anastasia—the mysterious lodger of whom no record could be found—from Prospa? It was shocking. But in a strange sort of way, it made sense.

"Sebastian loved her so much," I muttered to myself, "that he put on the Clock Diamond and went after her."

Estelle lunged at me. "How do you know about that foolish necklace? It doesn't exist! It is all lies!" She shook me rather violently. "You saw her, didn't you?"

I pushed the unhinged girl away. "Saw *who*, you mad cow?" I patted down my filthy apron with great dignity. "As for the *foolish* necklace, if I weren't sworn to secrecy, I would tell you that it certainly exists and that there is every chance that Anastasia's story was utterly true."

"You are as deranged as she is!" she spat.

"The child will have no name," said Baron Dumbleby sadly.

I saw panic flash across Estelle's face. "He is half asleep. His mind is confused."

But it was already too late. "Anastasia was with child?" I asked.

"Don't be absurd," said Estelle.

"I didn't see her after it was over," said the old man, his voice shaking, "but I heard her, for she would not stop that haunting—"

"She wanted money," said Estelle, silencing her uncle again, "and my mother knew that Sebastian would never have married her. Yes, she carried a child, but it could not have been his! And she was thrown out onto the street."

But I didn't believe her. I turned my back on Estelle and looked at her uncle instead. "Anastasia had the baby here, didn't she? That is what you meant when you said you didn't see her after it was over."

"Do not speak, Uncle," ordered Estelle. "She means to use your words against us."

But the Baron would not be stopped—he had a story, and he meant to tell it. "The baby was coming as she sat on the stairs, what else was there to do? She was taken down to the basement, where the child was born."

"And then?" I said eagerly.

"The only way to get her to speak the truth was . . ." Baron Dumbleby shuddered, closing his eyes. "It was cruel, but the newborn was the only weapon. If she would just tell us what had *really* happened to Sebastian, she could have her child."

I was shaking my head in disbelief. "You took her baby away?"

"What else was my mother to do?" said Estelle, pacing about the bedroom. "This girl claimed to be from another world, she claimed she and my brother had married there, and that he had perished. She was clearly insane and had no business caring for a child."

My legs seemed to give way, and I found myself slumping on the edge of the bed. "The baby—you gave it back to her, didn't you?"

Estelle offered no answer.

"McCloud was our very best maid!" cried the Baron. "She took the infant away with two hundred pounds and orders not to return until we sent for her."

My heart was a mallet trying to crack open my chest. Was such cruelty possible? But of course, it was. "Where is the child now?"

"McCloud promised to love it as her own," said the Baron meekly. "She had longed for a baby so the child would be well cared for. . . . The child would not suffer."

"They settled in Wales," said Estelle stiffly. "Mother did not wish to correspond with her, but I wrote this past winter and received a note back saying that McCloud and the baby had left there seven years ago, leaving no forwarding address."

"And Anastasia," I said. "What of her?"

"How should I know?" snapped Estelle. "Mother told her that as soon as she confessed the truth about what she had done, we would return her child. She went on her way, and we haven't heard from her since."

"But surely—"

I stopped. My mind was circling back. To just a few minutes before. Something I had heard, but not listened to. It was as if the words were threads that had looped themselves into just the right holes, until it was possible to step back and see the finished tapestry. I jumped up off the bed and crouched down beside the Baron.

"Listen to me," I said urgently.

The old man opened his eyes.

"You said you could not bear to hear her—you were speaking of Anastasia, weren't you?"

"She would not stop," cried the old man. "Her voice carried up from the basement."

"Be silent, Uncle!" Estelle came up behind me, trying to wrench me away. "Leave him alone. He is old and feeble of mind."

I freed myself from her grasp with a small amount of slapping. Kept my gaze firmly on Baron Dumbleby. "What was it she would not stop, dear? What did you hear that haunts you so?"

"Hush, Uncle!" cried Estelle.

The Baron did not heed her, for he was somewhere far away. His dry lips, which had been sunken into his mouth, pushed out. Then a shaky but unmistakable melody came up and out of him.

"Mmmm mm mmmm mm," he hummed.

"Sleep and Dream, My Sweet." The very tune I had heard day and night from my cell at Lashwood. They had separated Anastasia from her baby, then locked her away in Lashwood all these years.

I wanted to weep, but there wasn't time.

"You heard her, didn't you?" Estelle pulled me roughly to my feet, seizing my shoulders. "You heard her humming when you were at Lashwood?"

"Yes," came my faint reply.

"And you wonder why my mother had her locked away?" Estelle's eyes were wild and ferocious. "Every week for twelve years my mother would visit her and ask for the truth—offering her freedom if she admitted what she had done." She lifted her head defiantly. "And now I do the same."

"What you are doing is horrid! A child needs its mother, and a mother needs her child!" I pulled my arm free and took a shaky breath. "Your brother is dead, dear. You must accept it and stop punishing Anastasia—she did not kill him, I know that for a fact."

"She took him away, and she must pay the price," came the cold reply.

I walked past the hateful girl and headed for the door. "I will tell the world what you have done. Anastasia does not belong in that place any more than I did."

A door banged down below. Then the sound of raised voices. Followed by hurried footsteps.

"She is here!" cried Estelle at the top of her lungs. She lunged at me, grabbing my wrist. "Please, hurry, she has threatened me with a knife!"

I pulled free and ran.

26

My escape was of the daring and death-defying variety. The house was swarming with orderlies from Lashwood, as well as a constable or two. Clearly, when Estelle went to fetch a nightdress for me, she had sent word to the asylum. Or the police. Probably both.

They came charging up the main stairs, following Estelle's wicked cries for help. Being breathtakingly canny, I took the servants' stairs down. Came out by the kitchen door. I could hear a cook shrieking that she wasn't hiding a fugitive in her larder.

I picked up a vase from a gilded table and threw it down the hallway, where it shattered against the far wall. This set them all into action. I hid around the corner as they spilled out of the kitchen, while others came rushing down the back stairs—all of them charging off in the direction of the broken vase.

Then I burst into the kitchen, sidestepped the cook, leaped over a toppled chair, and charged out the back door. The cook, being a jolly good sport, didn't even sound the alarm.

Highgate was wonderfully deserted. The plump quarter moon had vanished—probably behind a cloud—the sky capping the city like a black shroud. I didn't slow until I was six or seven blocks away, turning into Crumble Avenue and walking in the shadow of a fine apartment building.

There was so much in my head, I simply didn't have room for it all. It churned with such fury that I couldn't hold a thought for more than a moment or two. But the silence was rather soothing. So soothing that I didn't sense the figure darting out from the shadows. Or the hands reaching for me. I was yanked from the footpath and thrust into a doorway.

"You are a hard person to catch, Miss Pocket."

"Miss Frost!" I cried.

"Hush," she whispered firmly, "we do not wish to wake the whole of Highgate."

The Mistress of the Clock began to remove her black gloves. She was just as I remembered her. Dark dress. Freckled face. Flaming red hair. "You need a bath," she said, looking me up and down.

"How did you find me?"

"With some difficulty," came the tart reply. "I tried to intercept you when you first broke out of Lashwood, but you seemed rather more interested in leaping onto the back of a carriage."

"That was *you*?"

She nodded. "I called to you, but apparently the carriage wheels obscured my voice."

I was frowning now. "If you knew I was being kept prisoner in Lashwood, why did you not get me out?"

Miss Frost smiled faintly. "I have kept as close an eye on you as was possible—and to be frank, as unpleasant as Lady Elizabeth's revenge was, in some ways you were safer in there." She glanced down the empty street. "Miss Always has led me on a wild goose chase—she is up to something, though I am yet to discover the particulars."

It was hard to deny that despite everything, I was rather delighted to see Miss Frost. But then I remembered the Snagsbys and Anastasia, not to mention Rebecca, and my heart hardened. There was so much to say. Naturally, I began with a firm scolding.

"You sent me to the Snagsbys knowing they would start using the Clock Diamond again, didn't you?"

"I knew it was a distinct possibility."

"How could you do such a thing?"

"The Snagsbys deal with people at the end of their journey here in this world," she explained coolly. "Who better to use the stone? The Clock Diamond's work, though unpleasant, is of the utmost importance."

"It is murder! Mr. Grimwig would have been next, and he was perfectly healthy!"

"Do stop shouting, Miss Pocket," was her calm reply. "It is most unbecoming and is likely to attract the attention of the gentlemen currently combing the streets looking for you."

"The Snagsbys are nutters," I said, lowering my voice.

"Murderous nutters. Now that they have the stone all to themselves, they will kill half of London before they're done."

"What a feverish imagination you have."

Then Miss Frost did the most remarkable thing. She reached into the sleeve of her dress and pulled out the Clock Diamond. Fixed it around my neck and tucked it under my dress. The stone began to glow like a lantern, warming against my skin. Its pulse was urgent, but within moments had slowed to match my heartbeat.

"I suppose you had to kill them for it?"

Miss Frost rolled her eyes. "We discussed the matter like mature adults, and after some *persuasion*, they relinquished the necklace."

"You should never have given it to them in the first place," I snapped.

"Shortly after I began my tenure as Mistress of the Clock, I was able to retrieve the necklace from a rather unpleasant fellow in Istanbul. As my time in your world is rather limited, I needed a collaborator, someone who would use the stone in the most *ethical* way."

I huffed. Scowled. Gave every indication that I violently disagreed.

"I searched all of the places that might have access to the old and the sick—hospitals, funeral parlors, poorhouses—and came upon the Snagsbys."

"But how could they be so willing to kill?" I said, shaking my head.

"The Snagsbys couldn't give their daughter a second chance, but they knew that for every soul they captured here, a hundred would be cured of the Shadow in my world." Miss Frost placed her finger under my chin and lifted it. "This plague of which I speak is a horror that I cannot describe, and children are particularly vulnerable."

"But what of the children from this world?" I pushed her hand away. "I have seen Rebecca. Why must she suffer so that children from Prospa can live?"

"Rebecca chose her fate," came the heartless reply.

"What are they doing to her in that ghastly place?"

"Once a soul crosses into Prospa, their very touch has great healing power," said Miss Frost, her gaze slipping from mine as she searched for the right words. "We call them Remedies, and they are treated with the greatest reverence. But this new life comes with conditions, and I freely admit that there is a cost."

"Well, the cost is too great, you cold-blooded fruitcake. Rebecca has the look of someone haunted, and poor Mr. Blackhorn seems to be fading away."

The Mistress of the Clock nodded her head soberly. "A Remedy's healing power is not infinite. Eventually it wears out."

"Which is just a nice way of saying they die all over again."

"They fade," said Miss Frost softly. "They fade away. I wish there was another way to help my people, but there is not."

I desperately wanted to hate Miss Frost. Or at the very least, stomp on her foot. But I couldn't. I may not have agreed with her methods, but I could see that she used the Clock Diamond reluctantly and that she understood the awful price.

"Come," said Miss Frost.

We walked swiftly along the street, taking refuge around the side of a stately mansion. Moments later, a pair of orderlies from Lashwood hurried past without spotting us. Miss Frost was peering into the night with a great deal of interest.

"Your new *friend*, Miss Dumbleby, will have the entire city looking for you by morning."

"They cannot lock me up again," I whispered firmly. "I'm not bonkers."

"You, Miss Pocket? Never." But there was mirth in her voice. Beastly dingbat!

The mention of Estelle's name brought the horror of what her family had done rushing back. I looked hard at Miss Frost. "I know that Anastasia Radcliff came from your world. What I don't know is *how*."

For the first time, the former governess appeared to falter. Finally she said, "Anastasia was my friend—a younger sister, you might say. Her mother is someone of high rank in Prospa, and Anastasia's future was mapped out for her. I suppose she yearned for the freedom of a simpler life, where she would be able to choose her own destiny."

"You helped her cross, didn't you?"

She nodded. "Anastasia only asked for three months— three months to live as an ordinary young woman in London." Miss Frost sighed, and the sound was plump with regret. "So I arranged for her to stay with the Snagsbys and fulfill her wish."

I knew the next part well enough. "She fell in love with Sebastian and told him the truth about where she was from."

"Correct. When Anastasia returned home, Sebastian was heartbroken. He went to the Snagsbys and pretended to be interested in the necklace, asking to see it. Foolishly they agreed, and when Sebastian saw it he—"

"He put it on, just like Rebecca," I said softly.

"Sebastian knew it was the only way he would see Anastasia again." She cleared her throat. "Against great odds, they found each other in Prospa and were married in secret, though Sebastian met the same fate as all others who used the stone. Anastasia found out she was to have a baby, and fearing that her mother would do something unspeakable to the unborn child, she crossed back to this world without telling a soul."

"Which is when you came looking for her."

"Tell me, Miss Pocket," said the grim Mistress of the Clock, her eyes still trained on the street, "what did you learn about Anastasia? Do you know where she and her child fled to?"

I did not answer. For Miss Frost grabbed the side of her neck suddenly. Pulled from it a small silver dart. Then fell to her knees.

I crouched beside her. "What should I do, dear?"

"Leave," she said, and her voice was horridly pained.

"I won't."

With what strength Miss Frost had left, she pulled me close. "The Rambler Inn in Hammersmith," she whispered. "Go there."

Then she slumped to the ground in a heap.

It felt treacherous leaving her lying there. The victim of a poisoned dart. I ran out into the street, fearing a similar fate. Was poison not fatal? It certainly was in every high-quality penny dreadful I had ever read. I charged through the gloomy streets of Highgate as if I were in a race for my life. Which was true enough.

My legs picked up speed as I dashed around a passing carriage and practically flew up onto the footpath. I plowed on, darting through a rabbit warren of streets, not at all sure if I was still in Highgate. I quickly decided to wait at the London library until morning and seek Miss Carnage's assistance. Coming to the end of the path, I turned the corner sharply, running straight into something. No, *someone*.

He pulled me up by the arms.

"Well, well, what have we here?" He was dressed in the same black-and-white uniform worn by all the orderlies at Lashwood.

I kicked his shin and whacked him in the stomach. He both doubled over and hopped about. Which is difficult to achieve. Then I took off again. The orderly blew his whistle and sprinted after me. I charged across the street, quickly running out of breath.

"You won't get away!" He sounded within striking distance.

I swerved, changing direction. Began running down the middle of the road. I heard carriage wheels rumbling in the distance. As I got to the crossroads, my legs turning to jelly, a carriage roared in front of me. And stopped.

The door flew open and a woman stuck her head out. "Hurry, Ivy!"

It was Miss Carnage!

"Stop her!" The orderly was a shadow's length from me now. "She's a runner from Lashwood!"

CALEB KRISP

I jumped. Flew through the air in glorious style. And tumbled into the carriage. The driver whipped the horses eagerly, and they took off, leaving the orderly shouting gibberish and throwing his whistle upon the road.

"Oh, Ivy, are you all right?" Miss Carnage looked at me from across the cabin in horror. "Whatever has happened to you?"

I took a few frantic breaths. "Locked in the madhouse, dear."

"You poor girl—are you hurt?"

"Not me, dear. Strong as an ox."

The dreary librarian was beside herself. I'm almost certain she hadn't had this much nervous excitement since she'd read *Jane Eyre*. Which raised an interesting question.

"What are you doing here, Miss Carnage?"

Thick layers of shadow lay in patches inside the carriage. Every time we hit a pothole and Miss Carnage jilted back, her face would vanish as if she were a headless ghost.

"I have been looking for you, Ivy," she said, and her soft voice was feather light. "I used your library card details to find your address and went to see your parents. At first your mother denied even knowing you. Then she said you were no longer welcome in her home."

Which was to be expected. And not even a *tiny* bit hurtful.

I turned and looked out the back window. "Can we tell the driver to turn around?" I said. "I *must* see if Miss Frost is all right."

"Who is Miss Frost?"

"A friend . . . well, I think she's a friend, it's hard to be sure. But she's been hurt—a poisoned dart, no less."

The driver whipped the horse again, and our pace increased. But I wasn't looking out the window anymore. I was looking at Miss Carnage.

She smiled, but there was coldness in it. "Something wrong, Ivy?"

Yes, something was wrong. I just didn't know *what* exactly.

"How did you know where I was?" I asked.

Miss Carnage sighed. "A friend told me."

"Who? Who told you?"

The librarian licked her lips. She sighed again and leaned back against the seat, her head slipping behind the veil of shadows.

"I think we are much alike, Ivy, you and I—all alone in the world and trying to find our way."

Miss Carnage's hand flew to her face, vanishing in the gloom. When it emerged, her fingers clasped a nose. Yes, a nose!

It was monstrously bent. And unmistakably hers.

I gasped. "What are you *doing*, Miss Carnage?"

Her other hand lifted to her face. Then emerged from the shadows holding a set of large teeth. Next a monstrous chin. These hideous pieces of her face were dropped into her lap as if they were hairpins. Next, her thick glasses were removed and set aside. She fished out another pair and appeared to put them on.

"Miss Carnage, are you falling apart? If so, I suggest we go to the nearest hospital."

She sat forward, the light slipping over her face like a mask. Only it was the opposite—for the mask had come off. There she was. Plain features. Round spectacles. Hungry eyes.

Miss Always giggled wickedly and pulled the gray wig from her head. "I do love a surprise."

27

She was back. But, of course, she had never gone. All this time, Miss Always had been there. Disguised as a perfectly dull librarian. Was it *too* much to ask that I might have one ordinary friend? Someone who wasn't barking mad or trying to deceive me!

"You look stunned," said Miss Always brightly. "Poor Ivy."

I shrugged. "Not really, dear. Miss Carnage was monstrously dull and gave off a rather foul odor. I suspected it was you all along."

"*Clever* girl," said Miss Always doubtfully.

I lunged for the door. Miss Always's foot flew at my hand as I reached the handle, knocking me away. Then Miss Always pulled a dagger from her pocket. Pointed it at me.

"Must we play these games?" she said softly. "I do not wish to hurt you, but I certainly will if I have to—if you doubt me, just remember Miss Frost with a poison dart in her neck."

"Is she dead?"

"I hope so," said Miss Always with a faint smile. "You still believe she is on your side, but *I* am the one who has opened your eyes. *I* am the one who wrote the rules that allowed you to reach Prospa."

I was frowning. "You are Ambrose Crabtree?"

Miss Always let out a dry laugh.

"You *wanted* me to reach Rebecca? You wanted me to help her?"

"What do I care about that foolish girl? What I *wanted* was for you to understand your power." She shrugged. "I also planned to have you snatched before you reached Prospa House, saving me the bother of dragging you there myself—but as I was never certain *when* you would try and cross, my underlings failed to intercept you."

I was no longer shocked by Miss Always's treachery. But I was puzzled. "Why would you want to capture me, when I was right under your nose at the library?"

"You are no good to me here, Ivy," came the playful reply. "I need you in Prospa so that you can fulfill your destiny—with my guidance and protection, of course."

Oh, that again. "You still think I'm the Dual?"

Before she could answer, I jumped up and reached for the carriage door again, desperate to escape. In a flash, Miss Always pinned me against the seat, the dagger at my throat.

"You can travel to Prospa as easily as walking from one room to the next," said Miss Always eagerly. "You healed my wrist back at Butterfield Park. You wore the Clock Diamond and survived." She looked at my face with something like bewilderment. "Out of the millions of girls who roam this world, you are the *last* I would pick to be the Dual, but fate has decided otherwise."

Which gave me a rather brilliant idea. I am prone to such insights during times of crisis, having all the natural instincts of a pig with a wolf at the door.

"Get off me, you hideous jackal!" I said, pushing her away.

Miss Always released her hold on me and sat back in her seat. Waved the dagger in my general direction. "I know what you are thinking, Ivy, but it will not work."

I folded my arms with tremendous petulance. "*What* am I thinking?"

"That you can escape this carriage by crossing into Prospa."

"You said so yourself, dear—I have *great* power. I could cross this instant, and you couldn't stop me."

"Probably not," came Miss Always's startling admission, "but if you hoped to reach Prospa House, you would be sadly disappointed. In fact, you would find yourself in the white woods, and I can promise you, it would take great luck to make it out of there alive."

"So long as I focus on Rebecca, I will reach Prospa House."

Miss Always laughed coldly. "To start with, I highly doubt that she is still there—not after your failed attempt to liberate her. As for the rest of it, you only know what I wanted you to know. Prospa is not somewhere out in the universe; it sits *here* beside your world, and when you cross, you reach the same point in my world as you have just left in yours."

I had never heard such poppycock. So I rolled my eyes and shook my head.

Miss Always sat forward in her seat. "A girl stands by herself in a room with four walls, no windows, no doors, no furniture—is she alone?"

"Well, of course she is, you homicidal bookworm!"

"But what if the wall on her left is a partition, and on the other side of it sits another girl just like her? Both girls believe they are alone, but they are actually standing in the same room. What separates them is the partition, or as we like to call it in Prospa, the *veil*."

The carriage lurched to the left, and we were jiggled about. Miss Always looked out at the black night and seemed pleased with our progress.

"The first time you reached Prospa House, I suppose you thought it was mere chance that you wound up on Winslow Street? Did it not feel as if you were being pulled there?"

I didn't nod. I didn't want to give the horrid wretch the satisfaction.

"You will only find Prospa House in that spot, for that is where it stands in my world," said Miss Always.

Naturally, I didn't want to believe it. But it *felt* true. Hadn't I returned to Winslow Street on my second crossing to Prospa House? Perhaps, without realizing, I had known it all along.

"Cheer up," said Miss Always, kicking me with her boot. "I have the most wonderful news. Tomorrow night is the new half-moon, and we will travel to Prospa together."

I looked past Miss Always and focused on Prospa. Within seconds the cabin began to shudder with an insistent buzz. Then the Clock Diamond bloomed into life and began to throw out great pulses of honey-colored light.

"What are you doing?" said Miss Always urgently.

My gaze shifted to her. I let all thoughts of lifting the veil fall from my mind. After all, that had never been the plan.

I fished the stone out from beneath my dress.

Miss Always was scowling up a storm. "You were trying to cross, weren't you?"

"Heavens no." I looked into the stone. It was churning with a golden light, nothing more. But I wasn't about to let Miss Always know that. "The Clock Diamond tends to bring attention to itself when it has something to show me." I gasped. Looked at Miss Always with considerable alarm. Looked back at the stone. "It's you, dear."

There was trepidation on her face, though she tried to mask it. "Do you take me for a fool?"

"I'm afraid it's true, dear—your hair is awfully gray, and you have aged with all the enthusiasm of a sun-dried tomato, so I can only assume this is a vision of the future. *Your* future."

Miss Always stiffened. Adjusted her glasses. "I will not play your silly games, Ivy."

"You are walking through a crowd of people with two men at your sides." My eyes widened with great commitment. "Oh, my . . . they are leading you up to a podium—perhaps you are getting an award?" Then I looked at her with as much sympathy as I could muster. "Oh, Miss Always, it is to the hangman's noose they are taking you. The crowd seems rather delighted, cheering and carrying on, but you should be terribly proud, dear, for you are putting up a marvelous fight."

Miss Always could stand it no longer. "Show me that," she snapped, reaching for the necklace.

Which was when I made my move. Kicking her right in the stomach. She flew back with an almighty growl, the dagger dropping from her hand. I leaped up and threw open the door. Cold wind flew into the carriage like a tempest.

"No!" cried Miss Always.

She lurched across the cabin, grabbing my arm. Now or never, came the voice in my head. I yanked myself from her grasp and jumped.

The ground was a dark blur beneath me, the only light thrown by the lantern near the driver's seat. My arms thrashed about. My legs kicked. I hit the road with a thump. Stumbling madly. Flying forward. My hands skidded along the ground. Knees scraping the hard earth. If there was pain, I didn't feel it.

The carriage came to a sudden stop. The horses reared up. The carriage wheels skidded across the gravel. Pushing up, I found my feet and started running, just as Miss Always bounded out of the cab.

We were somewhere outside London, though I did not know exactly where. The quarter moon had emerged from behind its cover, dropping pockets of pale light upon the landscape. It was a barren place, with barely a tree to hide behind. But up ahead there was a factory of some kind, with lights in the windows and smoke billowing from enormous chimney stacks.

My legs were tired. *I* was tired. But I bolted toward the building, hopeful that I might find refuge within it. I just had to reach *it* before Miss Always reached *me*.

"I can outrun you, Ivy," yelled Miss Always, rather cheerfully, from behind me.

"Stuff and nonsense," I cried back.

The factory was surrounded by a fence. At the front was a set of large gates. They appeared to be chained together and padlocked. Which was most unhelpful. I came to a sliding stop before them and gave them a good rattle. Miss Always was only a short distance away, galloping like a stallion.

I took a few steps back, then ran at the gates—leaped up, gripping the fence with fingers and boots. I began to climb like a crazed monkey, reaching the top in no time. Being magnificently athletic, I swung over and clambered down the other side. With Miss Always nearly upon me, I leaped from the fence and landed lightly in the dirt. Safe at last!

I raced across the yard toward the building. Stopped a sensible distance from the gates and turned back.

"I will alert the workers to my plight," I called out, "and you will be locked away. I would make a hasty retreat if I were you!"

But Miss Always did not do that. She had stopped about ten

CALEB KRISP

feet from the gates. Her arms were out and her head thrown back. I gulped. For I knew what was coming. She let out a hideous cry that seemed to make the very ground tremble.

Then they came. Emerging from the thick shadows around her skirt—three locks on either side. Impossibly short. Dark robes. Hoods shrouding their hideous faces. They began to spin in furious whirls, charging the gates like six small hurricanes. Great gusts of dirt churning around them.

I shivered. Began to back up.

The metal gate rattled furiously as the locks closed in. Then it simply blew off its hinges, flying over my head, and hitting the factory with a deafening clang. The frightful little villains stopped spinning as easily as they had begun. They stood in a line facing me, as Miss Always took her place in the very center. The dirt and dust fell around us like rain.

"Must we go through this every time?" said Miss Always softly.

"I'm afraid so, dear," I said, continuing to back away. "You see, I'm rather fond of my freedom. Rather allergic to insane supernatural librarians. Also, I'm almost certain I'd be horribly bored as your prisoner and puppet."

"You shall have plenty of time to find out." Then she smiled sweetly.

The locks moved quickly, surrounding me in seconds. Miss Always took slow steps, the dagger once more in her hand.

"The carriage is waiting, Ivy," she said. "Our destination is not far, so I apologize in advance for the brief burst of pain you are about to experience. I won't deny that there is another way, but you have rather tried my patience, and I find that I want very much to hurt you." She sighed and came to a stop. "Bosom friends have these little quarrels, but we shall be chums again tomorrow."

The locks flew at me. Hissing like steam pipes. Their claws extended. I put up a valiant fight, showering kicks and punches, but it was no use. I felt the skin on my arms split as talons swiped my flesh like blades. Then the real pain began, as two of those vile little devils grabbed my wrists. That was when I cried out. For it felt as if my arms were being wrenched from my body.

I caught sight of the light from the corner of my eye. It glowed in the night sky like a blue moon. And it appeared to be moving at some speed toward us. The locks noticed it too. I could tell, because the searing pain in my shoulders eased.

"Did I tell you to stop?" hissed Miss Always.

But there wasn't time for an answer. The ghost swooped down and flew through the breach where the gates had been, a great ball of luminous blue gas. Miss Always spun around. The locks seemed dazzled by the light and froze.

"Move, child," a voice whispered in my ear.

I pulled free and ran. Miss Always gave chase. But the ghost's mouth had begun to open, and it did not stop until it was a vast, churning hole with teeth like glass.

The locks scattered as the ghost flew up, then pounced. Swallowing them as if they were an evening snack. She collected three in one go, then a pair. The last lock she seemed to suck into her mouth, for it lifted from the ground and shot straight into the abyss.

Miss Always let out an almighty screech, her head flying back—no doubt to produce more of her hooded henchmen— but was rather quickly silenced when the Duchess of Trinity devoured her in one hungry bite.

The Duchess twirled, turning upright, a ginormous blubbery ball of sapphire hovering just inches from the ground. Inside her immense belly were Miss Always and her little henchmen. The locks were stumbling about in that ghoulish bubble, while Miss Always found her feet and stood looking through the luminous skin imprisoning her—right at me. Her stare was of the fierce and hateful kind.

"Close your mouth, child," said the ghost. "You look like a puddle."

"You . . . you ate them," I said rather feebly. "You ate them for *me*."

"It is a meal of the temporary kind." The Duchess of Trinity's voice had lost its music and sounded terribly strained. "I cannot hold them for long, so be on your way."

I was frowning now. Remembered that the dead woman had tried to use me again for her wicked deeds—poor Mr. Grimwig! Not to mention the fact that she had not come when I had called her in the madhouse.

"Do not think this signifies some affection on my part, child," warned the Duchess. "It is simply that you are of more use to me *out* of Miss Always's clutches."

"I'm terribly grateful," I said as a thick gray mist lifted from the cuts on my arms and legs (I had almost forgotten I could no longer bleed). "But I won't be helping you with another of your vengeful schemes."

"Hush, you foolish girl," said the ghost, her dark eyes twitching with the strain of holding her captives. "Miss Frost told you where to go, so for once do as you are told."

I didn't ask how she knew this. I had another, more pressing question.

"Do you know if she is alive?"

The dead woman shook her head. "I do not."

The locks had begun to spin around in her swollen belly like a ring of fire. Miss Always threw back her head and shrieked as a fresh army of locks flew from the folds of her skirt, swelling and churning inside the Duchess like a storm.

The Duchess's face grimaced in pain. Great plumes of dark smoke poured from her nostrils and seeped from her hair. "Hurry, child."

And that is just what I did.

The road stretched on into darkness, flat and empty. I had no idea how to reach Hammersmith (I had never been there before), or even if I was walking in the right direction. All I did was run—

keeping to the side so that I would not be discovered should Miss Always's carriage come past.

I didn't know if the Duchess had released her prisoners yet. Or if they would come looking for me in this direction. The wind blew hard and I hugged my shoulders, bending my head against the cold.

Then the ground rumbled. In the dim light I saw horses approaching. Without hesitating, I leaped behind a bramble bush and cowered. Prayed they hadn't seen me.

The carriage wheels slowed. Coming to a stop. Which was most alarming!

I didn't dare take a breath.

"I expect you have your reasons for hiding in there," came a deep, pleasant voice, "but if you'd like a ride, I'd be happy to have you along."

Was this Miss Always's driver pretending to speak like a dim-witted farmer to fool me?

"If not, I'll be on my way," he continued.

I peeked above the brambles. What I found was a wagon stacked with logs and a driver who didn't look even slightly deranged. In fact, he looked like a man who cut down trees for a living, with a thick wool jacket and a slouch hat.

"Tell me," I said, approaching the carriage, "are you going anywhere near Hammersmith?"

"Close enough," came the reply.

I stepped up into the wagon and took a seat beside the amiable stranger. Looked at him carefully. "Are you crackers in any way? Also, do you have any desire to steal souls or imprison perfectly innocent people in madhouses?"

The driver gave his horses the signal, and the wagon took off. "Not lately," he said with a chuckle. "Looks like we'll be traveling together a spell. I suppose we should swap names—Jonah Flint, pleased to meet you."

Being well versed in manners and whatnot, I said, "My name's Esmeralda Cabbage."

Mr. Flint looked at me sideways with a half smile but made no further comment. Instinctively, I started to cover the gashes on my arms—but when I looked down, the wounds had healed. All that remained were the rips in my sleeves and skirt.

The wagon jolted about a great deal and the seat was agony on the buttocks, but we were making good ground, and I began to relax.

"I'd duck if I were you," announced Mr. Flint suddenly.

I looked back and saw a dark carriage barreling toward us. It was Miss Always! I jumped down and crouched under the seat. The roar of the carriage filled my ears. But it didn't slow. Instead it went around us and thundered down the road.

I did not get up until Mr. Flint gave the word. And when I did, the woodcutter did not ask me a single thing about who they were or why they might be looking for me.

"I reckon we might take the back road. What do you say, Esmeralda?"

"I think that's a fine idea," I replied. I was about to compliment Mr. Flint on not being nearly as stupid as he looked. But as he didn't look at *all* stupid, I held my tongue.

The wagon slowed and then veered off to the left. Mr. Flint urged the horses on, and the carriage rolled swiftly beneath a canopy of elm trees, which arched above us like a cathedral. The moonlight splintered down through the web of branches, piercing the black night like shards of luminous ice. Despite its strange beauty, I shut my eyes tight. Praying that Miss Frost was still alive. And that I would find her at journey's end.

28

"Do you know where I might find the Rambler Inn?"

"Who wants to know?" The baker eyed me with considerable suspicion.

"That would be me, you chinless buffoon." I said this brightly, so as not to cause offense. "I am looking for a friend, and she told me to meet her there."

"Who did?"

"My friend."

"What's your friend's *name*, you cheeky imp?"

Mr. Flint had dropped me on the edge of Hammersmith,

directing me to follow the main road into the village, where I was to locate Oscar Bonson's Baked Delights—he seemed certain that the baker would be awake at this unseemly hour (it was a quarter to four in the morning) and would help me find the place I was looking for.

"My friend's name is none of your concern," I declared. "Our business is of a clandestine nature."

Strangely, this seemed to satisfy the gangly fellow. "There's a bank across the road," he said, kneading a great ball of dough with ease. "Go around the side, and you'll see a little green house at the back—that's the place you're looking for."

I found it easily enough. Even in the fading moonlight, I could see that it was a ghastly place. Peeling green paint. Broken eaves. Two of the five steps leading up to the front door missing.

A jolly woman with wispy gray hair and the roundest face I'd ever seen opened the door—inviting me in without so much as a hello.

"I'm Mrs. Spragg," she said, stepping over a pile of books in the middle of the narrow hall. "Excuse the mess, my husband is a great reader, though the dear man is burying us alive." She

The Rambler Inn

pointed to the unspeakably narrow stairs. "You go on up, it's the first door on the left."

My throat dried up as I knocked gently on the door.

I heard rapid footsteps. The door opened just a crack. I couldn't see anything inside. But I heard a voice. "I knew you'd make it, chatterbox."

When the door flew open, I was rather startled to see Jago standing before me. He had changed into a fine tan suit, and his dark hair was combed in a most pleasing fashion.

"But . . . ?" was my only question.

Jago shut the door gently and said, "I've worked for Miss Frost on and off since I was just a wee boy. It was her who sent me into Lashwood to get you out."

"Blimey," I muttered for the first time in my life.

We were standing in a poorly furnished sitting room. A doorway led off to another room that appeared to be dimly lit.

"Miss Frost?" I said urgently.

The boy's brown face looked utterly grim as he nodded. "Come on."

I followed Jago quickly into the next room. The window

was drawn shut. Miss Frost lay upon the bed, her hands crossed over her stomach. Her dazzling red hair fanned out across the pillow. Her eyes were closed, and her skin had the color of death upon it.

"She won't let me send for the doctor," said Jago. "I've been using the cloth to cool her head, but she's only getting hotter, seems to me."

"Fetch some more water," I said as I sat down on the bed and picked up the damp cloth.

Jago took the bowl and hurried off downstairs.

"Can you hear me, dear?" I said softly. I unbuttoned the top of her dress, which was damp with perspiration, and applied the cool cloth to her neck.

"Yes, Miss Pocket," came her faint reply. "I am pleased . . . that you could join us."

The poor creature was dripping. "You are positively burning up."

"That is the poison doing its job," she whispered, her eyes opening.

I laid the cloth across her forehead. "What can I do, Miss Frost? Please tell me what to do."

"I am . . . afraid . . . there is nothing to be done," came her monstrous reply.

"Stuff and nonsense. There must be *something*."

Miss Frost gulped and took a shallow breath. "There is a . . ." She shuddered with pain. "In my pocket . . . an address of a cottage near Weymouth . . . in Dorset . . . go there with Jago . . . stay until . . . until you hear from . . ."

"I will do no such thing," I said firmly. "Now I really must insist that you stop this dying business and snap out of it."

A smile crept onto her face. "Excellent advice, Miss Pocket." She closed her eyes. "But I fear . . . Miss Always has won the day . . . but hopefully not the war."

I pulled the cloth from her forehead. Set it aside. Used the edge of my apron (the only part not covered in grime and dust) to dab her face and neck. Though her freckled flesh was a ghostly white, dark circles smudged her eyes like bruises.

"Tell me . . . about Anastasia and her child." Each word seemed to be pushed from her mouth with great effort. "Where did they go?"

For the briefest of moments, I considered lying to her. But

if there was ever a time for the plain truth, it was now. So I told Miss Frost all about the wicked conspiracy that had ensnared Anastasia. About how mother and child were cruelly separated. About the woman in the madhouse humming her endless lullaby, and about how that sad creature was none other than Anastasia Radcliff.

Miss Frost listened, her eyes fluttering open then closing again. Her brow knotting and unclenching as I spoke. When I paused to dab her forehead again, she said, "I knew they were hiding something awful." She faintly shook her head. "But not *that* . . . not such malice."

"Estelle's mother was without pity," I said softly, "and she has bred that same hatred in her daughter. When I think of Anastasia rotting in that horrid cell while—"

"The baby . . ." Miss Frost struggled for breath. "What became of the baby?"

"A maid was paid two hundred pounds to take it away—they went to Wales, apparently, though Estelle claims they left there years ago, leaving no forwarding address." I walked quickly across the room, drew back the curtains, and opened the small window.

"When you are well again, we must return to London and liberate Anastasia from Lashwood. I have a perfectly brilliant plan in mind."

"What do you know of the maid?" said Miss Frost.

I shrugged. "Her name was McSomething or other, but they called her McCloud because she had a birthmark under her eye shaped like a cloud."

Miss Frost cried out suddenly. And though it didn't seem possible, she paled even further. For a moment I worried that another poisoned dart had stuck her.

"Could it be . . . ?" she whispered.

"What is it?"

"Miss Pocket, are you *sure* of what you are saying?" Her dull eyes were fixed on my face.

"About what, dear?"

"The maid who took Anastasia's child . . . and the mark on her face."

"Yes, quite sure. Do you know her?"

A faint, sad smile pulled at her pale lips. Then she called me close.

"I haven't much time, Miss Pocket, but I have . . ." Her eyes shut. She gulped. "I have something to tell you . . ."

"Is it a deathbed confession?" I folded my arms. "Because if it is, I do not wish to hear it. You are not going to die, I simply will not allow it."

"Listen to me . . . hear what I have to say . . ." Among the beads of perspiration tracking down her face, a vale of tears bubbled up. I had never seen her shed a tear. I didn't know she could! Her hand flew up to cover her eyes, as if in shame.

I reached over, pulling her hand away and holding it tight. With my other hand, I stroked her cheek.

"Cry if you need to, dear," I said softly. "There's no harm in it, is there? But do not fret about the past. I'm almost certain you've done some awful things—most pretend governesses are devious by nature—but I feel that despite all the times you have lied to me and been unforgivably stern, you are good at heart. You are good, Miss Frost."

The Mistress of the Clock was frowning. Then her eyes opened wide. And a gasp flew from her lips.

"Miss Frost?" I said.

Her pale skin began to glow, the color returning to her

cheeks as if she were blushing furiously. Her lips were suddenly red and bright. But it was her eyes that told the tale—they were clear and attentive and intense. I could feel her hand, which had been limp, tighten inside my own.

"Miss Frost?" I said again.

She lifted her head off the pillow and looked about the room. She peered up at me with something like wonder on her face. "I feel much improved. In fact, I feel remarkably well."

Miss Frost managed to sit up, then carefully swung her legs around and sat on the edge of the bed next to me. She tucked her long hair behind her ears. Then she nudged my shoulder with her own. "It seems I owe Miss Always an apology."

I was still rather befuddled by Miss Frost's remarkable return to health. But in no time the penny dropped. "When I touched your hand, did I heal you as I did Miss Always at Butterfield Park?"

"So it would seem," said Miss Frost crisply. She rose to her feet. Swooned slightly, reaching out and grabbing the wall. But soon steadied herself. "We must prepare to leave—Miss Always is probably on our heels, and we have far to travel."

Feeling it was only proper, I told Miss Frost the treacherous tale of Miss Carnage and the great disguise. Miss Frost showed a begrudging respect for Miss Always's abilities. Though she did look at me as if I were some kind of village idiot for not seeing through her disguise. The nerve!

By then Jago had returned with fresh water—and the poor boy was rather gob-smacked by Miss Frost's return to health.

"Blimey," he muttered.

Miss Frost invented a perfectly plausible explanation for her recovery. Then she ordered the boy to pack up their things for our departure. Without her saying it directly, it was clear that Jago would be traveling with us.

"Here," said Miss Frost, pulling a frightfully dull auburn dress from the closet, "this should be satisfactory for the journey ahead. There are several others waiting for you at our destination."

"Do you think we will be back in London by tomorrow?" I said, shooing Jago from the room so I could change.

"We are not going to London," declared Miss Frost, knotting her hair into a bun before the mirror.

I buttoned my dress and scowled. "Anastasia needs our help—surely you do not wish to leave her a moment longer in

Lashwood? We must break her out!"

"*We* will do no such thing," said Miss Frost, turning to face me. "*I* will see to Anastasia, and in time we will find her lost child, but not now. Miss Always will be on your trail, and with Lady Elizabeth and Estelle Dumbleby both baying for your blood, London is no longer a safe haven for you."

I would have offered a sharp rebuke, but Jago came flying back into the room, followed by Mrs. Spragg.

"There's a woman downstairs asking about a girl, and the description sounds an awful lot like that one," announced Mrs. Spragg, pointing to me. "I told her I would come up and ask Mr. Spragg, as he sees to all the guests."

"How did she find me?" I said, turning to Miss Frost in a shameful display of the jitters.

"What does this woman look like?" asked Miss Frost.

"Short and fat," declared Mrs. Spragg.

"Then it's *not* Miss Always." I said this calmly, with no sign of stupendous relief.

"Miss Always would no doubt have minions scouring the countryside," said Miss Frost. "Mrs. Spragg, tell her that the girl was here, but she received a note shortly after arriving, then asked for directions to the Chester Tavern. And here is something for all your trouble."

Mrs. Spragg took the coins from Miss Frost's hand and hurried out.

The Miss Frost turned to Jago. "Have the carriage brought around the back. We leave immediately."

The sun was just waking, blowing purple and orange breaths into the dark sky, as the carriage spirited us away from the Rambler Inn. Miss Frost insisted that the curtains be drawn, so the cabin was awfully stuffy. There was much shaking about. And a great deal of silence.

Jago drifted off to sleep, but as tired as I was, my mind was much too busy for me to rest. So I decided to make use of it.

"Why were you so interested in the maid who took Anastasia's baby away?" I asked Miss Frost.

"Anastasia was my friend," came her reply, "and I spent a great deal of time searching for her and the child. Naturally, I was curious to know what became of them."

Miss Frost did not look at me.

"How is it that Anastasia is able to live here? Didn't you say that it was ill health that forced her to return to Prospa in the first place?"

"I suspect that carrying a baby whose father was from this world created a tolerance in her, though I cannot be certain."

"But you made a great fuss about the maid's birthmark, and you seemed awfully—"

"Tell me about your travels to Prospa House, Miss Pocket," she interrupted. "I am very familiar with the place, and it astounds me that you were not captured."

"Oh, they tried, but I'm rather good at creeping silently about—having all the natural instincts of a fox in a henhouse." I stuck my nose in the air rather proudly. "But I confess, it wasn't easy, as I'm shockingly well known in your world."

"What an imagination you have," said Miss Frost with a most dismissive sigh.

"It's true enough," I shot back. "The guards took one look at me and said, 'It's her!' Right before they tried to capture me and bring me to Justice Holiday."

"Hallow," corrected Miss Frost. "Justice Hallow."

"Never heard of him."

"*She* runs Prospa House, and more besides." Miss Frost suddenly looked very interested again. "Did they say anything else, Miss Pocket?"

"There was one thing. The man, an unsightly brute with appalling manners, said something like 'She's awake.'"

"Did he indeed?" said Miss Frost faintly.

And though I had wondered about this before, now, after all that had happened, I suddenly felt the strangeness and the weight of it. How was it that they recognized me in a world that I had never been in before? Was it just a case of mistaken identity? Or something more?

"Once I have rescued Rebecca, I will look into it," I announced.

"You will do no such thing," said Miss Frost swiftly. "Rebecca is beyond your reach, and as for this other matter, it signifies nothing, and you shall leave it alone. There is enough to contend with in *this* world, without troubling yourself with Prospa. Have I made myself perfectly clear, Miss Pocket?"

With a great show of defiance I crossed my arms (and my legs). "Are you utterly bonkers, woman? There is a secret about me in your world, and I intend to find out what it is. Besides which, Rebecca is not even a *tiny* bit lost, not to me—I will fix my mind on her and I will find her, wherever she is. I am going back there as soon as I return to London, and you cannot stop me."

"Oh, but I can," said Miss Frost, and she was suddenly very calm. "In fact, I am utterly certain that you will forget all about this foolish mission."

"Never!"

Miss Frost lifted her pale, freckly hand and placed it gently under my chin. She was rarely this tender with me, so naturally I looked at her with great suspicion.

"Why should I forget it?" I snapped. "Give me one reason why I shouldn't go to Prospa right now and solve this wretched puzzle!"

"Because, Miss Pocket, I fear you would pay for the answer with your life."

Then Miss Frost blew at me as if I were a candle. Silver dust billowed up from the palm of her hand and flew at my face, engulfing me in a sparkly mist.

And then . . . darkness.

29

It was the ocean that brought me back. I awoke to the sound of the sea. The crashing of waves upon the rocks, somewhere nearby. When I opened my eyes, the brightness dazzled and stung them. The room was white. Very pretty. Two small windows. A patchwork quilt upon the bed. A wardrobe and chest of drawers. Even an armchair with a fetching blue cushion.

Miss Frost stood at the end of the bed. Jago came in and out, carrying a jug of water and an apple and knife upon a plate, which he set down next to my bed.

I knew it was gone from the moment I awoke. But I held my peace.

"Thought you'd never wake up, chatterbox," said Jago, tucking his hands into his pockets.

"Miss Pocket was exhausted," said Miss Frost. "It is no surprise she has slept a full day and night."

I sat up in the bed. Wiped sleep from my eyes. "Are we in Dorset?"

"We are," said Miss Frost, walking to the window. "When you feel ready to get up, you will see that our cottage is very remote—perched on a cliff near the outskirts of Weymouth. So we shall be quite safe here for the present."

Jago was staring at me. "You don't remember falling asleep then, chatterbox?"

I shook my head.

"What a foolish question," snapped Miss Frost, glaring at the boy. "Miss Pocket was overcome with fatigue, she fell into a deep sleep in the carriage, and I carried her inside. I would be shocked if she could recall a single moment of our journey from Sussex."

The boy looked chastened and set about peeling the apple for me.

"You are right, dear," I said. "It's all a blur."

But of course it wasn't. I remembered every moment. How we had argued about Rebecca. And about my intention to return to Prospa and solve the mystery about why those guards had recognized me. Miss Frost had said I would pay for the answer with my life. And then she had blown that devilish powder in my face. Clearly, she wanted me to have forgotten our little chat. So I let her have her wish.

"I have employed the services of a housekeeper," said Miss Frost, "who will tend to the cooking and cleaning. I trust her implicitly and expect you to do just as she says when I am gone."

Jago was frowning. "Don't see why I can't come with you."

"If you wish to stay in my employment, Master Jago, you will do as I ask without protestation. I have left five pounds in the larder under a sack of kidney beans—you are to use it *only* in an emergency."

"Are you not staying?" I asked Miss Frost.

"I have some urgent matters to attend to," she said crisply, walking back to the end of the bed, "but hopefully it will not take long. When I come back, we will discuss the future, Miss Pocket—I trust that is all right with you?"

"Perfectly."

Miss Frost turned and walked to the door. When she was almost past the threshold I called her by name and said, "Where is the Clock Diamond?"

Miss Frost paused, but did not turn around.

"I felt it was safer for everyone if I placed it somewhere out of harm's way. Perhaps when this is all over, I can return it to you, but for now . . . I hope you understand."

I wanted to cry out, "But what of Rebecca? And what of the answers I seek?"

Instead, I said, "It's not as if the stone was mine—it comes from your world, and you may do with it as you wish."

Jago let out a small gasp. "I thought you'd blow your top."

How much he knew about the necklace, I wasn't sure.

"Your wisdom is admirable, Miss Pocket," said Miss Frost.

Then she left. I heard her boots on the stairs and the opening and closing of a door. Jago watched from the window as she mounted her horse and galloped across the cliff tops.

I got out of bed and stood next to him, looking out. Then walked over to the armchair and sat down. "What did you and Miss Frost do here yesterday?" I pushed the hair from my face. "There isn't anything about for miles."

"She likes it that way," he said. He leaned against the window ledge. "I brought logs up from the basement and cleared out the chimney—it was awful blocked."

"And Miss Frost," I said casually, "what did she do?"

Jago shrugged. "Wrote letters, mostly." He scratched his head. "Oh, and she dug up some lavender from the heath and planted it under the kitchen window. Said it'd make the place smell sweet and such."

I patted my belly. "I'm frightfully hungry. Be a dear and rustle me up some eggs and a pound or two of potatoes." I got up and walked over to the wardrobe, opening it. There were six rather plain dresses in shades of blue, white, and yellow. "I will get changed and be right down."

"After breakfast we might go hunting for rabbits," said Jago.

I smiled sweetly. "Brilliant."

Nightfall. I was on my knees in the front garden. Beneath the kitchen window. The cottage fast asleep. A half-moon shone high in the sky, sprinkling silvery light upon the flower beds.

The lavender bush came out of the dirt with ease, its fragrant scent a burst of sunlight in my nose. I set it aside and thrust my hand down, scooping the soil in great clumps. It had to be there. I knew it as surely as I knew my own name.

The hole was soon up to my elbow, little hills of dirt stacked around the rim like watchtowers. Then I felt something. It was soft but rough, all at the same time. I clenched it with my fingers and pulled it up. A small cloth sack caked in dirt, fastened with a length of rope.

I pulled at the cord greedily. A smile broke across my face as I pulled it out. Held it in my hand. Inside the magnificent stone was a churning white mist. It parted, offering a delicious glimpse of the night sky above Dorset.

I fixed the Clock Diamond around my neck and took off into the darkness.

Epilogue

"Are you traveling all the way to London on your own?"

"Yes. Quite alone."

"Haven't you any family? A guardian?"

"I did have," I replied brightly. "A charming older couple who sold coffins and loved me to pieces. But they turned out to be murderous tricksters. All very tragic."

The prim-looking woman whose name I did not know looked vexed. She sounded vaguely American. Muttered something about this sort of thing being highly irregular. And it was true—it had taken all of the two pounds I had stolen from under the bag of kidney beans to convince the coach driver to take me to London. With no luggage. And no parents.

"I take excellent care of myself," I told her.

The woman glowered. Then leaned forward. "Now, I'm not normally one to stick my nose in where it's not wanted—but what business have you in the city?"

There were six of us in the carriage. The inquisitive American. Myself. Three older women (all sisters) snoring in near-perfect unison. And a rather dashing fellow who had his head buried in *David Copperfield*.

I felt a generous sigh was in order. "Well, I have to rescue a slightly disturbed though highly musical woman from a madhouse. Also, save my friend from certain death—she's suffering terribly, and I must bring her home before she fades away." I sighed again. "Then I'd very much like to find a child who vanished over a decade ago. And if I have time, discover exactly who I am."

The woman didn't look even slightly unconvinced. Though she did have concerns. "A mere child has no business doing such things!"

"Why not? I'm brilliant in a catastrophe. Everybody says so."

"You're a child! A little girl! How on earth do you expect to succeed?"

"Courage, dear," was my earnest reply. "Great bucket loads of it. The kind that causes spontaneous applause, fainting spells, and national monuments."

The curious American looked suitably impressed. And rather confused. Which managed to shut her up.

Through the dusty window I saw a patchwork of green and gold fields rippling beneath the morning sun. The stagecoach hurtled across a rickety bridge, causing the cabin to leap and tremble. I leaned back in my seat, strangely content, and watched the world hurry by.

In no time, sleep came to claim me—but I did my best to resist. It occurred to me, then, that yet *again*, I was bound for London and an uncertain future. But I did not despair or worry. I felt confident that, no matter what befell me, I would be perfectly all right. Rebecca would be saved. Anastasia liberated. Miss Always defeated.

I felt a pang of guilt for leaving Dorset and Jago under such circumstances. I knew deep down that Miss Frost was *trying* to do good, but that did not make her right. She was monstrously wrong to separate me from the stone. To try and make me forget what I had heard those guards in Prospa House say.

But the mysteries swirling around me were nothing more than questions yet to be answered. I would get to the truth. Somehow.

After all, I was a girl of excellent character. Stupendously pretty. Heart-stoppingly smart. It was true that I didn't *exactly* have a place to call home. Or a family to belong to. Or a penny to my name. But surely that wouldn't last forever? Nothing ever does.

At last I surrendered to sleep, falling gently into splendid dreams of dancing monkeys and brighter days. And all the while, the stagecoach spirited me swiftly toward the shadows and intrigues of London.

And destiny.

THE END

Acknowledgments

Ugh. Is it that time again? Another round of unbridled gratitude with a side order of grovelling. Didn't I *just* thank these people? Still, it must be done. So here it is:

Madeleine Milburn is a literary agent. Actually, she's *my* literary agent. Which shows great courage and fortitude on her part. And I thank her. In her bustling office are Cara Lee Simpson and Thérèse Coen, and I thank them as well. Thanks also to Cara's pal Harriet Orrell for her invaluable assistance with London locations.

I do not write for my own benefit. If I did, this book would be a three-hundred-thousand-word opus expanding on the widely held view that I am the new Dickens (and quite possibly the old one too). But as I write books for *other* people, a publisher is required.

Which brings me to Greenwillow Books. The following people had a great deal to do with creating the book you have in your hands—Virginia Duncan steered the ship with ease, Katie Heit assisted most ably, and Sylvie Le Floc'h provided wonderful art direction. Barbara Cantini's dazzling illustrations have again brought my story to life in all its whimsical glory. So I thank all of these talented people.

Thanks also to Michelle Kroes at CAA for all her efforts in the film world.

On the home front there is a group of people who frequently overlook how wonderful I am. Which is infuriating. That said, I should probably thank my parents for being hugely supportive and only occasionally regretting the day I was born. Paul, as ever, did all the printing and helped with computer-related stuff. Christine offered frequent encouragement. Carol allowed me to bend her ear on many occasions, and is often the voice of reason. Peter hasn't read any of my books, because they don't involve three men in a raft, climbing Mount Whatsit and eating their own arms for sustenance, but he always asks how my work is going, which is nice. My nephews and nieces—Nats, Ant and Liz, Josh, Ben, Thomas, Dylan, Shannon, Olivia, Kaelin, Jack, and Charli— provide a welcome distraction from the peaks and valleys of a writing life. Jacqui is the closest thing I have to a lifelong friend, and is one of the best people I know (which isn't all that hard, as I know a great many awful people).

Lastly, thanks to you, dear reader. Though, to be honest, it's you who should be thanking me. After all, the fact that you chose my book speaks very well for your future prospects. A great many of my keenest readers have gone on to thoroughly successful lives upon release from juvenile detention. So well done, you.

Until next we meet . . .

A PREVIEW OF SORTS

By The Author

Here we are again, dear reader. Book Two has ended and I must now whet your appetite for Book Three. Drop clues and hints like bread crumbs. Fill you with the sort of anticipation that often leads to spontaneous explosion. Or at very least a mild headache and a crying fit. If you fear that waiting another whole year for the next Ivy Pocket book will be complete torture, robbing your life of meaning, excitement, and happiness, you are completely correct. Sorry about that.

The fault is all mine, of course. I could have ended the book you have just read in a less thrilling fashion. Perhaps with Ivy dedicating her life to growing carrots. Or running away to join the postal service. Instead, I left our magnificently infuriating heroine on the very brink of her greatest adventure. Bound for London—and destiny.

Oh, but *what* destiny?

Excellent question. But how can I answer it without giving away the best bits? *Bring Me the Head of Ivy Pocket* is the final book in the trilogy, and as such is positively bursting with outrageous plot twists, hair-raising escapades, epic battles, and answers to all the important questions. It is a book so delicious, you may very well wish to eat it. Which I wouldn't recommend. Not without a pound of butter, a handful of nutmeg, and a good blender.

But back to Book Three and what you can expect. You have read this far, dear reader, and you deserve something solid. A big, juicy hint about what fate is going to befall Ivy once she reaches London. So here it is—Ivy will head straight to the Snagsby's funeral home and beg them to take her back. Mother Snagsby will agree, on three conditions: 1) Ivy must hand over the Clock Diamond. 2) Ivy must never speak again. 3) Ivy must spend her every waking moment cleaning. Naturally, Ivy agrees, and what follows is several hundred pages of Ivy's silent battle to rid the viewing parlour of dust. It's a thrilling read!

Actually, it's complete nonsense. What *does* happen is an epic journey between worlds as one girl-with-attitude tries to find out who she really is. I am up to my neck writing this final adventure and the story has taken even me by surprise. I warn you, the road ahead for Ivy is treacherous. Villains lie in wait. Secrets abound. Freedom has its price. And fate can be cruel.

My suggestion is that you proceed immediately to your nearest bookstore—bring a blanket, a change of clothes, some cheese and whatnot. Find a snug corner and set up camp. Refuse to move an inch until *Bring Me the Head of Ivy Pocket* is released. You know it makes sense.

Until then, farewell.

Caleb Krisp

a prized stallion

a junior Sherlock Holmes

a prima ballerina

a Buddhist monk

"For I have
all the instincts of . . ."

a writer of
penny dreadfuls

a stockbroker

a princess in a tower

a five-star general

a coffin maker's daughter

an assistant librarian

a physician

a sedated cow

a caterpillar

a postmaster's daughter

a highland hermit

a secret agent

a startled rabbit

a lion

a trapped miner

a cheese-maker's niece

a startled rabbit

a lion

an assistant librarian

a five-star general

"For I have
all the instincts of ..."

a highland hermit

a Buddhist monk

a junior Sherlock Holmes

a prized stallion

a cheese-maker's niece

a sedated cow